THE RANGER
Concho Book One

A.W. Hart

WOLFPACK
PUBLISHING
— EST 2013 —

WOLFPACK
PUBLISHING
— EST 2013 —

Text copyright © 2021 A.W. Hart
Special thanks to Charles Gramlich for his contribution to this novel.

Published by Wolfpack Publishing
5130 S. Fort Apache Road, 215-380
Las Vegas, NV 89148

Paperback IBSN 978-1-64734-714-7
eBook ISBN 978-1-64734-713-0
LCCN 2021937259

THE RANGER

AUTHOR'S NOTE

Eagle Pass, Texas, Mall de las Aguilas, and the Kickapoo reservation outside of Eagle Pass are real places inhabited by real people. Although the author has tried to represent the town, mall, and reservation as realistically as possible in a physical sense, certain liberties have been taken for fictional purposes and to avoid misrepresentation of actual individuals. For example, while the Kickapoo Tribal Police Force has a large staff in reality, it has been reduced to only three officers in this work. *All* characters are fictional and are not based on anyone living in Eagle Pass or on the reservation.

PART ONE
THE RANGER

CHAPTER 1

It was a poor excuse for a dirt road, and a waste of a
beautiful morning. The F-150 jarred and jounced under Concho
Ten-Wolves as he drove away from the site along White-Tail Creek,
which he'd been investigating. An anonymous call to the Texas
Ranger headquarters had reported a shooting along the creek over
the last few days. They had said it sounded like a war.

Concho had found about what he'd expected to find. No sign
of a crime. Someone had been taking target practice, several
someones by the look of the vehicle tracks and boot prints.

Yet, something bothered him about the site. The targets were
unusual. Not cans nor bottles nor a rusted-out automobile. But
dolls, all representing the female form. They ranged from Barbies
to china dolls to mannequins—with a blow-up sex doll thrown
in. All had been shot to shreds with high impact ammo. Concho
suspected an AR-15 in .223 caliber for some of it. But the empty
casings had been picked up. That was unusual, too, although plenty of locals reloaded their own ammo.

The main highway loomed in front of Concho and he pulled to
a stop. From down the road to his left, a glint of light grew steadily.
He waited for the oncoming vehicle to pass while yellowish dust
settled over his truck. Across the road stood a single dead oak.

Three vultures watched him from its silvered branches.

Texas is full of straight highways and fast drivers. A black Dodge Charger blew past Concho's unmarked vehicle doing better than a hundred miles per hour. Concho glanced back at the vultures and stabbed a finger at them like a baseball coach pointing at a player to say, "you're on deck." He was reaching to flip on his siren when the radio crackled.

"Concho! Come back!"

Concho plucked up the hand-held speaker. "Here," he said, keying the mic.

"An emergency at Eagle Pass Mall," the dispatcher said. "You're closest. The Captain wants you there."

"What emergency?"

"Hostage situation. Looks like terrorists, though it's not clear. Local cops are on the scene. FBI has been called. Captain Keller said to tell you you're backup. No lone wolf tactics."

"What about Ten-Wolves tactics?" Concho asked.

The dispatcher sputtered as he realized what Concho meant. "Captain's orders, man. Support only!"

"One riot, one Ranger," Concho replied.

He cut off the radio, hit the siren and lights. Wheeling onto the highway, he punched the gas. The big Ford seemed to hunch down as it gathered itself, then leaped forward with a squeal from the tires. The engine cranked to a roar; Concho had done the fine tuning himself. They ate the highway.

The driver of the speeding Dodge heard them coming. He slowed, put on his blinker to pull over. Still accelerating, Concho whipped past the Charger in the left lane. He gave the driver the same finger-point he'd given the vultures. Then he put everything out of his mind except the mall and the hostages.

He was fifteen minutes out, and bringing Hell with him.

CHAPTER 2

Concho shut off his siren and slowed a little as he entered the town of Eagle Pass, Texas. Eagle Pass had a population just south of 30,000 and was the county seat of Maverick County, which lay right on the border with Mexico. The Mall de las Aguilas, sometimes called the Eagle Pass Mall, particularly by whites, was off Bibb Avenue. Concho swung down Highway 375 and cut across parking lots to pull in behind one of the mall's smaller loading docks. It was 11:57 AM.

Officially, the mall's stores unlocked their doors at 11:00, though some locals always showed up earlier to exercise-walk. The terrorists must have entered just before the place opened, or maybe right after. Depending on the timing, they could have anywhere from ten to a few hundred hostages.

Concho neither heard nor saw any signs of villains or victims inside the mall. The place was silent as a funeral home. The parking lot was another world—and nowhere near quiet. Cop cars with blue lights flashing formed a bright noose around the area. Police officers ran back and forth on inscrutable errands. Radios crackled; voices jabbered. A helicopter swung back and forth in the clear morning sky with its rotors throbbing. The air stank of hot oil and asphalt.

Concho slid out of his vehicle and joined the crowd. No one had time to care, even from among the two news vans that had already shown up to disgorge cameramen and reporters. He threw open the door to the F-150's extended cab and started snatching gear. Speed was essential. The cordon around the building was thin, but more police cars and motorcycles were screeching in every second. The parking lot would be knee-deep in cops soon, and too many people would see Concho's actions and try to head him off.

Jerking a leather thong from the pocket of his blue work shirt, Concho tied back his longer-than-regulation straight black hair, a legacy of his Kickapoo mother. Stripping off the shirt revealed a dark T beneath. He transferred his badge to the top of the undershirt, then drew on body armor. Colt Double Eagle .45s already filled the holsters on each hip. He added extra magazines, knives, a few smoke grenades, and slung a Remington .30-06 hunting rifle with a Leupold VX scope over his shoulder.

Next came his own private weapon, non-regulation—a bow he'd constructed himself. He'd carved it from the wood of an Osage orange growing on the local Kickapoo reservation. It had been strengthened with deer hide and buffalo horn, and polished and oiled with sweat and not a little blood. The symbols etched on it meant something only to himself and a few others like him. There weren't many like him.

Setting the bow and a quiver of twelve homemade arrows across his back next to the more modern threat of the hunting rifle, Concho reached for a small yellow tin. He had one more task to complete before going into battle. Opening the tin and reaching in, he scooped up two fingerfuls of red ocher and smeared streaks of it beneath his right eye. He repeated the action beneath his left eye and resealed the tin, wiping his fingers on a handy towel.

A few police officers had noticed him by now. At 6'4", with shoulders as broad as those of an NFL linebacker in full pads, he was hard to miss. But they could all see the Texas Ranger's badge winking on his shirt and no one said anything as he started a brisk walk toward the loading dock that he'd picked to begin his assault.

A big delivery truck, as tall as a semi but not as long, was backed up to the dock. The driver was missing. Concho wondered whether he was a hostage, or if he'd been part of the crew who'd taken the mall. It didn't matter at that moment.

The dock doors were locked. OK. Gunmen were likely defending it from inside anyway. Concho had a plan. He scaled the hood of the truck, eased up onto the cab and from there onto the trailer. Above him lay the roof of the mall. It was a long leap but Concho had been an Army Ranger and had the muscles and training for it.

Taking half a dozen quick steps across the trailer, Concho jumped upward and caught the rim of the roof with both hands. He pulled himself up and over and dropped into a crouch. His fingers found the butts of his Colts without drawing them yet.

Motionless and waiting, he listened. No one confronted him. He wasn't expecting anyone to. A fitful breeze cooled his sweat and teased his nostrils with the smell of sun-softened tar. Staying crouched but moving swiftly, he worked his way along the top of the mall until he came to the spot he sought.

Sliding his legs over the side of the roof, he lowered himself a few feet onto the concrete railing of a small balcony. A dead fern stood next to him. He remembered the fern. It had been here the last time he'd set foot on this balcony. It had been alive then.

The balcony was narrow, barely three feet across. It opened off the office for the manager of the Mall de las Aguilas, Maria Marta Morales. She'd been employed by the mall for nearly ten years, and had run the place for the last two. Concho hoped she'd been late for work today; he knew she wouldn't have been. She was likely a hostage, which added a fresh level of 'personal' to the situation.

Almost a month had passed since Concho had spoken to Maria. She'd told him that trying to have a relationship with him was mixing matches with methane. He'd had to agree. He'd given her the fern as a gift after all, without noticing how she never kept any plants around. Gift giving wasn't his best skill. Afterward, she'd started referring to herself as "the thumb of death."

"Pretty thumbs," Concho murmured to himself, "be all right."

Concho stepped off the railing behind a concrete buttress at the edge of the office, then leaned his head to peer through the floor-to-ceiling window next to it. No lights were on inside and the Ranger's sensitive eyes picked up no movement. He nodded at the emptiness and stepped over to the door. His fist almost swallowed the steel latch as he took hold of it. It was locked but he exerted his strength, let it build until something in the mechanism broke with a crack.

Easing the door open, Concho drew his right-hand pistol and pushed inside. His nostrils caught the scent of lavender and honeysuckle. He didn't know the brand of perfume Maria wore but this was how it smelled. And, he saw her red purse lying in her desk chair. His teeth ground together.

The office had no outer door here, only steps leading down to the mall's main floor. He started in that direction and paused as a sound intruded. The door at the bottom of the steps had just opened.

Feet scuffed on the carpet in the stairwell, and a woman gasped, "Please!"

"Keep moving, bitch," a man's voice snapped. "Do what I say and you'll live through this." An ugly laugh followed. "You don't wanna end up like the rest of 'em will."

Concho didn't like the sound of the laugh, or the words. He holstered his Colt and flexed the fingers of his big hands.

CHAPTER 3

Two sets of feet came up the stairs toward Maria Morales's office, lighter steps in front, heavier behind. Maria had always preferred to work under natural light, hence the many windows in her office and why the ceiling fluorescents were turned off.

Concho pressed himself against the wall behind a bookshelf full of plastic folders of manuals and regulations. The shadows might hide him just long enough, if he were perfectly still. A faint smile turned up Concho's lips. He knew the patience of the hunt, whether it be for deer, or men.

Fresh perfume struck Concho's nostrils—lilac. A blonde woman stepped out of the stairwell and past the wall against which the Ranger stood rooted. A man followed; he thrust the butt of an AR-15 against the woman's back, shoving her forward.

She stumbled on her high heels, cried out. As she turned toward the man who'd pushed her, she saw Concho. Her mouth made a surprised "O". Her pupils dilated. The man with her, sensing something wrong, started to spin.

Concho's left hand snapped down to catch the barrel of the man's rifle and twist it to one side; he used his right arm like an ax—chopping down across the fellow's wrists. The blow was brutal. It broke the man's grip.

Barely an instant had passed but now Concho had the rifle in *his* hands. He brought it up and smashed the butt end squarely into the man's face. The nose broke and teeth shattered. The woman gave a little squeal of shock. The would-be rapist stumbled back, barely conscious.

Concho glanced at the hostage. She'd dressed in green this day, light cotton for the start of summer. She was young, pretty, terrified. But not stupid. He lifted a finger to his lips in a shushing motion. She nodded and put her hand across her mouth.

Concho leaned the AR-15 against the wall and grabbed the shirtfront of the terrorist, who'd fallen back against the opposite wall and seemed to be fighting for awareness. The Ranger jerked the man toward him, spun him about and snapped cuffs on his wrists. The fellow shook his head and made his first attempt to struggle. Concho spun him back around and slapped him hard, then pulled his biggest Bowie knife and pressed the wickedly curved tip against the fellow's cheek just beneath the left eye.

"Speak when I ask you questions," Concho said softly. "Otherwise, I take both eyes and your tongue and feed them to my dogs."

The man regained full consciousness. A look of horror crossed his face as he focused on the big dark-skinned man with the knife and the slashes of warpaint across his cheeks. Although he didn't dare nod agreement with the blade tip so close to his eye, it was clear he believed what Concho told him. Sweat began to bead on his shaven head and run down his cheeks and neck.

Concho studied the man. The tats on the bare arms were revealing—swastikas and runic SS lightning bolts, a skull embedded with an iron cross, the number 12, which among the members of one particular gang in Texas prisons represented the letters "A" and "B."

"Aryan Brotherhood," Concho said. "How many are you?"

Blood from the battered nose speckled the man's cheeks like freckles. He snorted to clear his airways before he spoke. "Ten," he said.

"How many hostages?"

"Not…sure. A bunch."

"Why?"

The gang member gave the faintest of shrugs. "Money," he said.

"I figure that's partly a lie," Concho said. "But we'll let it pass for the moment. Who's leading you?"

"Might as well tell you. He's not making any secret of it. Darrel Fallon!"

"Fallon! I heard he broke prison but didn't think he'd be stupid enough to hang around Texas."

The man bristled and Concho let the tip of the Bowie slide just a fraction of an inch closer to the eye.

"A fanatic, eh?" Concho said. "A true believer! Maybe you can see by looking at me, I'm not a sympathizer to your cause. Give me a reason to not cut you up."

"What's your name?" the fellow asked. "The Brotherhood wants to know."

"You'll hear about it soon enough. You can all gossip it back and forth when you get to prison. If any of you make it that far. Are there explosives?"

The man's bravado was coming back. He dared a smirk. "Yes."

"Where?"

"All around."

"On timers?"

"You'll know when they go off."

Concho grasped the man's chin with his free hand, forcing the mouth shut and the head back against the wall. With the razor tip of the Bowie, he made a tiny little slice in the dark circle of skin under the man's eye.

The gangbanger tried to cry out but only a whimper escaped his forcibly closed mouth.

"I'm just about to take the eye," Concho whispered. "It's a pretty one. Maybe I'll add it to my collection. I've got a whole jar."

A word that might have been "please" struggled from the man's mouth. Concho eased the pressure of his hand against the fellow's chin so he could talk.

"Not on timers," the man said, rushing his words as if they were the last ones he might get to speak. "Backpack bombs. But Fallon plans to detonate them at the end. To help us escape."

"And the hostages?"

"Fallon don't care if they die."

"Truth for sure," Concho said. "How many has he killed so far?"

"I don't know. A few. He needed examples."

"So, he made you an accessory to murder."

"No. I didn't shoot anyone. They were mostly Mexes anyway."

Concho banged the man's head against the wall behind him. "That word might piss me off," he said. "*If* I thought you had an opinion worth listening to. If the bombs go, you'll go with them."

Pain brought a quick retort to the terrorist's lips. "You won't be around to know. Soon as you take on the boys."

"We'll see. Any sound above breathing and I'll kill you right in front of our witness here. I doubt she'll report me."

Both Concho and the gang member looked over at the freed hostage. She nodded her agreement to the Ranger's words. Concho hid a smile as he sheathed his Bowie. Grabbing the man's arms, he twisted him down on the floor.

"Ma'am," he said to the woman. "Would you open the lower left drawer of the desk there and bring me the duct tape you find inside?"

The woman turned as she was bid, found the duct tape just where he'd indicated it in Maria's desk. She brought it to him. Concho nodded internally. Maria might not be able to grow plants but she knew the value of duct tape as a fix for just about everything else. Taking the roll of thick gray tape, Concho wrapped the man's legs together above the ankles. Next came taping the mouth. The man struggled, to no avail.

Concho rose, turned toward the woman. "What's your name?"

"Eliza."

"Eliza! Did you hear what the man said about the bombs? And about his crew?"

She nodded. "Ten of them. And the leader is…Fallon. Darrel Fallon. He has bombs everywhere."

"Yes, and you're going to need to give the policemen outside that information."

"There's…there's another one downstairs," Eliza added. "Watching outside the office door. They were going to…take turns."

"Thanks," Concho said. "I'll take care of him. Now, I want you to do me a favor." He pointed to a big clock on the office wall. "Wait fifteen minutes. Then go out on the balcony and wave your arms. Wave 'em high. Wave 'em a bunch. They'll send someone to get you. But I need just a little head start before more policemen come in. Can you do that, Eliza?"

The woman nodded. She seemed to be staring with a bit of shock at the crimson warpaint on his face. Well, shock was the purpose of it. Picking up the prisoner's assault rifle, Concho checked to make sure the safety was on. He handed it to Eliza. She took it reflexively, staring down at it with fear.

"It takes practice to master a gun," Concho told her. "But you're smart and I'm gonna give you a lesson of a lifetime in thirty seconds. This is the safety." He pointed. "You flick it this way to fire. Point and shoot. Do *not* put your finger on the trigger until you're ready to shoot. If I come back this way, I'll call out to you. But there might be other civilians who know about this office. Wait until you see your target before you shoot. And when you go outside to signal the police, leave the rifle behind. You got that?"

Eliza nodded again.

"You're doing well, ma'am. You'd think you were kidnapped every day."

A ghost of a smile flitted over Eliza's face and was gone. "If I have to wait here for long, I might put a stiletto heel in this bastard's eye," she said.

"If you do, I'll testify it was an accident," Concho said. "And the local judge owes me a favor."

"Do you really have…" Eliza started, and stopped.

"Have what?"

"A…a jar of eyes?"

"Ma'am!" the Ranger protested. He grinned. "I'm planning to start my collection today."

Eliza grinned back. Concho figured she would.

CHAPTER 4

Concho drew his bow over his shoulder and strung it, then nocked an arrow and started carefully down the stairs from the office. The carpeted floor deadened the sound of his boots. The door at the foot of the steps was closed. It opened outward, and according to Eliza, another Aryan Brotherhood member waited outside. The man must not have heard anything of the altercation above—or if he had, maybe he thought it was just his friend playing rough—else, he would have already come inside.

Concho pushed down the door latch and shouldered the door quietly open. He stepped through in one smooth motion, bringing up the bow as he did so. The second gang member had his back to the door but heard it click and turned. His actions were casual; clearly, he expected his friend.

"Finished alread—" the man started to say. His pupils dilated as he saw who faced him. His mouth opened and his hands tightened on his gun.

The outlaw wore body armor to cover his chest and belly. Concho bypassed it, shooting the fellow in the throat with an arrow at a range of less than five feet. At that distance and backed by the Ranger's considerable strength, the flint-tipped arrow slashed all the way through the neck and caromed off the wall behind the gang member.

The man gagged as blood and tissue sprayed out the back of his neck. He let go of his rifle to grab for his throat, but Concho was already stepping toward him and caught the weapon before it could hit the ground.

His eyes wild, the terrorist clawed for breath. He tried to speak but nothing resembling words came out, and no sounds loud enough to be heard outside the closed corridor. Concho slid an arm around the fellow's shoulders and lowered him slowly to the ground.

A dying hand snatched at Concho's arm as he released the fellow and started to stand. It caught at the Ranger's wrist for an instant, then slid away to leave a slick smear of blood like reddish tar against Concho's dark skin. He didn't bother to wipe it off. There'd be more gore before this day was done.

Concho checked the terrorist's rifle. It was another AR-15, in good working order, with an extended magazine holding thirty rounds. He slung it over his shoulder. The gangbanger was dead by the time Concho leaned over and pulled a walkie-talkie from his belt and attached it to his own. It looked like standard police issue. If the Brotherhood members were using these for communication inside the mall, maybe he'd overhear something important.

Having been to Maria Morales's office plenty of times, Concho could visualize exactly where he was in the mall. It was a perfect starting point for a counter assault on the terrorists. The corridor ran behind a couple of shops and was hidden from anyone who wasn't specifically looking for it. There were several offices besides Maria's, and customer restrooms at one end before you entered the public area of the mall.

In the other direction along the corridor, just behind Maria's office, stood the door to another small loading dock. Concho checked on it and found it rolled down and chained. The criminal he'd just killed must have been set to watch the door, but when the

Ranger checked the man's pockets, he found no keys to fit the big locks on the chain.

He needed bolt cutters and didn't have them. And time was fleeting. He'd asked the woman, Eliza, to give him fifteen minutes, and several of those had ticked away. Keeping the bow in his hands, Concho started quickly down the corridor toward the main part of the mall. He passed two more empty offices on the ground floor before reaching the bathrooms.

Going to his belly, Concho crawled the last few feet and peeked out into the main area of the mall. To his right stood a set of three glass doors leading to the outside. They also had been chained shut. Across the open area from him was a marine recruiting office and an H&R Block. Movement in the recruiting office caught the Ranger's eye. A well-armed gangbanger fidgeted as he watched the outer doors.

As he turned his head to the left, Concho saw a looted Kay Jewelers. Beyond stood a Krispy Crème kiosk with at least seventy hostages seated on the floor around it. Most of these appeared to be children and women, with a few old men. He saw no sign of Maria Morales. Two more gunmen circled the group, like sharks in the ocean scenting blood.

Putting down the bow, Concho slid both the AR-15 and the hunting rifle off his back. He'd have to take out the sentry in the recruiting office first. Fortunately, the glass front of the office had been smashed in. He could get a shot. The terrorist inside had the same bristle-cut hair and tats as the others. He carried a 12-gauge shotgun and was clearly nervous as he paced back and forth, continually wiping sweaty hands on his military-style camouflage pants.

A faint snick of sound drew Concho's attention. He turned his head, watched as the door to the woman's restroom started to inch open. He rolled silently to his right and came up into a squat against the wall next to the bathroom. A Colt filled his right hand.

The bathroom door opened wider. A dark-haired head appeared

barely a foot above the floor, with gold-rimmed brown eyes peering out above a sharp nose and a wispy beard. Concho grabbed the head by the tightly curled hair, shoving the face down against the floor of the hallway to silence the mouth. He brought his pistol to bear against the man's temple but held his fire. This wasn't one of the bad guys. His skin was black, for one thing, though lighter than Concho's own. He was also young, probably not even eighteen.

"Quiet!" Concho hissed. "Who are you?"

"Nate. Nate. Nate Taylor. Please don't kill me!"

"I'm a Texas Ranger," Concho said. "I'm not going to kill you." He drew the pistol away from the boy's head and let go of his hair. "How did you get here?" he demanded.

The boy cautiously turned his head to stare up at Concho. "Was…was just walking in the mall," he said. "I heard gunshots. Figured it was terrorists. Or a mass shooter. I was tryin' to hide."

"Smart," Concho whispered. "It's the Aryan Brotherhood. Worse than any mass shooter. But I'm here to take care of it." He pointed down the corridor toward the administrative offices he'd just passed. "Stay in the bathroom with the door closed until I take out the three A&Bs here. Then run down this corridor. There's a door and steps leading up to an office. You can escape the building there. But be cautious. There's probably still a woman in the office and she might shoot you unless you let her know very clearly who you are, and you go in slowly. You understand?"

The boy nodded. "Thank…thanks."

Concho nodded. He went back to his belly and made a slow, crawling return to his bow and rifles. Though it wasn't the usual way things seemed to work for Concho, the gangbanger in the recruiting office had just made the Ranger's job easier. He'd stepped out of the confined space into the main hall. A red-tipped cigarette dangled from the corner of his mouth as he tried to calm himself with quick puffs of nicotine.

This man was young, early twenties. He probably had a mother somewhere. He surely had at least a few people who loved him.

But here he was carrying a gun in service to a man who'd made it clear he wouldn't leave this mall without killing innocent people. Those people also had mothers and loved ones.

Concho picked up the bow, nocked an arrow. He worked his way into a crouch. The smoking man heard something, or sensed it. He turned his head in Concho's direction and saw the Ranger. In the one second before the man could shout an alarm, Concho drew and released.

The whisper-swift arrow punched through a mouth opening on a cry of warning. The man staggered backward, went down. His shotgun dropped with a loud clatter to the decoratively tiled floor.

CHAPTER 5

As soon as he fired the bow, Concho swung it over his shoulder and took up the Remington .30-06. The two Aryan Brotherhood members who were watching the hostages at the Krispy Crème kiosk heard their companion's shotgun clatter on the floor. Both turned toward the sound. They couldn't see the man Concho had put an arrow in because he'd fallen backward into the recruiting center.

One of the gang members called out a name, a nickname no doubt: "Skittle!" He hefted the rifle in his hands and started walking toward the recruitment center. "Skittle!" he called again.

The other gang member began to curse. He knew something was wrong. He stepped toward the hostages, hoisting his own weapon in a clear threat. It looked like a Streetsweeper 12-gauge semi-automatic shotgun, a rare piece known mostly for its high capacity drum magazine, which held twelve rounds. Though it was a cheaply made weapon, at close range it would chop through flesh like a threshing machine.

Concho realized the man was going to grab a hostage to use as a human shield. He wasn't going to give him the chance. Since all the terrorists seemed to be wearing body armor, a headshot was his only option. Centering the crosshairs of his scope on the fellow's forehead, Concho squeezed the trigger, felt it collapse as the butt of the rifle slammed back into his shoulder.

The roar of the big hunting rifle sent reverberations bouncing from the building's walls. The gangbanger's head exploded as most of the back part of his cranium came off. Hostages screamed in shock. The second gang member spun toward Concho, saw the Ranger, swung his rifle up, and pulled the trigger before his barrel was leveled. The weapon must have been adapted to full auto. Bullets sprayed, striking the floor and walking their way toward the crouching Concho.

The big Ranger knew he couldn't risk wounding the terrorist. The man might turn his rage on the hostages if given the opportunity. He took an instant to aim, ignoring the scope and using the iron sites beneath it.

A pair of slugs ricocheted away from Concho's feet just as he pulled the trigger on the .30-06. The jacketed hollow-point shell ripped the lower part of the criminal's skull off. The man's fingers spasmed, sending two more shots into the floor before he collapsed. Concho was up and running for the hostages.

"Police! Here! This way!" Concho shouted as he waved his arms.

His deep voice cut through the screams of the hostages. They heard him, began to scramble in his direction. He glanced back, saw Nate Taylor, who hadn't run as he'd been told. The brave young man was standing in front of the escape corridor, waving the hostages toward him with one hand while he held something in the air with his other. *A smartphone*, Concho realized, though he didn't have time to consider why.

A woman carrying a baby fell nearly at Concho's boots, and he picked her up and set her on her feet before she could be trampled. Another child stumbled and lost his grip on his mother's hand. "I'll get him," Concho shouted to her. "Keep running!"

He plucked up the towhead under one arm and brought up the rear. The hostages reached Nate Taylor and milled around him like disturbed ants. Voices babbled, children cried, sweat and fear showed on every face. Concho handed the little boy he was carrying to Nate, who pocketed his phone.

"Take them out the way I told you," Concho said to Taylor. "Keep them behind you. Remember the woman in the office with a gun. Be careful. The police will be coming in, too, after those shots."

The teenager nodded, though he looked half sick with fear. He held the little boy up in the air and called the hostages to attention. Concho heard Taylor start to explain the situation but had no time to wait. He headed back toward the center of the mall. There might be other hostages. Surely there were more terrorists. And Maria Morales was still missing. He wasn't leaving without her.

Yanking his cellphone out of the pocket of the black BDUs he habitually wore, Concho hit his contact list and brought up Pete Bishop. Pete was a cop in the Eagle Pass police department, and a good friend. He was almost certainly in the cordon locking down the mall. The phone rang only twice before Pete answered.

"Concho? What? Man, this is not a good time."

"Pete! Listen! I'm *in* the mall. Tell whoever's in charge. A bunch of hostages are in the corridor near the management area. They're safe for the moment. The doors near the army-marine recruitment center are clear of hostages or living terrorists. You guys can come through there. No problem."

"By the recruitment center? Down near the H&R Block?"

"Right."

"What's happ—"

Concho terminated the call, turned off the phone and stuck it back in his pocket. "Sorry, Pete," he murmured. "No time." He ran over to the last criminal he'd shot.

Hooking his .30-06 over his back, he leaned over the dead man to pick up his rifle. Although it also fired the .223 Remington round, this was no AR-15, which was the go-to weapon for most preppers, survivalists, and militia members. This was a military-grade rifle, an M4A1 carbine like those carried by most US

Special Forces units. Concho had carried one in the Army Rangers, long before he'd become a Texas Ranger.

Concho knew the Aryan Brotherhood had connections, but they should not have had access to such weaponry. It scared him to think what other kinds of military ordnance they might have. He checked the magazine. It had been nearly emptied—at him. But there were at least half a dozen more of the thirty-round magazines in a web bag at the gangbanger's waist. Concho stuffed a fresh mag up the carbine's pipe and slipped three extras into the pockets of his BDU's.

Two big retail stores, Bealls and Ross, were nearest to him. Using their entrances for cover, he started working his way quickly up the mall, trying to maintain a balance between caution and speed as he watched for both terrorists and more potential hostages. The terrorists, depleted in numbers, would now be aware of a wrench in their plans. And Maria was still here somewhere.

Concho was giving some thought to what Darrel Fallon's plans might be when he became aware of a sound that had suddenly stopped. He'd been hearing it faintly since he'd entered the mall, a high-pitched whine, almost a vibration.

Like an industrial strength drill! Concho thought. And, *the bank!*

IBC had a branch in the Eagle Pass Mall. As far as Concho knew, it was a relatively small branch and not likely to have huge funds on hand. Maybe the Brotherhood members were just taking what they could get, as they had with the jewelry store. Or maybe they knew something he didn't.

Behind him came a deafening crash of glass, which probably meant SWAT—Special Weapons and Tactics—had just come through the doors he'd told Pete Bishop about. They'd follow their protocols, though, clearing every store and room as they advanced. He had some time.

The walkie-talkie he'd taken from the white supremacist in Maria's office gave a little crackle. Concho plucked it off his belt and turned up the volume. A voice came through clearly, an educated voice, an articulate and precise voice, an arrogant one. But beneath its external smoothness, Concho detected pent up rage and brutality. This could only be one man, the neo-Nazi leader of the local Aryan Brotherhood—Darrel Fallon.

Concho Ten-Wolves had never met Darrel Fallon. He'd seen him in the news, had read articles about him. He knew the capsule history of the man who'd come from nowhere. Born in Maverick County, Fallon had moved with his mother, a single parent, to San Antonio when still a boy. He'd attended East Central High School, earned respectable grades, and been a standout on the football team as a quarterback.

Texas A&M had offered him a football scholarship but he'd turned it down. No one knew why, except maybe his mother. She wasn't saying. Fallon attended San Antonio College and completed his associate degree in cybersecurity. He surfaced a few years later, arrested on drug charges and intent to manufacture and deliver methamphetamine.

He'd been sentenced to ten years at the Eastham Unit prison outside of Houston, where the Texas Aryan Brotherhood had been founded. They'd recruited Fallon right away, although there was some suggestion he might already have become involved with right-wing extremist groups. He'd certainly risen quickly through the ranks. After serving four years of his sentence, he and some of his "brothers" had broken out, killing two guards and a civilian doctor in the escape. Now he was back in Maverick County, and on the two-way radio with Concho Ten-Wolves.

"I'm sure someone has taken a radio from one of my men," Darrel Fallon said. "I'm sure he's listening to my voice. To whoever that is, to whoever killed one or more of my brothers, I say you've accomplished nothing except to create martyrs for the cause. But perhaps you've acted out of ignorance, out of the lies you've been told about me. Why don't you answer? Why don't you learn?"

Concho did not stop moving forward but he pressed send and whispered into the radio, "Give yourself up, Fallon. It's the only way you'll live through this."

"Ah," Fallon said back. "The proscribed command from the orchestrators of the ordinary. How disappointing. Is that truly who you are? Don't you wish for more?"

"Afraid I wouldn't be allowed in your club. Even if I hated myself enough to want it."

"You see the lies you've been told? There is always room for the superior. If…they can prove they deserve such."

"I see, Fallon. Is killing innocent people how you proved that you deserved it?"

Over the radio, Fallon's chuckle sounded like a lawnmower chewing gravel. "You *must* be some kind of policeman. Surely you don't believe in innocence. But, since you know my name, may I know yours?"

"I'll whisper it in your ear in a few minutes," Concho said, before breaking the connection.

CHAPTER 6

Movement closing on his position made Concho turn off the walkie-talkie and return it to his belt. He stepped through the open doorway into Ross's department store and crouched behind a display of women's dresses. The IBC bank was not far ahead. He heard no sound of work coming from there now. If the gang had been robbing the bank, they must have finished.

In the open corridor of the mall just in front of him was another kiosk. From the variety of smells, they sold perfumes, deodorants, soaps, and the like. Across the way was a shoe shop and something called Crazy 8. He had no idea what such a store might carry.

A man came darting past Crazy 8 and crouched. He wore body armor and what looked like a security guard's uniform, but was no cop. His gaze was focused mainly down the way Concho had just come. The gun in his hands was shorter than an AR-15, with a huge magazine stack sticking out of the bottom. It looked like a MAC-10 or some knockoff, basically a machine gun in pistol size. You didn't want to be in front of that thing when it fired.

Concho went to his belly and inched back toward the department store's door with the M4A1 in his hands. He pulled a smoke grenade from his belt but did not ignite it. Instead, he hurled it underhanded toward the perfume kiosk. It hit and bounced just short of the small structure.

The crouching gangbanger heard the sound and did what Concho hoped for. He opened fire on the kiosk. Bottles shattered; plastic containers seemed to grow wings; the hail of bullets tore away wood and signage. The kiosk collapsed in on itself as a cloud of intense smells blossomed from the carnage.

Concho took careful aim and touched off a three-round burst from his carbine. All three slugs punched into the terrorist below the edge of his armored vest and flung him back in a smear of blood. He began to scream.

But now the enemy bit back. The store's glass walls exploded over Concho's head, raining shrapnel down as an unseen gunman opened fire. Concho ducked and scrambled backward as he closed his eyes against flying pinwheels of glass. A stinging fragment cut his cheek, another his forehead.

The Aryan Brotherhood member emptied his rifle's magazine into the store, spraying it like a hose. Ricochets buzzed past Concho. Something bounced off the side of his bullet-proof vest hard enough to leave a bruise behind.

Silence fell as the terrorist's gun clicked on empty. Concho heard the clatter as the man let the empty magazine fall and stuffed a fresh one up the rifle's well. Footsteps tapped on the floor as the man approached.

Concho jerked another smoke grenade from his belt and ignited it before hurling it out the door into the mall beyond. A cloud of purple-dyed potassium chlorate billowed upward. The gangbanger cursed.

Next to Concho stood a wheeled cart hung with men's long coats. The Ranger rose to a crouch behind it and gave it a tremendous shove. It rolled straight out the door and into the smoke. The Brotherhood member opened fire, thinking Concho must be behind the cart.

Following the cart instead, Concho burst into the open and saw the gangbanger firing an AR-15 into the coats, which flapped wildly as bullets whipped through them. The terrorist's eyes widened, and he started to swing his weapon toward Concho.

The Ranger charged straight into the man, chopping brutally down across the fellow's neck with his left hand. The muscles spasmed all along the right side of the man's body. He dropped his rifle and Concho slammed him in the face with his M4A1.

The man staggered back, blood on his lips and cheeks. But he wasn't out of the fight. He dropped a hand to his waist and came up with a flashing knife. Concho had hoped to capture and question the man but it was taking too long. He shot him in the head at point-blank range. Expecting more fire, he dodged behind a decorative wall buttress at the corner of Ross's department store.

No more bullets came Concho's way, and the man he'd shot in front of Crazy 8 had stopped screaming. He could see the fellow's body lying still with a thick film of blood spreading around him on the tile floor. Seven of ten of the Brotherhood were down—if the terrorist Concho had interrogated had been telling the truth. Where were the last three? Where was Darrel Fallon? Where was Maria Morales?

The thump of an explosion thudded through the wall where Concho leaned. It sounded controlled, sounded deep, as if it were under the mall. He didn't know what to make of it. He ducked around the buttress, sprinted toward the IBC bank. The front of the place was blown out, and the inside was a shambles. He stepped past the wrecked counter into the rear section of the room. The vault was open, which meant little to him, considering he had no idea what might have been inside.

A smaller explosion shattered glass just around the corner from Concho. That would be the mall's main entrance, which had probably been chained shut and had to be blown open. No doubt, SWAT was coming through. The Mall de las Aguilas had taken a lot of damage but they'd be insured. It was the people who needed worrying about.

Concho stepped to the busted front of the bank. Down the mall from his right came several SWAT members in blue and black uniforms, wearing helmets and goggles, with the lower part of their faces masked with fire retardant balaclavas. They moved like soldiers, half crouched to lower their target profile, and with their carbines swinging from left to right as they searched for trouble.

The Ranger leaned his own carbine against the wall of the bank and stepped into the clear with his hands up high and his badge glinting on the front of his shirt above his body armor. He didn't want to get shot by his own side.

Voices yelled at him to "Get on the ground!"

He didn't, only called out in response. "I'm Texas Ranger. Texas…Ranger!"

The Texas Ranger Division had its own SWAT team, complete with a bomb squad, under the designation "Special Operations Group," but they were housed in Austin and couldn't have been on the scene so quickly. This was a local unit, independent of any authority Concho had. They wouldn't treat him any differently than any other police officer.

A SWAT officer approached warily, his gun aimed and dead steady. Another SWAT member backed him up.

Concho lowered one hand slowly and tapped his badge. "I'm Concho Ten-Wolves. I'm sure you were told I was here."

The officer nodded, then slowly straightened. His backup joined him. He had the expression of someone in charge and the attitude of one who wanted everyone to know it.

"Yes, Ten-Wolves. We were informed you were here, where you're not supposed to be. You're going to leave. Now!" He pointed back down the mall the way they'd all come. "Out! It's clear that way and officers there will make sure you're appropriately received."

"Not until it's over," Concho said, almost gently. "There's at least one hostage left."

"Our job! Not yours!" the SWAT commander snapped.

Concho wasn't going to argue; he just wasn't going to obey. The issue became moot as gunfire erupted from the direction of the main entrance. Concho drew one of his .45s and began to run toward the sound.

CHAPTER 7

The two SWAT officers had no choice but to follow Con-
cho. The three reached the corner, turned it, and saw at least eight
other SWAT members with their weapons aimed toward the doors
of the public restrooms—or, more precisely, aimed at the terrorist
in a ski mask who must have sprung out of the men's room.

The man stood swaying against the wall, holding a bloody left
arm against his chest. A rifle lay at his feet. Whoever had shot him
must have fired to wound, to capture him. They were yelling for
him to "Get down, get down!"

Instead, the gangbanger dropped his hand to the hilt of a machete at his waist. He drew it. The officers stepped back, continu-
ing to shout at the man to give up.

"He's about to die for his cause," Concho said to the SWAT
team member next to him.

"Death to the mongrel races!" the Brotherhood member
screamed.

He leaped forward, swinging his machete. Half a dozen rifles
vented quick bursts of fire, the sound like bubble wrap being
popped in a giant's hands. Shot to rags, the man dropped his
machete and crashed hard to the tiled floor.

Eight terrorists down, Concho thought. Where were the ninth and tenth? And was this one Darrel Fallon? Or was it the other? Would Fallon sacrifice himself so dramatically?

Everyone milled around. Concho waited for someone to pull the ski mask off the dead criminal. He'd seen mugshots of Fallon, and knew he'd recognize him. But all such thoughts were vacuumed from his head as a SWAT officer came barging out of the men's bathroom carrying an unconscious body in his arms.

It was a woman's body, with dark strands of hair falling across the face. Concho couldn't see the woman clearly for all the policemen in the way, but Maria Morales had long dark hair. His heart started to drum.

"This hostage is barely alive," the SWAT officer shouted. "I've got to get her to an ambulance. They blew up the floor in the bathroom. I think they're trying to get into the sewers. At least one of them is down there already. Maybe more!"

The man pushed through the crowd of his fellows, who jumped back to get out of the way. Several SWAT members rushed at the bathroom. Concho hesitated. If it *were* Fallon trying for the sewers, he couldn't be allowed to escape. But if the injured woman was Maria, he had to know if she were all right. Maybe his part in today's affairs was done. Let someone else get Fallon.

The SWAT officer carrying the woman began to run toward the door to the outside. Her left arm dangled, completely limp. She was unconscious, or dead. Concho started to yell "wait," but snapped his mouth closed. If Maria was injured, seconds might count. He started after the man and his burden while thoughts of Darrel Fallon fled.

A ring of police officers waited outside, various troopers and local sheriff's deputies. They parted for the SWAT officer and Concho followed him through the cordon. The cameras of reporters glinted and flashed in the distance. A couple of choppers worked back and forth above the crowd. The sun hung overhead like a great heated stone; the air stunk with the sweat of many bodies.

Beyond the police line, a dozen ambulances waited in a row between police cruisers, whose blue lights fractured the light of early afternoon. None of them seemed to have any business yet, which was about to change.

The SWAT officer ran toward the nearest ambulance. Concho rushed after him, but not to catch him. For the first time since he'd entered the mall, he murmured a quick prayer to any spirits who might conceivably be listening. To be on the safe side, he used all three dialects of the Algonquian tongue—his own Kickapoo, and the Sauk, and Fox.

The officer must have heard the footsteps behind him and glanced over his shoulder. Most of his face was hidden by his balaclava. His blue eyes were visible through his goggles as they arced with sunlight. Something chilled Concho, and not the fact that he could see the woman hostage clearly enough now to recognize Maria Morales. For an instant, the Ranger's steps faltered.

The officer's glance slid away from Concho; he ran harder for the ambulance. He was almost there. A paramedic rushed to meet him, arms out. Concho jerked the walkie-talkie off his belt, twisted it on and hit send as he mouthed a single word.

The SWAT member also wore a walkie-talkie. It crackled, and Concho's voice came through clearly.

CHAPTER 8

The walkie-talkie Concho spoke into had been taken from an Aryan Brotherhood member inside the mall. Darrel Fallon had called the Ranger on it, had spoken with him for several moments. And now Concho's voice came like the harsh call of a crow out of the radio carried by a man dressed in a SWAT uniform.

"Fallon!" Concho shouted.

The SWAT officer froze. The paramedic, who looked to be of Vietnamese descent, had reached him, concern written on his face for the woman the man was carrying. The officer abruptly hurled Maria's unconscious body into the paramedic's arms. The man caught her, surprise flashing in his eyes.

Darrel Fallon pulled the SWAT issued semi-automatic pistol from his belt, pointed it between the paramedic's eyes. His thumb cocked the weapon's hammer. Concho hit him from behind with the blade of his shoulder. At the impact, Fallon's arm flung wide. The gun fired, the bullet cracking wild into the sky.

The paramedic cried out and fell backward to the ground with Maria's body on top of him. Concho couldn't see if Maria or the man had been hit and had no time to check. His lunge into Fallon had driven the Brotherhood member into the side of the ambulance. The pistol clattered away.

Now Fallon's elbow snapped back, catching Concho a lucky blow right in the throat. The Ranger choked for breath; his grasp on his opponent loosened. Fallon twisted around in Concho's hold and blasted an open-handed blow into the Ranger's chest. The punch did no damage against his body armor but did knock him two steps back. Fallon dropped to a crouch, whipped his leg across and swept Concho's feet from under him.

Concho crashed down, the back of his head thumping on concrete. Brilliant lights flashed in his brain. Fallon lunged toward him, tried to curb-stomp him with a heavy boot. Reflexes saved Concho as he caught the boot just above the ankle, stopping it an inch from his face. He twisted and shoved. Fallon stumbled back and Concho rose. The two faced each other.

Concho shook his head to clear it. He was 6'4" but Fallon was also a big man, only a couple of inches shorter. He must have spent plenty of time in prison working out because the biceps bulged beneath his tight black shirt. He was fast, too, and trained. But he was desperate.

The terrorist leader must have planned to commandeer the ambulance taking Maria Morales to the hospital. If not for Concho, it would have made for a simple and effective escape. But now help would be coming to the Ranger in moments. No one was coming to aid Darrel Fallon. And he knew it.

Fallon launched a vicious attack, with feet and hands flashing. Concho blocked. Bone and flesh smacked together. They fenced like two swordsmen, using their bodies for weapons instead of rapiers. Fallon tried to circle Concho, to get out of the corner he was pinned into by the ambulance at his back. The Ranger kept imposing his big frame in Fallon's way.

Fallon's desperation grew. He tore off his goggles and threw them in Concho's face. He charged, trying to get in one decisive blow to end the fight and give him a chance to flee. A kick to the Ranger's side might have broken ribs if he hadn't been wearing his bullet-proof vest. The knuckles in a backhand cut Concho's lip; a closed-hand punch grazed his chin. But he caught the hand, forced its fingers open. He broke two of them with a twisting motion, with a sound like a sodden stick snapping.

Fallon cried out but did not let up. His free hand hacked into Concho's shoulder right at the point behind his vest. Concho's right arm went numb for an instant. Fallon tore his hand free from the Ranger's grip, and tried the leg sweep again. Concho got his knee in the way, then exploded an open hand into Fallon's chest. The fascist leader stumbled back against the side of the ambulance, gasping for breath, his eyes darting in search of an escape. Concho allowed him none.

Every blow taken and given had strengthened Concho while they weakened Fallon. Now the Ranger readied for the finish. He stalked forward. Fallon rained blows against him. Concho blocked some, shook off others. He caught an arm, snapped Fallon's wrist.

The gang member howled, launched a kick that barely registered against Concho's focused rage. The big Ranger snapped a knee up into Fallon's thigh. The man sagged in his boots as the muscle there spasmed. A flurry of bladed hands rocked the terrorist from side to side and back and forth. The man's arms dropped; he slid to his knees. Concho stood over him, looking down at the bloody face, the busted mouth, the swelling cheekbones.

"No…no more," Fallon whispered.

Concho cocked his fist.

"Please!" begged Fallon.

Concho glanced over at the paramedic and at Maria Morales. Her eyes fluttered open, then closed again, seemingly without awareness of her surroundings. But Concho felt as if her heartbeat reverberated in his chest.

"She's going to live," the paramedic said into Concho's gaze.

The Ranger opened his fist. Fallon slumped into a sitting position with a sigh of relief. Concho stepped to one side, glanced at the half dozen police officers with nightsticks to hand who'd come up behind them while the two battled.

Looking around, Concho said, "Doesn't look like the press is filming us quite yet."

He turned to move toward Maria as the officers closed in on Darrel Fallon, and the terrorist began to scream.

CHAPTER 9

"She was drugged," the paramedic said, as Concho squatted beside them. "But she's starting to come out of it."

"How do you know?" Concho asked.

The paramedic pointed to the crook of Maria's elbow, marked with a little red spot and a dried flake of blood. "You can see where the needle went in," the man said. "Some kind of anesthetic. Probably chloral hydrate. But her heartbeat is good and her breathing is getting deeper."

Concho nodded.

Two other paramedics, a man and a woman, came up pushing a lowered stretcher. Concho could only watch and feel helpless as the three professionals lifted the dark-haired woman he'd once dated onto the stretcher, then raised it up to transfer into the ambulance.

As the first paramedic climbed into the back of the ambulance with Maria, he smiled at the hovering Concho. "We'll take good care of her. I'm sure she's going to be fine."

"Where...." Concho cleared his throat of gruffness. "Where are you taking her?"

"Fort Duncan Regional Medical Center," the man said. "She'll probably be waking up by the time we get there. You might even be able to see her in the emergency room."

The man pulled the ambulance doors shut and the vehicle started off through the milling crowd, which quickly parted to let them pass. Concho watched, and, as if a switch had been flipped, the world came snapping back into existence. Once more he heard the helicopters circling overhead. The heat and humidity of the Texas midday began to hammer at him. He smelled engine exhaust and oil and sweat and blood.

Turning around, he watched a bruised Darrel Fallon with his hands cuffed behind him being led away. The white supremacist's head hung down. Freedom hadn't lasted very long for him. He'd soon be back in prison, and watched much more careful for any future escape attempts.

A restlessness possessed Concho. He picked up his bow and the .30-06 he'd dropped when he launched himself into Fallon, and slid them again over his shoulders. He considered following the ambulance to the hospital but didn't think Maria would be glad to see him when she awoke.

She had family, who didn't care much for Concho. She'd want *them* around her, not someone who'd become almost a stranger, who certainly felt as if he didn't belong. Taking out his cell phone, he entered a *67 before tapping in a number from memory. The phone rang five times. Someone answered in Spanish.

"Hola."

"Mrs. Morales," he said slowly, knowing her English was weak. "I need to tell you. Your daughter, Maria, is being taken to Fort Duncan Regional hospital. They say she's going to be OK."

"Maria! Hurt! Who…is these?"

Concho hesitated a moment, then said, "A friend," before disconnecting. He'd only spoken to Maria's mother, Rosa, a few times. And only in Spanish. He didn't think she'd recognize his voice when speaking English, and he'd blocked his number from showing on her phone. He wasn't sure why.

Tucking the phone in a pocket, Concho started toward the back of the mall to check on the hostages he'd sent out that way.

Someone moved to confront him and he stopped to wait. The man was probably around 5'10" and nearing fifty but looked fit in a black jacket labeled SWAT.

"Concho Ten-Wolves," the man said, his voice brisk and measured.

Concho nodded as he noticed the insignia the man wore. "Captain," he said. "If you're here to give me shit for entering the mall ahead of you, may I suggest you get in line?"

The Captain looked suddenly amused. He held out his hand and Concho shook it.

"Adrian Lastra," the man said. "And yes, I'm going to give you shit. You tossed a whole lot of rules out the window today. Officially, you're in a world of trouble."

"So, if I say I'm feeling all cut down to size, will that make it better?"

Lastra chuckled as he eyed Concho's big frame. "Seems like cutting you down to size would take some doing."

"The bigger they are...."

"The harder they fall?"

Concho let a small grin curve his lips. "I was gonna say, the bigger they are, use a chainsaw."

"Let's hope the coming chainsaw doesn't cut too deep," Lastra said. He gestured over his shoulder at the mall. "You did some amazing work in there. Freed seventy-two hostages, killed seven well-armed terrorists, and recaptured a fugitive wanted for all sorts of crimes. And all while the FBI were waiting for a phone call from Darrel Fallon to tell 'em how high he wanted 'em to jump."

"Six terrorists, sir," Concho said.

"What?"

"I killed six terrorists. Captured one alive. Besides Fallon."

"Right," Lastra said. "Six."

"I believe there were ten in total. Your guys killed one. Fallon made nine. Did you catch the tenth?"

"We did," Lastra said. "They blew a hole in the floor in the bathroom trying to access the maintenance tunnels under the mall and use them to get to the sewer. The one we caught was quite talkative. Maybe even a little disillusioned. Said using the sewers was Fallon's plan to get his people out safely. Of course, we know Fallon had a different plan, one he didn't share with his followers."

"Did you find any more hostages?"

Lastra's smile faded. "We found five male hostages dead. Fallon separated the younger men from the women and children early. According to the gang member we caught, Fallon personally executed the five we found before the first police officer arrived on the scene. Two security guards were among the five. A third security guard and another man were still alive. They claimed that Fallon told them he was going to shoot them in front of witnesses to emphasize the seriousness of his demands. He never had time. The 'Rangers' arrived."

"And what were their demands?"

"Money. Safe passage. The release of other Brotherhood members still in prison. They also had backpack bombs and even a few grenades. Seems they were going to use the negotiating period to get their explosives set. Supposedly to bring down the mall on the hostages and to cover their escape through the sewers. You going in early threw their timing off. You saved a lot of lives and some expensive property today."

"Maybe you should tell it to my Captain," Concho said.

"I will," Lastra said. "*Unofficially*, of course."

"Naturally," Concho agreed. "You take care, sir. I'm going to go check on those other hostages."

"One last thing," Lastra said. "I looked over several of the AR-15s most of the gang were carrying. Half of them had been converted to full auto. All the serial numbers were filed off. We recovered some other military-grade weapons. These scuzzballs were well supplied and armed for bear."

The morning he thought he'd wasted flashed into Concho's

head. What if the makeshift shooting range along White-Tail Creek had been more than just a place for locals to take target practice? Could it have been a staging area for today's raid? He'd have to make sure someone took a closer look. He said as much to Lastra.

The SWAT Captain's eyes filled with speculation. "Thanks for the info," he said. "I'll get forensics on it. Maybe they can match some tire prints or boot prints. Probably too much to hope for."

"You never know," Concho said. "I'll see if I can find any information on the gun trail. Whoever supplied Darrel Fallon has more. Maybe enough to arm another bunch just like this."

"Sounds like a good place to start," Lastra said. "I'll let you get back to it." The two shook hands again before they parted.

The parking lot behind the mall was even busier than the front lot. If that were possible. Concho didn't see as many ambulances; some must have already pulled out for the hospital with patients aboard. But numerous police officers were interviewing numerous hostages, many with blankets around their shoulders despite the morning's heat. Cups of coffee or bottled water seemed to fill most hands.

The young man he'd met inside, Nathan Taylor, was nowhere to be seen. The blonde hostage, Eliza, was talking animatedly to a police officer who seemed as intent on the woman as he did on her story. Everything looked under control.

Feeling the inevitable let down of an adrenaline high, Concho returned to his F-150. He unloaded the .30-06 and returned it to its rifle case, then carefully wrapped his bow and quiver of arrows in an oilcloth and tucked it in the back of the Ford's extended cab. He'd used two of his dozen arrows. He'd have to replace them. It was important to keep the number at twelve.

He had wiped off his warpaint and was taking off his body armor when he heard footsteps approaching. Turning, he saw Pete Bishop walking up. Pete stood close to six feet, with a craggy, clean-shaven face and short brown hair laced with a few gray strands. He was closing in on forty and still a patrol officer. This had more to do with his "seldom-by-the-book" attitude than it did with his abilities. It was probably why he and Concho got along so well.

"Quite a few of those hostages are singing your praises," Bishop said as he shook Concho's hand.

"What can I say," Concho replied with a shrug. "An angel's gotta fly."

Bishop laughed heartily. "Right!"

Concho smiled. "Everything good?"

"Some nervous exhaustion. A sprained ankle for one woman. A couple were roughed up a bit by the terrorists before you pulled 'em out. The ambulances took half a dozen to the hospital for routine precautions. The rest are good. In amazingly fine shape considering the circumstances. We actually found three other people hiding. So far. The number of saved continues to grow."

"Glad to hear it."

"I didn't see Maria."

Concho explained about Fallon attempting to escape by using the woman as a distraction.

"Glad you got the son of a bitch. Sounds like Maria's going to be OK. You going to see her?"

Concho shook his head. "I called her mother. She's got a lot of family. There'll be a crowd. No one will miss me."

Bishop shook his head. "You ain't that smart are you, Ten-Wolves?"

The big man shrugged. "Never said I was."

The radio in Concho's truck squawked. The Ranger dispatcher asked for Concho to "Come back."

Pete tipped an imaginary hat to his friend and turned away with an "Uh-oh" and a "see you later."

Concho grasped the speaker and said, "Here."

There came a moment of silence. A voice that was not the dispatcher's came on the line. Max Keller, Concho's commanding officer in the Texas Rangers, spoke as he if were chewing each word twenty times before uttering it.

"You *were* told," Keller said. "That you were backup. Right?"

"I was told," Concho agreed.

"So, you disobeyed a direct order?"

"I improvised in a fluid situation."

A fresh silence lingered. Then, "Don't bother coming into work for the next week. There's going to be some discussion about your future in the Texas Rangers."

The radio went dead. Concho slid into his truck and drove away from the Mall de las Aguilas.

CHAPTER 10

Some eight miles southeast of Eagle Pass lay Kickapoo Village, a reservation site for the Kickapoo Tribe of Texas. Many of the members had dual citizenship in both the US and Mexico. The one hundred and twenty-five acres upon which the village sat had been purchased by the tribe in 1984 and was sometimes called Nuevo Nacimiento. The reservation's administrative offices had been built there. The new Kickapoo Lucky Eagle Casino and Hotel stood there. Many tribal members had homes in the village, though many also kept residences in Mexico at the original Nacimiento, near the town of Múzquiz, in the state of Coahuila.

Concho lived outside Kickapoo village, in a new trailer placed on the site of the old trailer where he'd grown up with his grand-mother. His mother had been a full-blood Kickapoo. Local gossip, weaponized against him as a kid, claimed she'd sold Concho as an infant for a fix of heroin. According to his grandmother, his moth-er was dead but there was no truth to the rumors about her. He had no memories of his own to contest the two stories; he'd always assumed the truth lay somewhere in between.

His father had been black, described at various times by various people as a drug dealer, pimp, gangbanger. His grand-mother, who quite possibly had never met the man, had just said she didn't like him, that she didn't know what he did and didn't care. To her, Concho was a Kickapoo and nothing else. For a long time, she'd seemed the only tribal member who thought that way, though over the years he'd earned acceptance, oftentimes grudging, from a few others.

After leaving the mall site, Concho drove around for a while. He called the hospital to check on Maria and found she was conscious and soon to be released. Happy for that but still feeling an unaccountable melancholy, he finally turned toward home.

Pulling up in his yard, he shut off the engine. His truck windows were down. A little breeze teased him, then fled. He climbed out of the Ford. The yard was about half dirt and rock and half various species of dry-land grasses and shrubs. A stand of mixed mesquite and juniper trees grew just behind the trailer, on the edge of an old arroyo. Prickly pear clustered at each corner of the house.

Under a blue sky, low hills dotted with dull green sage and other brush stood off at a distance behind the gray trailer. The trailer itself, a double-wide, sat upon a concrete slab, with a set of six wooden steps leading up to a postage-stamp-sized porch and the door. As Concho approached the steps, a vicious rattling sound came from underneath them.

"Just me, Maggie. Just me," Concho murmured.

Someone cleared their throat behind Concho and he spun swiftly. About twenty yards from his front door grew a very large mesquite tree with wide spreading limbs to provide rich shade in a shade-poor land. Beneath the tree, two nylon chairs sat next to a small firepit where Concho sometimes spent his evenings. One of the chairs, a green and white striped affair, was occupied.

Concho felt his eyebrows arch. He'd been in the army special forces. He wasn't easy to sneak up on. But either the man had been sitting in the chair when Concho pulled into the yard, or he'd come out of the brush behind it and seated himself while the Ranger's back was turned. Whichever it was, Concho had missed it. At least he knew who the man was, and he wasn't a danger—to him.

"Uncle," Concho said as he walked up to the man. "You honor me with a visit."

The man snorted. "I know your heart, Ten-Wolves. You insult this old man."

"Yes, I remember insulting him last week with two fresh rabbits. Proving the great Meskwaa is too old to hunt for himself."

The man Concho called Meskwaa, meaning "red" in Kickapoo, smiled with a full set of teeth, which were mostly still white, albeit crooked. Concho did not know this man's true age. When asked, Meskwaa often claimed to be more than a hundred, but the Ranger guessed it was closer to seventy. He wore a faded red cotton shirt and a new blue neckerchief tied loosely about his thin neck. His trousers were of fringed buckskin. The broad-brimmed hat on his head had once been gray but was now called "the hat of many stains." One stain looked like it had been made by mustard, though how it had gotten on the crown of the hat, Concho had no idea.

"Rabbit," Meskwaa said. "Good eating with dumplings. I remember honoring you by accepting your offering to your betters. And in return, I offer you…"

The old man pulled a small sack of red-dyed doeskin from his shirt pocket and opened it to reveal a jumbled pile of gleaming white cigarettes from which the filters had been pulled.

The offering of a smoke was no medicine ritual and Concho refused with a polite "Thanks, but no."

Meskwaa shrugged, took a cigarette for himself and returned the sack to his pocket. Striking a match with a thick yellow thumbnail, the old man lit his smoke and inhaled gratefully. Shaking out the match, he stuck it in the pocket beside the sack. The harsh smell of tobacco warred with the sweeter scent of the mesquite that shaded them.

The old Kickapoo was sitting in the biggest of the two lawn chairs, the one Concho normally sat in. He slipped carefully into the other chair, which creaked dangerously under his weight. It was a tight fit.

"I remember," Concho said, "when you used to hand roll your tobacco in corn-husks. Looks like you're smoking store-bought now. Or casino bought, I imagine. Reckon it saves time."

"Time! You sound like a white man."

"Humph," Concho snorted. "Saves effort then. It's easier."

"Easy. Yes." Meskwaa shook his head. "Such an awful thing. Easy. The sweet moments of life should not come easily. You do not appreciate them. That is what is wrong with the young ones today. Everything comes too easily."

"You counting me as young, old man?"

Meskwaa nodded. "It starts precisely at your age. And all those younger than you. Who knows what will become of the people? Even I may not be able to save them from their follies."

"So why are you smoking the *easy* cigarettes?" Concho asked.

Meskwaa shrugged again. "I am an old man. I do not want to die while waiting around for a little pleasure. Besides, I'm lazy."

Concho chuckled. "So tell me why you're here. You didn't come to lecture me about my age."

"I came because I had a vision. Only a short time ago."

"What vision?"

"Many people running. Screaming. Evil men threatening women and children and stone wickiups full of pretty white man toys. But the great hero came riding. He saved the day."

"Really!" Concho said. "And where do you think this vision came from?"

Waving his cigarette around, Meskwaa sketched a circle of smoke in the air. "It came from the sky. As all visions do."

"From the sky? You mean, you saw it on the TV news."

Meskwaa spat out a bit of burnt paper and grinned. "Indeed. I did not lie. A 'special bulletin,' the pretty lady called it."

"And you actually saw *me* in this special bulletin?"

"Surely there are not two in the world so monstrous as you."

Concho shook his head. "I wonder where they got the footage?" But as soon as he asked the question, he knew. The boy, Nathan Taylor. He'd been holding up his phone when Concho started herding the hostages toward him. Now the Ranger understood why. He'd been filming the scene. Probably uploaded it immediately to YouTube, if he hadn't sold it directly to a news station.

"It'll just give people around here more reason to complain about me," he said.

Meskwaa's cigarette had burned to nothing but a glowing nub. He pinched out the ember with a callused thumb and forefinger and tucked the remnant in his shirt pocket. He always saved the last shreds of tobacco from one cig to roll into another. Waste was not a part of his life, or the lives of most Kickapoo.

"People complain about the summer heat, too," Meskwaa said. "But the heat is inevitable. Better to learn to live with it."

"So," Concho said, "I'm like the heat, eh? I cause a rash and just have to be tolerated?"

"Meh," Meskwaa said. "The heat is not so bad." He gestured to the mesquite over their heads. "Not if you have a little shade. *I* am like the shade that makes the Ten-Wolves' heatwave tolerable."

Concho laughed as the little old man rose from his chair with remarkable spryness.

"By the way," Meskwaa added, as he turned to go. "My vision held more. This did not come from the TV news."

Concho frowned. From the old man's tone, this was not a joke. "Tell me," he said.

"Two men dead." He slashed his hand through the air in a flat line. "Hanging. I think the great hero's work is not quite done. He should be careful. There are things hidden. And those exposed. It is not always easy to tell which is which."

Without waiting for comment, the old man turned and walked away. His gait was that of a much younger person. The Ranger let his gaze follow him, then leaned back in his chair and closed his eyes for a few minutes to calm his thoughts. He remembered the last time Meskwaa had shared a vision with him. He remembered the havoc it had brought.

CHAPTER 11

Concho unlocked his front door and stepped into his liv-ing room. The trailer was clean and neat and still relatively cool from the morning. Bookshelves lined two walls in the large room. In a back bedroom were more shelves. Those were full of nonfiction works on language and history and law, but the books in this room were fiction and poetry.

He recognized the authors from the spines on the books: Poe and Bradbury, Hemingway and Steinbeck, Harjo and northSun, Brackett and Moore, Jackson and Atwood, Momaday and Angelou, Thomas and Baldwin, McMurty and McCarthy, MacDonald and McBain, Burroughs and Howard. As a boy and a young man, he'd escaped into many of those worlds—escaped from poverty and gossip and too much real-life conflict. It would be nice to pick up a book and fall into it. But he didn't have the luxury.

Against a third wall in the room stood a flatscreen TV and an old stereo, which included an ancient turntable that still worked. Meskwaa said he'd seen the story about the mall attack on a special bulletin, but Concho doubted he'd find it easily on the television. He headed toward the rear of the house.

The master bedroom lay upfront but there were two more small bedrooms here, a guest room and one which the Ranger had turned into a home office. He entered that room with its three walls of bookshelves and flicked on the computer, then took a quick bathroom break while the machine booted up. His internet connection was satellite based. Loading Google, he typed "Eagle Pass Mall, terrorist attack" into the search line. The first hit was a replay of the video Meskwaa had mentioned.

As Concho had expected, the scene had been filmed using a phone camera with a video app. It was surprisingly sharp, though, with good sound quality. He could see it had already been shared numerous times.

"Guess this is what 'trending' means," he muttered to himself.

Concho watched himself take out two Aryan brotherhood members, one of whom was threatening hostages and the other who was shooting at him. The kill he'd made with his bow was not included. Probably a good thing.

His interactions with the hostages were almost lovingly featured. Picking up and carrying the small boy who'd fallen would play particularly well with the public. Concho felt a momentary surge of anger toward Nathan Taylor. He wished he'd realized what the young man was doing and smashed the kid's phone. Too late now. He was famous and he never wanted to be.

At least, he thought, *maybe it'll only be fifteen minutes before the public moves on to someone else.*

The only good thing that might come out of the publicity is how hard it would be for Max Keller to fire a hero cop. Keller and Concho had history, and not of the pleasant sort. Keller didn't like Concho and would be happy to see him gone. Concho didn't like Keller either, but he liked a lot of things about being a Texas Ranger. For now, one came with the other.

His cell phone rang. He didn't recognize the number but it was listed as KVAW—Channel 16, the main local TV news station. Concho hit the hang-up button. Almost immediately, the cell rang again. He hung up a second time and put the phone on vibrate. Next, they'd be looking for him in person. But not many people knew where he lived. It would take the newshounds a while to find him.

So, what should he do in the meantime? The core truth he'd discovered during his days in Army Ranger training was simple. He'd follow it now. Eat and sleep when you can, because there'll be a time when you can't.

***

Concho habitually rose at 6:00 AM. At 6:30 he got another call. This one he took.

"Sheriff," he said into the phone. "What can I do for you?"

"Concho," Isaac Parkland said. "Hope I didn't wake you." Parkland was the Sheriff of Maverick County. Concho had worked with him on local cases and respected him. The respect seemed to be mutual.

"Been up a while," Concho replied. "What's going on?"

Since quitting smoking, Parkland had developed a habit of chewing on a toothpick. Over the phone, Concho heard the sound of the man switching the splinter of wood from one side of his mouth to the other.

"Got a situation you might be able to help me with," Parkland said. "A murder. Two of 'em actually."

"Considering I've been 'offered' a leave of absence from my job as of yesterday, I've got some time. Where do you need me?"

"It's down by the casino. You know the fence between the Rez and the rest of Maverick County. You'll see the lights."

"Gotcha. Be there in twenty."

"Appreciate it."

Concho ended the call, threw on his clothes, buckled his gun belt, and rushed to his truck through the early morning's light. It seemed like Meskwaa's vision of "two men dead" had already come true. But who were they and why did he wish that he didn't have to find out?

CHAPTER 12

As Sheriff Parkland had suggested, flashing blue lights guided Concho to the crime scene, which lay down a short dirt road branching off the main highway and leading to the Kickapoo reservation. It was barely three-quarters of a mile from the Kickapoo Lucky Eagle Casino and Hotel.

Concho pulled to the side of the road and slid out of his truck, leaving his own dash-mounted police light flashing. Only two other vehicles were here so far. One was Parkland's dark blue Chevy Tahoe with "Maverick County Sheriff, To Protect and Serve" painted on the side; the other was a black and white Dodge Charger Police interceptor. The latter would be driven by Terrill Hoight, one of Parkland's deputies.

Deputy Hoight, immaculate in black jeans and a brown uniform shirt worn tight enough to emphasize his gym-built physique for the ladies, leaned against his car talking into the microphone attached to his collar. He offered Concho a two-fingered salute and the Ranger acknowledged it with a nod of his head.

Sheriff Isaac Parkland stood across the roadside ditch on a patch of seared brown grass next to a barbed wire fence and two bodies. Parkland's white, long-sleeved western-style shirt was tucked into crisp new blue jeans; a white ten-gallon hat rested on his nearly bald head. Eschewing the more standard semi-automatics that were popular with most law officers these days, Cortland carried a Colt Trooper with a four-inch barrel in a holster riding high on his right hip. The sheriff stripped off the blue latex gloves he was wearing and shook Concho's hand.

"Good work at the mall yesterday," Parkland said.

"You'd have done the same."

Parkland chuckled. "Twenty years ago and fifty pounds lighter maybe. But probably not even then."

Parkland was a short man, about 5'7", and, as he'd said, fifty pounds heavier than his ideal weight. He could still handle himself.

"Thanks for getting here so quickly," Parkland added.

"Nothing better to do. What have we got?"

Parkland stepped to one side and gestured for Concho to have a look. The Ranger shook away a wince. The bodies of two men had been displayed like a museum exhibit. They'd been hung up facing forward, with their arms hooked over the top strand of the barb-wire fence and their hands tied to their belts to keep them from sliding down. The deaths were recent, and there was no smell of decay. There weren't even any flies yet—despite the blood smear on one of them.

The body on the left was a Kickapoo, a man in his early sixties dressed casually in a checked cotton shirt, faded jeans, and moccasins. The gray hair was cut short. A small feather earring dangled from the left earlobe. The throat had been hacked open with something barely sharp enough to do the job. The edges of the cut were torn and ragged.

"You know that's Ben Deer-Run, I guess," Concho said, pointing to the body. "Chief of the tribal police here."

"I know Ben," Parkland agreed.

"Must have been off duty," Concho added. "He's not wearing his uniform. Did you call Daniel Alvarado?"

Parkland shook his head. "Wasn't sure who to call. There's a lot of turnover in Ben's office. Don't know his current deputies. Or their phone numbers."

Concho nodded and took a deep breath. "Alvarado is next in line. And not an easy man to get along with. I'll give him a call in a few minutes."

"Appreciate it," Parkland said. "Knew you'd be of help. What do you make of the scene?"

Concho glanced at Parkland from the corner of an eye. Surely, the sheriff wasn't testing him by asking such a question? But the older police officer seemed intent on the body and Concho realized the man just wanted confirmation of his own thoughts.

"Well, considering how the blood sprayed in a fan shape across the ground in front of the body, and how those barbs of the fence are buried in Ben's arms, the cut was made *after* he'd been bound here. And it was done from behind."

"What I figured, too," Parkland agreed.

"Whoever did it, seems he wanted Ben to suffer. Looks almost like he used a saw blade."

Parkland winced himself. "Yeah, yeah. Looks the same to me."

"Any idea who the other guy is?"

"Nope. Was hoping you might. Given the location."

Concho stepped closer to the second body. The man was late-middle-aged, maybe a few years over fifty. He wore khaki pants and a striped sweater. He was African American, standing a little over six feet but weighing shy of two hundred pounds. Skinny, with gray-peppered hair clinging close to his scalp, he had an oval face with even features. For a moment, the shape of the face brought a feeling of familiarity. It didn't last.

"Don't know him," Concho said. "Is the coroner on the way?"

"Yep," the sheriff said. "I expect he'll get a DNA sample. And we'll take fingerprints. We should know pretty soon who it is."

"OK, let me give Alvarado a call. He'll be pissed if he doesn't get a chance to see the scene laid out like it is."

Parkland sighed. "Whoever killed 'em wanted to complicate my life, it appears. Set 'em right here on the border between the reservation and the county. The jurisdiction issues alone are going to give me ulcers."

Concho studied the surroundings. Low, rugged hills covered in mesquite, juniper, desert willow and saltbush loomed on one side of the scene. There were few roads and fewer houses into that area. In the other direction lay the casino, less than a mile away across a stretch of prairie. Its glass windows gleamed with the newly risen sun. The victims could have been walked from there last night. Or they could have been brought in by the main road. If they'd been walked, footprints would confirm it.

"The perps didn't much try to hide it," Concho said to the sheriff. "Anyone driving by in the daylight would likely see it. Who reported it?"

"A sales fellow coming along the road about five this morning."

"In the dark?"

"Yeah. But he didn't report 'em specifically as bodies. Just said he'd seen something odd. Hoight was on patrol and drew the assignment. He called me. We'll run a check on the guy, of course."

"I don't see any wounds on the second man," Concho said. "No marks on the throat. Any idea how *he* died?"

"Not sure. Not by bullet or knife. Or strangulation. Working on the assumption it's a drug overdose. The coroner will be able to tell."

Concho nodded, then strode a few steps away from the sheriff as he pulled out his cell phone and selected a never-used number in his contact list to punch. The phone rang seven, eight, nine times, before a voice slurred with sleepiness answered.

"Ten-Wolves! What the hell do you want? This better be good."

"It's not good, Alvarado. Not good at all. Drive over toward the casino and follow the lights. Your boss is dead and it ain't pretty."

CHAPTER 13

The throb of a heavy-duty exhaust system vibrated through the morning and Concho watched as a bright red Ford Mustang came wheeling along the highway and turned in at the murder scene. The vehicle pulled over to one side behind Concho's truck and the engine died. The morning grew quiet again.

Sheriff Parkland glanced over at Concho and lifted an eyebrow. The car was a Mustang GT Premium with the 5.0 tag on the side indicating a 5-liter V-8 engine. It looked like a 2020 model and both Concho and Isaac Parkland knew these vehicles were expensive—probably in the $40,000 range. It was true the casino paid monthly dividends to the tribe but this car still wasn't within reach of most members. It certainly wasn't in Concho's reach and he received the same check as the Mustang's driver.

Daniel Alvarado, the number one deputy in the Texas Kickapoo Tribal Police Force, climbed out of the car. He was a big man, almost as big as Concho, with long, straight black hair hanging down his back, with the front strands pulled back and held behind his head with a silver and turquoise clasp. Alvarado wore his uniform, black pants and a dark brown short-sleeved shirt, but over the shirt he'd thrown on a fringed buckskin jacket. The gun at his hip was a Glock 40, a big, powerful semi-automatic chambered for 10 mm rounds.

Alvarado crossed the ditch toward Concho and Parkland. He didn't even glance at Concho but focused on Parkland for a moment, examining the sheriff as if the man were a leftover sandwich he was trying to decide whether to eat or discard. Parkland offered his hand and Alvarado shook it, then stepped past and stood studying the body of Ben Deer-Run. His black eyes missed nothing. After a couple of minutes, the big deputy walked over to the second corpse but didn't spend much time studying this one before turning back to Parkland.

"The coroner on the way?"

"Yep," Parkland said. "Should be here any minute."

"I'll expect a copy of the report."

"You'll have it right after I do."

Alvarado looked around. His eyes lingered on the casino across the way. "They could have been walked over from the casino," he said. "I'll check the video recordings."

"Good idea to check the recordings," Concho said. "But I walked the field myself. No sign of any foot traffic between here and the casino. Looks like they were brought in by vehicle."

Alvarado's gaze flickered briefly toward Concho and returned to Parkland. "Why is this man here?" he asked the sheriff. "And why would you have contacted him before you called me?"

"Wasn't sure who Ben's next in line was," Parkland said, shrugging. "Figured Officer Ten-Wolves here would know."

"*Officer* Ten-Wolves has no jurisdiction in this matter," Alvarado said. "In fact, considering that fence is part of the territory of the Kickapoo Tribe of Texas, neither do you."

"Can't agree with you there, Deputy Alvarado," Parkland said firmly. "The bodies are more on my side of the fence than yours. And my office took the call. Concho was invited in as a consultant on my part."

Alvarado took a deep breath. His obsidian-flake eyes glittered. The breeze stirred his hair. He seemed to be considering a bitter retort but came out with only, "For now."

"When was the last time you talked to Ben?" Concho asked.

Alvarado took another breath. "As far as I knew, he left three days ago for Nacimiento. He has a grandchild on the way."

"Nacimiento! Is that where his daughter lives?" Parkland asked.

Alvarado shook his head as if he were being confronted by idiots. "Let the half Kickapoo tell you," he said. "I'm going over to the casino to see if they have any video that might help. I want all the crime scene reports and photos as soon as they're ready."

He stalked away from the scene and back to his car.

Concho watched Alvarado go, saw him speak briefly to Deputy Hoight before getting in his car and leaving. The coroner's van pulled in as the new head of the Kickapoo Tribal Police pulled out.

Parkland glanced at Concho again. "I see what you mean about him being difficult. Appears you two ain't exactly bosom buddies. Anything I should know?"

Concho shrugged. "We grew up together. Went to school together. He was a couple of years older. Used to beat the shit out of me. Until it got to where I could beat the shit out of him. Appears he hasn't forgiven and forgotten."

"What was he talking about with Ben's grandchild and Nacimiento?"

"Ben's daughter lives here but Nacimiento is…well, a sacred place. If Ben was going there at this time, it would likely be to hunt deer. It's part of the naming ritual for a child. Normally the father makes an offering of four deer. But Ben's son-in-law. He's…no hunter."

"Obviously Ben didn't go there though. So why did he tell Alvarado he planned to?"

"If he did tell him?" Concho said.

Parkland looked startled. "You think Alvarado lied?"

"Daniel Alvarado speaks lies easier than he speaks the truth. But I don't know if he lied in this case. I need to speak to Ben's daughter, Estrella. She'll know if her father was going to Nacimiento. I'll have to tell her about Ben's death, too. I doubt Alvarado will."

"Those two don't get along either?"

"Not a lick. Though once upon a time, Alvarado sure wanted to get along with her."

"Good to know," Parkland said. "Just let me talk to the coroner a minute, and I'll go with you. I want to hear what she has to say."

"Might not be a good idea," Concho said.

"You mean, because it's on the reservation?"

"Yes."

Parkland considered. "How about if I'm just along but let you ask all the questions? Alvarado can't complain too much about that, can he?"

"He will, but he'll complain about *me* asking her questions even more. Just remember, Estrella won't talk about Nacimiento in front of a white man. No offense."

"Fine," Parkland said. "If I need to walk away at some point, I will."

"All right," Concho said.

"Gimme a minute to deal with the coroner."

Concho nodded. He turned back toward the dead bodies, but it was the black man he studied most. The feeling of familiarity came back. He could see no reason for it. It made him uneasy and he recalled Meskwaa speaking yesterday of his vision.

"Something hidden but now exposed," Concho murmured to himself. "Something rising from the past."

He'd read enough gothic novels to know that never ended well.

CHAPTER 14

Once the coroner and his assistants started their work at the crime scene, Concho and Sheriff Isaac Parkland climbed into Concho's truck and headed to the reservation. They drove in silence for a while.

"So," Parkland said after a bit, "what's the background on Ben Deer-Run's daughter and her husband?"

"Estrella is a teacher's aide for the Eagle Pass Independent school system," Concho said. "They're off for the summer now, of course. She's about six months pregnant."

"You said the husband was 'no hunter.' What's that supposed to mean?"

"Not really my place to say. There are things for which I do not respect him."

Parkland nodded. "Fair enough."

They took Lucky Eagle Drive past the casino and past a modern looking daycare and head start center with a nice green lawn and a fenced-in playground. A sign at the entrance to the center read: "All Visitors *Must* Check in at Police Headquarters ahead." Concho ignored it even though Sheriff Parkland was just such a visitor.

Soon, they reached Kickapoo village with its interesting mixture of buildings—old trailers and manufactured homes, cinder block-houses, and a number of new wood and brick frame structures. Another mile or so on a dirt road brought them to Ben Deer-Run's place. This, too, was built of cinder blocks, of once-white blocks weathered to gray. The wooden frame of a much bigger and more modern home stood under construction about a hundred yards away, although no workers were around today.

A stand of desert willow and a few oak trees offered shade for the cinder blockhouse. The yard was mostly dirt. Concho parked beneath the limbs of a large oak. The door and screen to the house both opened as Concho and Parkland climbed out of the truck. A woman stepped out onto the concrete steps, one of her hands resting on her swollen belly.

Parkland took off his big hat and held it awkwardly in front of him. Concho raised a hand in a wave. Estrella, the daughter of Ben Deer-Run, did not wave back. She had dark curly hair that barely reached her shoulders, and wore a loose, multi-colored dress and flip-flop sandals.

"Concho Ten-Wolves," Estrella said. "Why do you come here? And," her gaze shifted past Concho to Isaac Parkland, "with a white policeman? If you seek my husband, he is not home."

"I'm sorry to bother you, Estrella," Concho said. "This has nothing to do with your husband. I have…some other news for you."

Her lips pursed in a look of distaste. "Bad news, no doubt."

Concho nodded but refused to sigh in front of her. A few times he'd had to give people the kind of bad news he was bringing to Estrella. It never got easier. But he'd always found it best to be clear from the beginning, even if it meant coming off as blunt.

"Your father, Estrella. He's dead. He was murdered over near the casino sometime last night."

Estrella's eyes widened in shock. She shook her head, licked her lips. "No! That's not…true."

"I'm afraid it is. I saw him myself. I came straight from there to tell you."

Estrella swayed. Her hand grabbed at the door frame to steady herself. Concho stepped quickly toward her but she jerked her free hand up, palm out and facing him. He stopped at her gesture. After a moment, her legs seemed to strengthen. She let go of the doorjamb, then said with seeming calmness, "You'd both better come in." Then, she disappeared back inside.

The main door to the house stood open. The screen had closed. Concho pulled it back, held it until Parkland caught it, then stepped on into the house. Parkland followed and closed the door behind him. They were standing in a living room, a small square room packed with two couches and a big TV stand along one wall. Both couches were cluttered with toys and unfolded clothes.

A small girl of four or so stood in one corner of the room watching them with bright marble eyes. Estrella pushed some clothes aside on one couch and sat ponderously down. She glanced at the girl. "Go on out back and play. Now!"

The girl trotted quickly from the room, although she did not take her eyes off Concho and Parkland until she was gone. There weren't any other places to sit so Concho and Parkland stood— Concho easily, and Parkland uncomfortably as he twisted his hat brim around and around in his hands.

"How…how did it happen?" Estrella asked.

"He was knifed," Concho said. "There was another man dead, too. A black man. Looked about fifty. Very thin. Have you ever seen your father with such a man?"

Estrella shook her head.

"Deputy Alvarado said—" Estrella's head came up abruptly at the mention of Alvarado's name. Her brown eyes were direct and alive, and not yet ready to fill with tears. They seemed angry more than anything.

"Alvarado said your father was supposed to have gone to Nacimiento three days ago," Concho continued. "Did you know about that?"

Estrella winced and her hands tightened over her belly as if the baby had kicked her. She took a deep breath.

"He told everyone he was going there. To Nacimiento. Including me. But I did not think he had really gone."

"Why?" Concho asked.

"Unlike some other Kickapoo I know," she said bitterly, "my father was not good at lying."

"No," Concho said. "Your father was an honest man. What do think he really did? Or planned to do?"

Estrella shrugged.

"What about confrontations? Anyone who he had particular problems with lately?"

"The Bloods."

A series of flashbulb memories rocked Concho. His grand-mother's face, her smoker's voice, the old, beat-up El Camino that Concho had driven as a teenager, the one that had belonged to a grandfather he barely remembered. The distant sound of an ex-plosion, which he'd heard one day while catching birds in the scru-bland. And the aftermath—the flashing lights, sirens, the news that someone had planted a bomb in the El Camino and, for reasons unknown, his grandmother had decided to drive the car that day.

The Ranger's thoughts came back to the present. His fists were clenched and he forced his fingers to loosen. He glanced over at Parkland, who was looking confused. "Indian gang," Concho ex-plained. "They call themselves the NATV Bloods. But I didn't think they were much active on the Rez these days."

Estrella gave a strangled chuckle. "You would know something about that, Ten-Wolves."

Again, Sheriff Parkland looked confused. Now, Concho shrugged.

Turning back to Estrella, Concho asked, "So, the Bloods are making a comeback?"

"For a few months," the woman said. "And growing stronger of late. It had been giving my father night fits. As I think on it, perhaps it is why he lied about going to Nacimiento. Maybe he was looking into the actions of the Bloods and didn't want anyone to know."

Concho nodded. "Do you know the names of any of the gang members?"

"No. These things are not shared with the women."

"Thank you for the help you've given," Concho said. "I'm very sorry about your father. And you know I respected him."

"I know."

"It's not good for you to be alone," Concho said. "Where is Bearfoot?"

"My husband has not graced our home with his presence for nearly a week. When you mentioned the second man dead, I thought for an instant it would be him. But that would be too easy."

"You have someone to call?"

"As soon as you leave, I will call my clan. I will not be alone for long."

Concho nodded. "Be well, Estrella."

The Ranger turned to go and gave Isaac Parkland the nod to follow.

"Ma'am," Parkland said to Estrella as he trailed Concho outside.

Concho carefully shut the door to the house, then led the way to the truck. Parkland put his hat back on as he climbed in the passenger side.

"Terrible to have to bring such news to someone," he said.

"Yes."

"Her husband's name is 'Bearfoot'?"

"It's a nickname. Not a particularly fond one. It's usually given to dogs."

"Doesn't seem like she is all that happy with her husband."

"They've not had a smooth relationship."

"What about these NATV Bloods? I didn't know there was a gang out on the reservation."

"Didn't know they were back myself," Concho said. "Not sure why someone didn't tell me."

"Seems like you've had a run-in with them before," Parkland said.

"A long time ago."

"Are we working on the theory that they're responsible for killing Ben Deer-Run and our John Doe?"

"I don't like having a 'theory' so early in a case," Concho said. "Constrains the way you look at things. But we'll definitely want to find out the names of the members." He started the truck and backed out of the yard onto the road. "Alvarado will know. If he'll tell us. He'll probably want to chew on us first."

"I'll have to let you deal with that," Parkland said. "Sorry, but you better drop me off back at my vehicle. I want to call the coroner and make sure he puts a priority on this case."

"Good idea," Concho said. "Better make sure he keeps whatever he finds out of the news until we have a chance to process it, though. There'll be a lot of anger at the death of Ben Deer-Run. If we aren't careful, the reservation could explode. And it'll be the Kickapoo who get hurt the worst."

CHAPTER 15

After dropping Sheriff Parkland back at his SUV, which now stood alone except for some yellow crime scene tape on the access road where the murders had taken place, Concho headed back into Kickapoo Village. It occurred to him that he might have another source of information about the resurgence of the NATV Bloods than Deputy Alvarado, perhaps one much easier to talk to. He drove over to Meskwaa's place.

The old Kickapoo lived along another dirt road, in a small trailer that looked to have made a long, hard trek to get here. Unlike most other members of the tribe, Meskwaa said he had no plans to build a bigger and more modern house. He had, however, constructed for himself the typical summer wickiup of the Kickapoo people.

Concho had helped build such structures himself when he was younger, though he had not done so for years. Traditionally, there were four huts constructed by the Kickapoo: summer, winter, cook, and menstrual. The summer house was generally the largest.

One started with posts cut from local one-seed juniper or desert willow. These were staked deep into the ground, and walls of sotol stalks and cut saplings were constructed and bound together using pita twine made from the fibers of the maguey plant. A roof of overlapping mats of river cane and cattails was placed over this frame, leaving an internal rectangular area of some two hundred and forty square feet that was about six feet high right along the center.

The wickiup had no windows and didn't need a smoke hole because the loose construction of sotol stalks allowed for plenty of ventilation. It had just one entrance, always facing east, though it also had a sort of open porch or "ramada" attached at the front of the building. This was open on three sides, with one or two long wooden benches for sitting and sleeping. It was where the owners spent most of their time during good weather. The floors of both the wickiup and the porch were made of tamped down dirt, which was kept neatly swept using a homemade brush broom.

Concho found Meskwaa seated on his porch, with his back against the wall of his wickiup and his legs stretched out along a bench. One of his filterless cigarettes dangled between two gnarled fingers of his right hand. His left hand was busy as he rolled a quarter back and forth between his knuckles—around and around in a practiced motion that the old man often used to enthrall the young members of the tribe.

Without halting his coin rolling, Meskwaa said in Kickapoo, "Welcome to my wickiup. Sit at ease and drink." He pointed to a tin pail of water near the open doorway of his home.

Concho sat on a second bench and used the dipper protruding from the bucket to lift a cool draught to his lips. He sipped gratefully, returned the dipper and wiped the sweat from his forehead with the back of his hand.

"Thank you for hospitality," Concho replied in Kickapoo.

"Of course."

For a while, the two sat in silence. Concho let himself enjoy the moment, the profound peacefulness he found here, which seemed to be a product of more than just the quiet landscape.

Finally, Meskwaa began the conversation with, "Why do you visit this old man? You saw me only a day ago."

"I came because your vision of yesterday came true this morning."

Meskwaa nodded. "I am sorry to hear that. Ben Deer-Run was not a bad man."

"You knew it would be Ben? Why didn't you tell me when we first spoke?"

"I didn't know I knew until you mentioned my vision a moment ago."

Concho understood. "Another man was killed alongside him," he said. "It would be helpful if you knew who *he* was."

Meskwaa shook his head. "That I cannot help you with. I know he was not Kickapoo. I do not think it will be pleasant for you to find out, though."

"I have the same feeling. I don't like it."

The old man inclined his head. "You did not drive this far only to tell me what I already knew. What more of Meskwaa's wisdom do you require?"

"I spoke to Estrella."

"A beautiful woman. With a fool of a husband. You would do well to have such a wife. Perhaps it is not too late for you."

"It seems you've tried to marry me off to just about every eligible woman in the tribe at one time or another."

Meskwaa shrugged. "I simply do not want you to end like me. A lonely old man with no soft one to comfort me when I have bad dreams."

Concho laughed. "Now you're just lying," he said. "You've never lacked for female comfort."

Meskwaa grinned but said only, "What did Estrella say to send you here?"

"She told me Ben had been having trouble with the NATV Bloods. I didn't even know they were making a comeback. But I'm sure you know all about it."

"Certainly. I am their *Jefe*. They were here only moments ago taking their marching orders. Surely you caught a glimpse of their backsides as you drove in!"

"Afraid I missed it. Do you know who they are?"

"Do you think they killed Ben Deer-Run and this other man?"

"I don't know but it's worth investigating."

A nod came as Meskwaa lit another cigarette from the dregs of the first. "You will want to speak to one who calls himself Bull Knife."

Concho frowned. "Never heard of him. Who is he?"

"A young man who came here about a month ago from the Oklahoma nation of the Kickapoo. He came with others. He seems to have a certain…power. Our own young people are beginning to listen."

"The name doesn't sound Kickapoo."

"Bull Knife claims he is also of Apache blood. I do not know if it is true. He chose his name to reflect how the Apache fought so long against the white man. He sees himself as such a warrior. But the Apache were no more honorable or brave than we Kickapoo. No bravery could stand against the numbers our ancestors faced."

"Why hasn't anyone mentioned this Bull Knife to me?"

For a space of a dozen slow breaths, Meskwaa did not speak. Then: "You do not often sit on porches as you are doing now. To sit quietly and listen is the way one learns about such things."

"Somehow, I don't think sitting on porches would work as well for me as it does for you."

Meskwaa considered. "What I tell you now, I say as one who knew and loved your grandmother. Some of the people think you are too much in the white man's world. There are personal things they will *not* speak of to you."

Concho's first reaction was to bite back an angry retort, but he knew it wasn't justified. He swallowed and sighed. "The world must be dealt with as it rests on the table," he said finally. "It is good for us Kickapoo, and all Indians, to remember our history. But history is not a place to live. We have to make a future as well. And in that future, there will be others besides the Kickapoo on these lands. White, and Black, and even Apache. I do not apologize for looking to the future."

"Are you speaking to me? Or to yourself?"

"To both, I guess."

Meskwaa nodded.

Concho rose to his feet. "And now the world intrudes again. Where do you think I might find this Bull Knife?"

"On one porch, I heard he spends much time at the casino. On another, it was said he lives with the ghosts."

"I think I'll try the casino first," Concho said.

"Of course, *you* will."

Concho smiled. "Thanks, old friend. For everything."

Meskwaa's gaze met the Ranger's. "I knew your grandmother," he said. "So did you. Do not forget."

CHAPTER 16

Concho pulled into the parking lot of the Lucky Eagle casino and slid out of his truck. It had been a full day. Evening closed in. The western sky was yellow-orange with an almost translucent aquamarine above. The scene was peaceful, until he turned to look at the casino and saw the busyness of electric light and bustle. Reluctantly, he started in that direction.

A middle-aged white couple, obviously intoxicated, walked toward him in the parking lot, arguing vehemently about something or other. The woman grabbed the man's arm and swung him around to face her. He snapped words at her that Concho didn't hear, and she took a swing at him. The man ducked, and as the woman teetered off balance from her swing, he leaned in and gave her a shove that pushed her back three steps.

Concho stopped between them. His height and the bulk of his shoulders silenced them for a moment. He turned to face them both. They stared, with no words. Reaching into his pocket and taking out his billfold, Concho removed a twenty-dollar bill.

"It's a beautiful evening," the Ranger said to the couple. "Too beautiful to fight over something I doubt you'll even remember in the morning. Why don't you take this twenty and call a cab? Or an Uber. Or whatever you need to get home."

He stepped closer to the couple and pressed the twenty into the man's hand, who gazed at him rather owlishly.

"Maybe try," he continued, "not saying any *angry* words to each other until you get home. I think that would be a good idea."

The man glanced at the twenty, then back at the big Ranger, his face a blank slate upon which almost anything could be written. His wife stepped nervously toward her husband and slid her arm through his.

"I think maybe he's right, Len. Plenty of cabs by the casino. Let's get one. We can come back tomorrow for the car."

The husband took a deep breath and nodded. "All right, baby," he said. "I'm really pretty tired anyway."

Concho smiled and tipped an imaginary hat before walking on toward the casino's front doors. As he passed through the entrance, a security guard, striving to appear relaxed and unconcerned and doing a pretty good job of it, nodded at him but said nothing. He nodded back.

Passing through a small atrium, he came to the main gaming hall. If he hadn't already known where it was, he could have found it by the sound—the discordant jingle-jangle of slot machines working, the low hum of jabbering voices, with a shriller cry rising occasionally from someone who'd won big or lost bigger.

Most of the gamblers were white, middle-aged or older, locals and tourists. The wait staff was uniformly young and attractive and much more varied in heritage. Concho never stopped to watch this room when he came here. It reminded him too much of psychological articles he'd read in college about rats pressing levers in reinforcement chambers.

Toward the rear of the gaming area was a set of steps leading up to the second floor where several meeting rooms were located. After finding the room he wanted by the sound of Daniel Alvarado's laughing voice, the big Ranger stepped over the golden rope designed to keep out the riffraff and walked inside. Motion and sound ceased. Concho stood waiting.

A circular table rested in the middle of the room. Alvarado lounged in a chair directly opposite the door, with a man seated on either side of him and another man standing like a statue at his shoulder. The man standing up was Indian and Concho didn't know him, which meant he was probably Bull Knife or one of the others who'd come here from the Oklahoma tribe. Smooth faced, this one hardly looked old enough to be in the casino. He appeared to be acting as a bodyguard for Alvarado.

The other two seated men were white. The one to Alvarado's left wore jeans and a short-sleeved blue cotton shirt without a jacket or tie. His head was shaved. He was taller than Concho by a hair, and probably weighed a good forty pounds more. He was clearly muscle for the other man, who was lean and dapper and dressed in a gray suit with a light pink dress shirt and tie.

"What are you doing here, Ten-Wolves?" Alvarado demanded, setting down the shot glass of whiskey he held in his fist.

Concho waved a hand around generally to indicate the whole casino. "Came to check on my investment. I'm a shareholder, after all. Just like you."

"Not like me, Ten-Wolves. Never like me. I'm on the casino board and this is board business. A private meeting which you weren't invited to. So leave or I'll have you thrown out."

Concho smiled. He was getting a little tired of taking shit off Alvarado. "You must be drunk, *Deputy*. You haven't been able to throw me out of anything since you were fourteen and I was twelve."

The big white man who appeared to serve as muscle stood up slowly and squared his shoulders.

Concho glanced over. "You should sit down again before you get into a mess your boss can't get you out of."

The man took a step toward Concho, but the well-dressed other white man, who was clearly the boss in question, barked a quick, "Wayne!"

Wayne froze, then slowly returned to his seat. Concho looked over at the man who'd spoken. Short blond hair, carefully groomed. Eyes, a very pale shade of blue. The man made an expansive gesture by spreading his hands. One of the hands, carefully manicured, Concho noted, picked up an expensive bottle of 12-year-old Weller straight Kentucky bourbon and poured a shot glass full. The man capped the bottle and held up the glass, pointing it toward Concho before setting it down in front of one of the open chairs at the table.

"Why don't you have a drink with us, Officer Ten-Wolves. I'm sure we can all be friends."

Alvarado started to protest but the man laid a light hand on the deputy's wrist and he subsided.

"Who are you?" Concho asked the man.

"My name is Jacob Drake."

"German."

Drake arched an eyebrow. "What makes you say that? I know many Americans named Drake."

"Not the accent," Concho said. "You've lost it. Or you're masking it. But the cadence. The pattern of your words."

Drake smiled. "By the good god, you are quite the linguist to recognize such. Or would you prefer I say, 'Gott im Himmel.'"

"Doesn't much matter," Concho said. "And," he pointed to the whiskey, "I don't drink hard liquor."

"Of course," Drake said. "I understand…your people don't handle the hard stuff well." He turned to look at Alvarado and said with a false heartiness. "Except our good deputy here. He throws it back like a born German."

Alvarado smiled, seemingly unaware he was being made fun of. He picked up his own shot glass and tossed the liquor into his mouth.

"And," Drake continued. "Although I was, in fact, birthed in Germany, I moved to the USA when I was quite young and have been a naturalized American citizen since I was twenty-one. So, I'm quite sure I'm as much of an American as you are, Mr. Ten-Wolves."

"And what kind of business do you...Americans have with the Kickapoo tribal casino?" Concho asked, glancing from Drake to Alvarado and back.

"None of *your* business," Alvarado snapped. "I don't know how many times I have to tell you that you don't have any jurisdiction on the reservation, but I'm telling you again. Move along. You may be tough, Ten-Wolves, but there are enough men working for me in this casino to take you down."

"Probably enough," Concho agreed. "I guess we could always find out. Though they don't really work for you! But mainly I'm wondering if you've done anything so far to investigate the recent murder of your sheriff? That's Ben Deer-Run, if you don't recall."

"I've been reviewing the past week's videos all day," Alvarado retorted. "We're looking for any sign of Ben, or of the...African American man who was with him. If we find anything, I'll let the Maverick County Sheriff's office know. You can find out from them."

"Good to know you're on the job," Concho said. "Just one more thing and I'll leave you to your American friends. I heard Ben has been having run-ins with members of the NATV Bloods. Maybe like the new fellow standing at your shoulder. Would you know anything about such?"

Alvarado's response was unreadable but the young Indian man stiffened. His acorn-brown eyes darkened as his gaze darted around the room.

"The boy is going to run," Jacob Drake said.

"No, he's not," Concho said, as the youth's hand darted swiftly downward.

CHAPTER 17

As the Kickapoo man grabbed for something behind his back, Concho drew his right-hand Colt. He didn't fire; it wasn't a gun flashing into the fellow's fist. It was a knife. At almost the same instant, Alvarado lunged from his seat. The deputy smashed down at the younger man's arm, sending the knife flying. He twisted the boy against the wall, putting his body in Concho's line of fire.

"Don't shoot!" he shouted.

"Didn't intend to," Concho said, making a face. He returned his pistol to its holster. "But that's a mighty big reaction to a simple comment."

"You just accused him of murder," Alvarado snapped.

"If I *had*, I'd be the one holding him against the wall," Concho replied.

Alvarado murmured something in the boy's ear, then released him. The youth turned to face Concho, his eyes furious and embarrassed. Not a good combination.

"I was merely asking if either of you," Concho nodded at Alvarado and the boy, "knew anything about Ben's issues with the NATV Bloods?"

"He's no member of the Bloods," Alvarado said with a snarl. "I invited him here tonight. He intends to apply for the tribal police force in Oklahoma."

"Ah," Jacob Drake said. "You might say the young man's on an internship."

"Exactly," Alvarado agreed vigorously.

Concho glanced at Drake, who'd scarcely shown any reaction to the excitement of moments before. The man reached out and picked up the shot glass of whiskey he'd poured for the Ranger. He tossed it back, smiled.

Concho looked back at Alvarado. "Maybe the first thing your 'intern' needs to learn is some self-control. What's his name anyway? It wouldn't be Bull Knife, would it?"

Some look passed quickly across Daniel Alvarado's face. Again, Concho couldn't quite read it and was beginning to be troubled by that. Alvarado wasn't usually capable of controlling his emotions this well—especially while drinking. Maybe the deputy had been interning himself, getting some training in self-control. Maybe he'd been working with this Jacob Drake, who was a total cipher but certainly seemed to have no trouble modulating his own behavior.

"Joseph Big-Pine," Alvarado said. "That's his name."

"I can speak for myself," Big-Pine said.

Alvarado gave the boy a glare and he fell silent.

Concho walked over to where Big-Pine's knife lay on the carpeted floor. "I need to know where Bull Knife is," he said. "He needs to be questioned regarding Ben Deer-Run's death."

"Where did you even get that name?" Alvarado demanded.

"Not important. Where is Bull Knife?"

"I don't know," Alvarado said. "But I can find him. And he'll be questioned by me. Not you!"

Concho knew his legal options were limited in this situation. It was one thing to ask Ben's daughter a few things. It was something else to question a witness who might be involved in an actual crime. Any information a Texas Ranger got from an Indian suspect on the reservation could be easily dismissed by a good lawyer. It wouldn't matter if the Ranger was a Kickapoo as well.

After considering several responses, Concho decided on, "You'll need to keep Sheriff Parkland in the loop."

"If he shares with me, I'll share with him."

Concho nodded as he leaned down and picked up the knife, being careful to touch nothing more than the pommel.

"That's my blade," Joseph Big-Pine snapped.

Concho slid the bare blade into his belt next to his left side pistol. "Not tonight," he replied. He walked out of the room without another word.

Three minutes later, Concho opened the door to his pickup. He pulled the knife out of his belt and laid it on the passenger side seat. Then he turned to face the man who'd followed him from the casino.

"Klaus, wasn't it?" Concho asked Jacob Drake's muscle-bound guard dog. "Or, maybe it was Helmut? Something German, I think. Wulfsnizzle, perhaps?"

The big man, who'd been called "Wayne" by Drake, offered the Ranger a smirk that made his face look like a bulldog smelling a stink.

"Funny man," Wayne said. "And a very lucky one."

"How so?"

"Lucky Mr. Drake didn't want me to stomp you."

Concho took two steps toward the guy, stopped just within range of a punch. "How about now?" he asked. "No Drake here. Stomp away!"

Wayne smirked again. "And be arrested for attacking a police officer? I know these laws. I am no fool."

"I'll give you a free pass. No cop shit involved. Just a fight in a parking lot."

"And you with guns," Wayne sneered.

Concho stepped back toward his truck. The door was still open and he unbuckled his gun belt and stretched it across the driver's seat before returning to the other man.

"Got any more excuses?" he asked.

Wayne was getting a good workout for his sneering muscles tonight. He offered another one and said,

"It is a trick. No doubt you have cameras watching. But there will be a time." He pointed a thick index finger at Concho's face before stalking off.

Concho shrugged and returned to his truck. He buckled his gun belt back on, then slid into the driver's seat. Catching a glimpse of himself in the rear-view mirror, he shook his head. A touch of melancholy seeped over him. He'd wanted the fight with Wayne. Maybe he'd needed it to fill something inside that seemed empty today.

As he reached for the key to start the truck, his phone rang. Picking up the cell, he saw the name of the caller. A rim of ice coated his muscles. Then thoughts of yesterday set them afire. He listened to a couple more rings before swiping the answer button.

"Hello, Maria," he said.

CHAPTER 18

"Concho," **Maria Morales said through the phone.**
Her voice was just as he remembered it, a combination of gravels and honey. He took a deep breath.

"I'm…glad to hear from you."

"I understand I have you to thank for being alive," Maria said.

"Just…I'm…glad I could be there."

"I know why you didn't come to the hospital. At least I think I do. Hope I do. Too many people. Too much family. *My* family."

"They're not my biggest fans," Concho said. "But they're who you needed most. I'm glad you're OK. You are OK, aren't you?"

Maria laughed. It was good to hear. "Yes, I'm OK. And you can stop saying 'glad' now."

Concho felt his face flush as embarrassment swept him. He tried to fall back on humor. "Me heap good with words."

"Better sometimes than others," Maria said. "I…just wanted to say thank you. For me and for everyone in the mall. A lot of people owe you. And don't say you were just doing your job."

"All right, I won't say it."

"Sometimes, though…." Maria said, her voice suddenly pensive.

"Sometimes what?"

"Sometimes people come to resent those they owe. Right now, most everyone is in your corner. But that doesn't always remain. Be careful."

"You too."

A pause filled the connection. Concho heard Maria's breathing and was content with that. It couldn't last.

"Good night, Concho."

"Good night, Maria."

Silence.

***

Concho drove toward home. He drove slowly, with his windows down. The night scents of mesquite and juniper rolled into the truck. The radio interrupted his calm.

"Ten-Wolves. Come back."

Concho picked up the handset. "Here," he said.

The dispatcher's voice came through. "Hold for Captain Keller."

Concho gritted his teeth, but held. A moment passed. Keller's voice came on.

"Ten-Wolves. You there?"

"Here," he said again.

"You need to be at City Hall tomorrow by 10:30."

"Why?"

"Press conference at 11:00. The heads of all the police units involved in the Eagle Pass mall debacle are going to give statements and be questioned by the press. The FBI, local police, sheriff's office, and me. You're the only regular officer whose presence was requested. I'm not happy with it."

"I understand."

"I'd prefer to keep you out of the press's eye. They'll either eat you alive, or vice versa. I don't know which one would be worse. Fortunately, I've gotten permission for you to make just a short statement. Then the rest of us will take over."

"What kind of statement?"

"Don't worry about it. It'll be written and ready for you when you get here. You just stand up and read it. Think you can do that?"

"I *think* I'm suspended. Am I being reinstated?"

A sigh full of exasperation came through the radio. "I never said you were suspended."

"That's not what 'don't bother coming into work for the next week,' or 'there's going to be some discussion about your future in the Texas Rangers' meant?"

Keller's voice grew tight with controlled anger. "You don't know when to stop pushing, do you, Ten-Wolves?"

"I need to know whether I'm suspended or not."

"You're *not* suspended!" Keller snapped. "Be here tomorrow."

The radio went silent.

Concho rehung the mic and considered how hearing from his boss had darkened his mood—just as the day had darkened fully into night. He turned off the main road onto the dirt stretch leading to his house, then pulled into his usual parking spot. Coyotes howled off in the scrubland. A few night birds and crickets called from around his trailer.

He slipped the knife he'd taken from Joseph Big-Pine into an evidence bag and sealed it before climbing out of the Ford. The night was warm and close around him. A mosquito dive-bombed him. He slapped it away. A chuck-will's-widow vented its lonely song.

Concho started toward his door, took three steps and paused. Something wasn't right. He listened. He sniffed the air. Nothing seemed out of the ordinary but he knew it was.

The Ranger's free hand slipped to the butt of one of his Colt Double Eagles and drew it. He walked backward into the bulking shadow of his truck, letting it swallow his silhouette. When younger, he'd sometimes felt embarrassed at heeding the hunches he got. Like this one. He no longer felt that way. They had saved his life in the past.

Returning the evidence bag to the truck, he took out a flashlight and locked the vehicle. Then, with a swift, crouching move, he lunged toward the corner of his trailer and took shelter against its wall where a clump of prickly pear cacti broke up his outline.

An animal snuffled along the ground to his left. An armadillo, he was sure. An unseen beetle zipped past. He worked his way around the prickly pear to the back corner of his trailer. A small grove of mixed mesquite and juniper grew here. The smell was intense, more intense than it should have been. Something had moved through the grove, something big enough to break a few fronds and let the sap bleed into the air.

Deer lived in the low hills behind Concho's house, and feral hogs. Both were big enough to cause that kind of damage. However, the air fluttered with fitful breaths of wind that would have brought him those scents—particularly the hogs—if they had visited him. He didn't think they had.

He started along the rear of the trailer toward his back door. Another scent came to him, one he knew well—copper sweet blood. Staying crouched, he decided to take a risk and switched on the flashlight, letting its beam play across dirt and rock and clumps of dry grass.

His trailer sat up on blocks. He'd never put in back steps and the door here was a good four feet off the ground. Just at the base of the trailer, beneath the door, lay the severed head of a white-tail deer.

No sound moved the night except for the faint whisper of a breeze. No other smells made themselves known. He worked his cautious way over to the animal head and crouched to study it in the light. The fur around the cut was shredded. It looked like the head had been sawn off, much like the cuts on Ben Deer-Run's neck.

Pointing the flashlight toward his back door revealed something else—a symbol scrawled on the white paint in black blood.

It resembled a stylized half circle with a lightning slash of gore through the right side. *A cracked cup*, he thought. *No, a medicine wheel. Broken.* Concho did not consider himself a particularly spiritual man, though he had been taught well by his grandmother, but he understood the power of the circle, and the power of it broken. This symbol represented a curse. He was the target. Whether the person who'd done it actually believed in the magic or was just trying to scare Concho off wasn't clear. Easing to his feet, Concho ran a finger through the blood paint. It was still wet. Whoever had committed this act must have snuck along the old arroyo running behind his little grove of desert trees. He wouldn't be able to find tracks or any kind of trail in the dark, though. He'd have to investigate tomorrow. For now, he felt confident the deer killer had gone.

Concho clicked off his flashlight and holstered his pistol. He needed a shovel and a machete. They were inside the house. The deer had been desecrated and deserved a proper burial. It was the Kickapoo way.

CHAPTER 19

Concho managed a few good hours of sleep, but the
night had conspired with whoever had left the deer head to
cover their tracks. Around 11:00 PM, a huge storm cell moved
across Maverick County. Towers of cloud full of lightning and
thunder boiled over the area and the rain pounded down like
mortar fire. The arroyo behind his house soon careened with
a rush of water that tore away dirt and rocks and any small
bushes that dared to cling to its sides. A real "gully washer" the
old-timers would call it.

Concho watched the storm through his windows for a while,
hearing the wind rushing as it smashed through the mesquite and
juniper out back. Sticks and leaves flew. Lightning strobed the
darkness, searing its brief existence into Concho's retinas.

One of the few memories Concho had of his grandfather
involved such a storm. He couldn't have been more than four.
They'd been spending the summer in a wickiup. When the storm
first churned up, grandfather had taken Concho onto the ramada,
the wickiup's front porch. Grandfather had sat on a bench against
the wall and held Concho in his lap while the rain and thunder
and lightning roiled over them.

He remembered the excitement of the storm, the smell of the

rain, and all the wet scents of a land being ravaged by nature. And, he remembered his grandfather's calmness, how he'd merely sat and held Concho while the whole world seemed to shudder. Both had ended up soaked to the bone by wind-driven rain. Neither of them had cared.

By the time morning came to Concho's trailer, the storm was over, and there were no signs to find of whoever had decided to curse the Ranger. Some in his world might have called the unfortunate arrival of the storm "dark magic." Concho gave it no name other than bad luck.

After a shower and a breakfast of eggs and toast, Concho left the reservation and drove along freshly washed roads into Eagle pass, taking Highway 57 to Balboa-Jones Blvd and pulling up in front of the steel and glass building that housed the Maverick County Sheriff's Department. The officer at the front desk took his name and called back on the intercom to Isaac Parkland's office. Parkland himself came down the hallway a few minutes later and gestured for the Ranger to follow him.

The two entered Parkland's office and the sheriff motioned for Concho to sit. The Ranger closed the door before he did so, then placed a plastic evidence bag on the sheriff's cluttered desk.

"What's this?" Parkland asked.

"Ran into a young man who might be one of the NATV Bloods Ben Deer-Run's daughter was talking about. He had this knife, pulled it as a threat, but it didn't work out so well for him."

"You thinking it might be the knife used to cut Ben's throat?"

"Doubt it, actually. But figured it couldn't hurt to have it looked at. The man's name is Joseph Big-Pine. Young guy. I doubt he's twenty-one yet. He was on edge from some kind of stress but trying to hide it."

"You arrested him?"

"No. It was at the casino and Alvarado was there. Any arrest I made would be thrown out of court. Alvarado claimed the boy was 'interning' with him. I got another name of someone who might be the leader of the gang, though. Bull Knife. Ever heard it?"

Parkland shook his head, which was hatless for the moment. His chair creaked as he leaned back in it and crossed his hands over a belly that put a little strain on the buttons of his white shirt.

"Don't mean much what I've heard of, though" the sheriff said.

"Alvarado recognized the name Bull Knife. Said he'd question the man. And he'd report it to you. Might be a good idea to call him, stir him to action."

Parkland nodded. "I'll do it this morning. The fellow that reported the bodies checked out fine, by the way. Pretty sure he was just doing his civic duty."

"What about the coroner?" Concho asked. "Anything from there?"

"Not much. No identification on the second body yet. But toxicology tests indicated both heroin and meth in his system."

Concho mused. "Not a typical combination," he said.

"Nope. Best guess is he took one and was doped with the other. Probably the meth, then the heroin. In that order. Did you drive all this way just to bring me that knife?"

Concho considered telling Parkland about the decapitated deer's head at his doorstep. But he couldn't imagine what good it would do.

"No," he said. "I'm invited to a press conference this morning at 11:00. I hear you're attending as well."

"Afraid I am," Parkland said, shaking his head. "Wasn't looking forward to it. But it might be more entertaining if you're there."

"They've written a statement for me to make," Concho added. "Or so Max Keller told me."

"You gonna make it?"

"Depends on what it is."

"Don't let 'em get to you."

Concho pushed up from his chair, gave the sheriff a nod. "Guess I better get moving."

"See you there," Parkland said. "Just keep in mind, these things always go bad."

"Don't tell me that!"

"Too late."

CHAPTER 20

The Eagle Pass City Hall was located at 100 South Mon-
roe Street, smack in the center of a school zone that included half
a dozen elementary schools. Concho pulled into the parking lot a
little before 10:30. The press was out in force. Their vans clustered
in one group while the police vehicles from various local agencies
clustered in another.

Disembarking from his truck, Concho was almost immediately recognized. Ignoring all shouts for his attention, he walked
quickly and forcefully to the street and along the sidewalk to the
building, entering through a pair of doors next to a white sign
on the wall reading "POLICE." Only after he was inside did he
take a breath and relax.

Max Keller stood in one corner talking to the Mayor and other
city and law enforcement officials. Isaac Parkland hadn't arrived
yet and Concho was feeling pretty isolated until Adrian Lastra,
the SWAT captain he'd met outside the mall on the day of the
takeover, walked over to shake his hand.

"I was afraid they'd rope you into this," Lastra said.

"You think the press will be *more* or *less* vicious than the Aryan
Brotherhood?"

Lastra laughed. "Hard to say. You ever been through one of

these?"

"Not while being served up as a main dish."

"Some friendly advice? Volunteer nothing. Give your statement, answer your questions, don't ramble and don't speculate."

"Thanks."

"By the way, we may have gotten a hit from the tip you gave us about the shooting range along White-Tail Creek."

"Oh?"

"There'd been a lot of traffic in the area but forensics got a couple of clear boot prints and a set of tire tracks. We're running those down but one boot print looks like a match for what Fallon's chief lieutenant was wearing on the day of the mall takeover."

"Interesting," Concho said. "Let's hope the tire prints lead somewhere. Keep me informed if you would."

Before Lastra could respond, Max Keller appeared at Concho's shoulder. Keller was gray headed in his fifties but thin and fit in a gleaming white shirt with a yellow tie and tan trousers. His badge shone. His hair shone beneath a shining white western hat. Everything about him shone, including his teeth, which looked to be painted a porcelain white.

Concho introduced Keller to Lastra and the two shook hands before Keller turned the full weight of his personality on Concho.

"Ten-Wolves! I expected you to wear a tie and a hat for the occasion."

"Don't own a tie, sir. And the only hat I have is pretty battered and wouldn't look too pretty on camera."

Keller shook his head. "You're paid enough to afford better. I'll expect it of you from now on."

"I hear you, sir."

Keller reached into the pocket of his freshly pressed and starched shirt and drew out a folded piece of paper, which he handed to the big Ranger. "Your statement," the commander said. "I don't want you to vary from it."

"I hear you."

As if he'd noticed the lack of a "sir" this time, Keller gave him a glare. He might have said more but someone more important than Concho Ten-Wolves called him away. He strode off with military precision. Concho slipped the notepaper into his own pocket.

"My significant other tells me *I'm* uptight," Lastra said. "I'll have to show him a recording of this press conference and let him get a look at Max Keller. Can't believe the man doesn't squeak when he walks."

"You need to get your high-pitched hearing tested," Concho replied.

Lastra laughed a second time. "Well, see you on stage. Good luck."

The two shook hands again and Lastra disappeared into the crowd. Concho didn't like crowds. He glanced at the clock on the wall. *10:44 AM.* Where had the time gone already? He didn't want to do this.

Realizing he was nervous, Concho took a few deep breaths, then headed for the bathroom to relieve his bladder before the big moment. After washing his hands, he took out the "statement" he was supposed to read and started scanning it:

A Texas Ranger is entrusted with a sacred duty, to protect the innocent and the rule of law. We do this for the greatness of Texas and its people. We do this for every man, woman, and child who bears the title of Texan. These ideals are not options for a Ranger. They are serious, and even holy. And we stand for them with honor and with full knowledge of how we must uphold the glorious history of the Rangers....

The statement contained much more about the Rangers, words about justice and brotherhood and commitment. Much of it was good and Concho believed most of it, but it wasn't him. He stopped reading, folded the paper and tucked it back in his pocket.

As he exited the bathroom, someone from the Mayor's office called his name. For the next few minutes, he was introduced to the mayor and a dozen other city officials whose names he'd never remember. His hand was shaken, his shoulders slapped. Compliments were slathered over him like butter. He felt like a turkey being basted in the oven and wished they'd take him out of the heat because he was already pretty much done.

When 11:00 AM struck, the mayor took the stage, which had been set up just outside the front doors of City Hall. He spoke to the reporters for a bit, though Concho didn't really listen. Then Concho himself was called to the microphone to make his statement. Keller nodded at him as he passed on his way to the stage. Moving forward on automatic, Concho nodded back. Sheriff Parkland had arrived and gave him a thumbs up. He gave it back.

And then he was standing under the bright sun, under the three flags flying above the hall. Cameras were rolling. Cheers came. Forgetting where he was, he cleared his throat into the mic, hearing it reverberate in the air like the grunt of a buffalo. He stifled the urge to apologize.

He didn't bother taking the prepared statement out of his pocket. He had no intention of reading it. He spoke on his own, saying what he wanted to say. And he didn't care what Max Keller thought of it.

CHAPTER 21

"Like most of you here, I'm Texan," Concho said into the microphone. "I'm also a Texas Ranger and a Kickapoo. I'm proud to be all three. A couple of days ago, a group of homegrown terrorists known as the Aryan Brotherhood attacked us all. I did what I could to stop them. I did not work alone. Hundreds of other police personnel, as well as many civilians, played their part. And yet, some innocent lives were lost. I'm grateful for those who survived and saddened for the families of those who did not. Thank you and good day."

He started to turn away but could not get off so easily. Voices began to shout out his name, shout out questions.

"Concho! Concho Ten-Wolves—"

"I'm not planning to take quest—" Concho started.

But one sharp, loud voice cut him off. "What do you say to people who call you a hero?"

"I say to stop it," Concho said into the mic, and his voice carried, booming. A smattering of laughter followed his words.

"Is it true that Darrel Fallon called you the N-word when you two were fighting?" another voice called.

"I wasn't paying attention to what he called me," Concho replied. "I was just trying to hit him more than he hit me." Again came the laughter.

"Concho! The manager of the mall, Ms. Maria Morales, was taken hostage by Fallon when he was trying to escape. Didn't you and Ms. Morales used to date? And is that relationship still ongoing?"

"Ms. Morales and I are friends," Concho said. "Now, I really need to let some other people talk."

As he turned away from the crowd of reporters, he saw Max Keller striding toward him, and the stiff smile on the man's face indicated his unhappiness. Concho wasn't unhappy with that.

Someone at the back of the crowd shouted a question for Concho: "As a Native American, how can you justify working for an organization like the Texas Rangers, who have a long history of brutalizing your people?"

Keller's hand clutched down on Concho's arm. The Captain leaned past him to the mic and said, "We have a number of people who need to speak so we're not going to take more questions at this time."

Keller started to step away from the mic, his hand still on Concho's arm, exerting pressure. Concho didn't let the pressure move him. He spoke without the benefit of the microphone. He didn't need it.

"The Texas Rangers, like any organization, is made up of people. And people are complicated. Not all good or bad. The Kickapoo remember our history. All of it. But it's the present I'm more concerned with. History cannot be changed, but it doesn't necessarily represent the present, and it doesn't have to become the future. Thank you."

Applause roared. A few more questions came shooting from the crowd but Concho ignored them and made his way off the stage and back into the city hall building. Keller remained behind at the mic. Concho didn't hear what he said, or particularly care.

A water fountain beckoned and Concho leaned over it for a big gulp. The sweat drenching him came only partially from the day's heat. Footsteps approached and the Ranger turned his head. A man in an orange Texas Longhorns shirt walked up. Concho finished his drink and straightened. The man was staring at him.

"Yes?" Concho asked.

The fellow, in his late twenties, stood about six feet, with short dark hair. He wore jeans to complement his T-shirt. His face was clean-shaven, with even features, and his eyes were blue-gray. He stuck out a hand and Concho took it.

"I just wanted to thank you, Officer Ten-Wolves," the man said.

"What for?"

The man snapped his fingers. "That's right. You don't even know who I am. My name is Coleman Chase. My buddies call me Cole. I was workin' security at Eagle Pass Mall on Tuesday."

The light bulb went off for Concho. "Right! You're the guard who survived."

"Barely. And thanks to you. Believe me, that was a long stretch of time waitin' after being told to your face by Darrel Fallon you're gonna get shot."

"I can imagine."

"But it didn't happen." The man grinned. "You arrived. One riot, one Ranger. Ain't that the saying?"

"It is."

"I thought about tryin' for the Rangers one time," Chase said. "Never could get the timin' quite right, though."

Concho had no idea what to say in response and the conversation lagged. Finally, Concho asked, "Any idea why Fallon singled you and one other fellow out for special treatment?"

"Reckon for the other guy it was because he was…uh, of mixed blood. I know we don't use the term *breed* anymore. Anyway, he maybe had some Japanese or Chinese blood in him."

"And you?"

"My wallet," he said. The grin that came then was a little sly. "I been dating this black girl. Had a picture of her in there. Fallon didn't much like it."

Concho nodded. "I guess so."

The silence came again. This time, Cole Chase broke it. "Well, I won't bother you any further. Just wanted to thank you. Say, could I give you my cell number? In case you ever wanna let me buy you a beer or three?"

"Sure," Concho said.

He took his phone out of his pocket and swiped it on. Chase stood at his shoulder while he gave Concho his number and the Ranger entered it in his contacts.

"Thanks," the man said again. "Hope you give me a call sometime when you're free for a beer. I might even wanna ask you some questions about the Rangers. Maybe it's not too late for me to give it a go."

"Maybe not," Concho agreed.

The two shook hands one more time and Chase wandered off. Concho stuck his phone back in his pocket. Max Keller stepped inside the building and stalked toward Concho with fury written on his face. Concho waited, but Sheriff Isaac Parkland came through the door behind Keller and caught up with the Texas Ranger commander just as he reached Concho.

Keller turned in irritation but Parkland got his words in first.

"Captain Keller!" Parkland said. "I was hoping to ask you a favor."

"What favor?" Keller replied.

"I've got a pair of murders on my hands. Right on the border with the Kickapoo reservation. I wonder if you'd lend me Mr. Ten-Wolves here for a week or so to help me out. I'd be beholden."

Keller's mouth opened, snapped shut. He glanced from Parkland to Concho, who smiled politely, and then back to the sheriff. He shrugged, and maybe he was thinking this was a good temporary solution to his problem—his problem being Concho.

"All right," Keller said. "Send me an official request. Email will do."

"Right," Parkland said. "I'll get it off to you this afternoon."

Keller glanced once more at Concho before striding off without a further word.

Concho met Parkland's gaze and raised an eyebrow.

"Figured he was about to lay into you and I didn't want to see it. Besides, though, it *will* be better to have it official than you just 'helping me out.'"

"Appreciate the thought," Concho said. "But I'm not much worried about him 'laying into me.'"

"Right," Parkland said. "I also got some news on the case I wanted to relay anyway."

"Shoot."

Parkland held up his phone. "The coroner texted me the name of the black fellow we found. Wanted to run it by you."

"Glad to hear it."

Parkland called up the text, peered at it for a moment. "Looks like the guy had used various aliases but his real name was Donnell Blackthorne. Kind of a pretentious moniker for that skinny little fella."

Concho remembered what it felt like to get blindsided in football. This was much the same.

"Uh… Surely that's a mistake," he said.

"No, don't reckon so," Parkland said, frowning. "Looks like the fella was into just about everything—drugs, prostitution, gunrunning, money laundering." The sheriff was looking at Concho and seemed to realize the name had punched the Ranger in the guts. "You OK? You recognize it?"

Concho realized his breath was coming fast, and quickly made an effort to control it. His left hand tapped on his hip. "I think I've got something for you. But…I need to check on a couple of things." He sought Parkland's gaze again. "I'm…I'll call you this evening."

He turned without waiting for a response and headed for the back door to City Hall. He needed to get clear of this place, get somewhere in the fresh air where he could think.

CHAPTER 22

Concho made it to his truck undetected by the reporters, who were still gathered in front of the City Hall listening to various talking heads. A few minutes later, he was on his way back to the reservation. His mind lay elsewhere though.

At twenty-six, he'd returned home from Afghanistan with the rest of his Army Ranger Unit. They'd been sent to Joint Base Lewis-McChord outside of Tacoma, Washington, in the Puget Sound region. That land, with its wealth of lakes and rivers, the Sound itself, and its lush evergreen forests, it couldn't have been more different from the burned and barren drylands of Afghanistan, or from south Texas where Concho had grown up.

Flying in, the Army Ranger had been looking forward to exploring some of the forests, maybe doing some hunting and fishing. The attraction of the place was destroyed for him almost immediately. A lieutenant had been waiting for him when he got off the plane, had handed him a note ordering him to report immediately to the base commander's office.

He remembered: the damp, living air, thick with moisture that his skin seemed to drink gratefully, the smell of jet fuel and tarmac cut through by the scents of pine and cedar and spruce and fir, the jokes and laughter of his squadmates, who walked past him on their way to R&R (rest and recreation). And then, there was the note in his hand, which left a brassy, unpleasant taste in his mouth. He had no specific reason for the feeling, but he knew it wasn't good news.

On the jeep ride to the CO's office, the lieutenant tried to engage Concho in conversation about his duty overseas. The effort failed miserably. Concho didn't like discussing the war with anyone and wasn't talkative even at the best of times. This was not the best of times. By the time they reached their destination, the silence between them was as deep as the forests around the base.

A guard in a white helmet and white armband let Concho into the building once he'd seen the note signed by the CO. Another soldier led him down a hallway to a small waiting room where a male secretary tap-tapped at a keyboard. Concho barely had time to seat himself in an uncomfortably small chair before the door to an inner office opened and he was ushered inside.

The CO's name was Perkins. Leonard. His iron-gray hair, his clean-shaven face with a hint of a 5 o'clock shadow, and a uniform as neat and precise as his movements, gave Perkins the look of the kind of commanding officer one could order from Officers-R-Us. Concho saluted. Perkins returned it and waved for the big soldier to relax. They shook hands and, after, Concho tucked his hands behind his back.

"Welcome home, soldier," Perkins said. "Helluva job, over there."

"Thank you, sir," Concho said, but his gaze lingered curiously on the other guest in the room. He was a civilian, a dark-skinned man immaculately and expensively dressed in a gray suit, maroon tie, and various gold accoutrements, such as a watch, cuff links, and tie tack.

"This is Cyrus Abelard," Perkins said, pointing a hand at the civilian. "A lawyer. He has…. Well, I'll let him explain."

Abelard rose smoothly from his chair and offered his hand to

Concho. They shook.

"Concho Ten-Wolves," Abelard said. "I'm very happy to meet you."

"Why?"

Abelard didn't seem taken aback at all by Concho's abrupt tone. "I have a very important client. A very wealthy one. He's interested in meeting you. It involves your family."

"I don't have any family," Concho said. "My grandmother and grandfather are both dead. It was years ago."

"Well, this doesn't have to do with them," Abelard said. "And I'm not actually familiar with all the details. My clients hire me for my discretion but they don't always tell me why I'm being discreet. I *can* tell you that everything will be explained soon. If you'll just give me a little bit of your time."

Concho glanced over at Perkins, who said, "At the request of Mr. Abelard's client, you've been granted two days' leave to deal with family matters."

"As I said, sir, I don't have any family."

Perkins shrugged, and his tight-lipped smile made it clear he didn't like the situation either. "You know the army, soldier. There are ranks far above yours. And mine. Someone in those ranks apparently wants this leave to happen."

"And if I refuse?"

Abelard started to speak but Perkins held up a hand abruptly to forestall him. "Ten-Wolves," Perkins said. "You're a soldier under my command. If you decide you don't want to go with this lawyer, I'm not gonna order you. I'm sure you're aware, of course, there will be consequences for us both. Lord knows what those will be."

Abelard knew enough to keep his mouth shut, though he looked like he'd just chewed up a prune.

"All right, sir," Concho said to Perkins after a moment. "I'll be back in two days." He glanced at the lawyer. "Or sooner."

Abelard inclined his head slightly and spoke quickly into his phone. "Please, this way," he said a moment later to Concho.

The lawyer turned to leave the office, and Concho followed after saluting Len Perkins again and getting another salute in return. The white-helmeted guard opened the door and held it for Abelard and Concho. As they stepped outside, a copper-colored BMW SUV pulled up. Concho recognized the X3 model, but this wasn't the standard issue. After his stint in Afghanistan, he recognized an armored vehicle when he saw one, even if it had been disguised as no more than an upscale Bimmer.

A white man who wore his suit like a uniform and was probably ex-military slid from behind the wheel, opened the SUV's back door, and held it open. Concho leaned down a little to look in. The tall black man already sitting in the back seat was probably seventy but looked younger. His shoulders were broad, his body lean. The fit of his exquisitely tailored suit made Cyrus Abelard look positively disheveled.

"Mr. Ten-Wolves," the man said in a modulated voice that indicated professional vocal training. "I am most happy to finally meet you. Won't you join me?"

Concho knew a king wolf when he saw one. And this Bimmer was a pretty fancy den to be invited into. He wasn't wearing a sidearm, but there were a couple of knives secreted around his body. And the threat inherent in the situation seemed latent. Whatever the man wanted, it wouldn't be until after Concho turned him down that the danger would come. He figured he'd be able to get in and get back out again if he had to.

Concho slid into the back seat. The man offered his hand but Concho didn't take it. His defenses were up now. "What's this all about?" he asked.

The man didn't seem offended to have his offer of a handshake rebuffed. He leaned back in his seat and said, "Driver!"

The bodyguard returned to the SUV and Abelard climbed in on the passenger side. The Bimmer started up and pulled out toward the base's main gate.

The man looked once more at Concho. "My name is Hamilton Blackthorne."

"Am I supposed to recognize it?"

"Not really. But what about Donnell Blackthorne?"

***

Concho's reverie ended abruptly as he turned onto one of the reservation's isolated dirt roads and light exploded in his eyes. A black pickup with a piece of railroad tie strapped across the bumper like a battering ram whipped off of a side road in a pall of dust and lunged directly at him. Its headlights were on but they weren't what blinded him in the middle of the day. The truck had a spotlight, like a white incandescent spear. The glare punched Concho in the face.

Concho swerved hard to go around the vehicle, but the road was too soft. The rear of the Ford F-150 lost traction. The truck slewed sideways. Concho fought for control but now the black pickup plunged into his left-front bumper and tore it loose with a shriek and a shower of sparks.

The Ford's airbag went off in the Ranger's face. The F-150 came up on two wheels but didn't quite roll. It slammed back down, slid sideways on the road's loose dirt. The ditch seemed to reach for the vehicle, suck it in. The driver's side of the truck smashed against the wall of the ditch, jarring Concho from the toes up. The engine died.

Through a haze of shock and pain, Concho heard brakes squealing in the road. Vehicle doors were thrown open. Shouts roared. The Ranger knew what was coming next.

If he didn't get out of the truck, he was dead.

CHAPTER 23

The airbag snagged at Concho's body like a clammy blanket. The seat belt constricted like a python. Concho grabbed for the belt latch. It was jammed. The truck was tilted downward on the driver's side. He couldn't see the road. But whoever had run him into the ditch would be coming for him in seconds. With guns.

He fumbled with his left hand for the knife he always carried at his belt, pulled it free and slashed the airbag away. Stale air, smelling of plastic, erupted in his face. He grabbed the seat belt, slashed through it with the razor-sharp blade of the Bowie.

Footsteps thudded on the road. Someone racked the slide on a weapon. There was no way out the door on Concho's side; it was pressed closed against the wall of the ditch. But he'd been driving with his windows down, as he generally did on the reservation.

"Kill him!" someone shouted.

Twisting his body, Concho thrust himself through the window of the Ford. It was a tight fit but he made it just as more than one gun sprayed bullets into the passenger side of his Ford.

Metal shrieked, lead caromed, glass shattered and sprayed. Concho hit the ground hard behind the truck but held onto his wind. He couldn't get into the ditch itself but the cab of the truck hid him from the road. And he still had his pistols. He snapped the thong off his left-side Colt, drew it, opened fire over the hood. He couldn't see a target. He only wanted to let them know he could still bite, to keep them back.

Now Concho dropped his knife and drew his right-side pistol. Bullets pinged and ricocheted across his truck. One of the tires blew. For an instant there came a lull. He heard someone changing an empty magazine.

"Where is he?" a voice shouted. "Where the hell is he?"

"Here!" Concho shouted as he rose into a crouch.

Two armed men were in the road, advancing openly and foolishly on Concho's wrecked truck. They had bandanas tied across the lower part of their faces but one was a white man, the other an Indian. A third man, with shaggy blond hair, sunglasses, and a balaclava that hid most of his face, stood by the open door of the black pickup with a pistol in his fist. The vehicle's engine was running.

The white man had his rifle reloaded; it looked like an AR-15. He raised it as Concho shouted, and the big Ranger fired both his Colts into the man's body at barely a dozen yards distance. The gunman staggered backward, a look of surprise on his face. Before Concho could see the man fall, the Indian opened fire and the Ranger flung himself down. Something whipped through his hair, and yanked at it like a passing hawk swooping on a mouse.

"Let's go! Let's go! Let's go!" a voice screamed.

Concho didn't dare try looking over the hood again. Rolling to his right, he came up behind the attached toolbox sitting in his truck bed just behind the cab. He lifted his head just in time to see the Indian fling himself into the empty bed of the black pickup.

The driver wearing the balaclava revved the engine and slammed the vehicle into gear. Concho rose to his full height and opened fire. The pickup fishtailed away. Concho emptied his pistols, heard a few bullets ping against metal but couldn't see if he'd hit anything else.

When the Colts were empty, Concho ceased fire. The truck was out of range. The Ranger slipped the magazines out of his pistols and reloaded, then stepped around the Ford.

The man he'd shot still lay where he'd fallen in the middle of the road. An AR-15 rested next to him. One of Concho's bullets had struck him in the middle of the chest, the other in the meat of the left shoulder. The chest shot had killed him. The mask had come askew at one side. It was no one he knew.

The fellow had on a long-sleeved green shirt with the cuffs un-buttoned. Concho used the toe of his boot to push the sleeve up the man's wrist. The bottom of a swastika tattoo came into view. That made sense. This man was cut from the same mold as the white supremacists who'd followed Darrel Fallon. The Aryan Brother-hood might want revenge on him for taking down Fallon, but he wouldn't have expected them to try it on the reservation. And....

Sirens in the distance caught Concho's attention. He frowned. It was too soon for the tribal police to be on the scene. Some-thing was odd. Feeling exhausted from the fading adrenaline rush, Concho holstered his Colts and walked over to sag against his bullet-ridden truck. He checked himself over and found cuts and bruises he didn't remember getting. His scalp stung from a bullet that had passed close enough to yank out a knot of hair. Nothing permanent, though.

As he leaned there, wishing oddly for one of old Meskwaa's smokes, a white SUV with the Kickapoo Tribal Police emblem on the side and the siren flinging light and sound came barreling through the afternoon dust toward him. He stepped back into the road and raised a hand to stop them from running over the corpse. The vehicle slid to a stop and Daniel Alvarado bailed out of the passenger side, his Glock 40 in his hand. Roberto Echabarri, the only other tribal deputy at present, scrambled out from behind the wheel with a shotgun in his hands.

"What the hell, Ten-Wolves?" Alvarado shouted. "What the hell! You don't bring your white man wars onto this reservation!"

"Interesting," Concho said. "How would you know this was part of a 'white man war', Alvarado?"

The Kickapoo deputy hesitated before gesturing at the body in the road. "That's a white man, ain't it?"

"It is," Concho agreed. "And judging by his tattoos, probably an attempt at payback for the Darrel Fallon incident. But how did he get on the Rez? And why was there an Indian with him?"

"What?" Alvarado demanded. "What Indian?"

"A black pickup ran me off the road." Concho pointed toward his truck in the ditch. "Then they tried to fill me full of holes. Three men. Two were white. The other was an Indian who I'd never seen before."

"An Indian?" Echabarri asked. "Who you didn't recognize? On the Rez?"

Concho heard the skepticism in the deputy's voice and stared at him. Echabarri was new on the job, less than six months. He was one of the few local Kickapoo with a college education. Political science. Rumor had it he was saving money for graduate school, to be a teacher, and maybe a writer. Concho rather liked him and thought he might turn out all right if he stayed out from under Alvarado's wing.

"I wouldn't expect them to send someone I knew," he said, answering Echabarri's questions quietly.

"They might have," Alvarado disagreed. "If they didn't expect you to be alive to tell anyone."

Concho ignored the statement. "How did you get here so fast? I heard the sirens almost the instant the pickup took off."

Alvarado's dark eyes and face were unreadable. It was Echabarri who answered. "We were on…patrol," he said. "Chief Alvarado," he nodded his head toward his companion, "was showing me some of the ropes. I got a call on my cell phone. Didn't recognize the number or the voice. It just said there was a shooting in progress."

"A shooting in progress? Those were the caller's actual words?"

"Yes, why?"

"Because it sounds like a cop or someone who knows the lingo."

Echabarri's teeth clicked together audibly. His eyes showed his surprise.

"I tried to trace the call while Echabarri was driving," Alvarado said. "Looks like it was probably one of those burner phones."

"That didn't seem suspicious to you?" Concho asked.

Alvarado shrugged. "Not particularly. Some around here don't care much for the police knowing their business. But it almost seems like you're accusing *us* of something. You figure Echabarri and I are involved somehow? Maybe we were just waiting for the word that you'd been shot down to come rolling in here?"

Concho smiled, and it wasn't a nice one. "Not accusing Echabarri of anything."

Alvarado's face darkened as he flushed. His free hand closed into a fist. "Pendejo! I should throw you in jail."

"Seems like you have enough trouble as it is investigating Ben Deer-Run's death. And now with an attempted murder of a Texas Ranger."

"For all I know, you staged this yourself!" Alvarado snarled.

Concho shook his head. "Yeah. It's a little film project I'm doing. And this extra," he pointed at the dead man in the road, "even died on the job. So hard to get good help these days. Maybe, though, right now, you might want to call in a description of that black pickup. It was a Chevy. Older model. Some rust on the fenders. Oh, and it's got a few bullet holes in it. The license plate was too dirty to read."

Concho turned to walk back toward his truck as he heard Echabarri say, "I'll call it in."

The Ranger was standing beside his truck counting the bullet holes when a text came through. He pulled the phone out of his pocket and checked it.

One text, from an unknown source. It read: *Lucky boy. Almost had you. Next time.*

CHAPTER 24

Concho's eyes sought Alvarado. The deputy was bent over the dead man, studying the scene. Interesting how he'd mentioned "burner phones" just a few minutes earlier. These were cheap phones loaded with prepaid minutes so they could be used briefly for calls and texts and discarded. No one could trace them through a phone plan, and even if you were able to get a number it would not link back to any specific user. Criminals often used them, even purchasing them in bulk for just such a purpose. Concho was quite sure his text had come from such a phone.

But Alvarado had been in clear view when the text came in and couldn't have sent it. Roberto Echabarri was inside the SUV, though, out of sight. He *could* have sent the text but Concho didn't figure him for it. *Who then?* Not many had his cell phone number.

Except, he thought. That wasn't true. Or might not be true. On the day of Ben Deer-Run's murder, he'd called Alvarado on this phone, which meant the deputy had access to his number and could have given it to anyone.

He also considered the wording, "Lucky boy." Jacob Drake's bodyguard, Wayne, had recently called him a "lucky man" in the casino parking lot. Wayne might have reason to orchestrate this little gig, and he seemed like he might be sympathetic to the Aryan

Brotherhood's cause. But, he struck Concho as more of a 'straight-ahead' kind of fellow, and he probably wouldn't have taken any action at all without Drake's go-ahead.

Alvarado and Drake were friends, or at least business associates. The tribal deputy could have given Concho's number to Drake, who certainly seemed cold blooded. That didn't mean he was a killer, and even if he was, would he do it as a favor for Alvarado? It was all just speculation, though. Nothing but reaching. He'd taken an automatic dislike to Drake but had to accept he could be wrong. He'd been mistaken about people a few times.

Echabarri climbed back out of the SUV and stopped to speak a few words with Alvarado before coming toward Concho, who slid his phone back in his pocket. The Kickapoo deputy whistled at the condition of the Ranger's truck.

"Lucky you got out," the man said. "I called in the black pickup to the Sheriff's Office of Maverick County. I also notified security at the casino. I have to take your statement. Then I'll get back on patrol myself."

Concho didn't like how often the word "lucky" seemed to be getting thrown around these days, but it was probably just a coincidence coming out of Echabarri's mouth. It wasn't an unlikely term considering that Concho indeed felt pretty lucky.

"All right," he said

Echabarri took a pen out of the pocket of his uniform shirt and lay the notepad he was carrying across the hood of the F-150. He clicked the button on the pen and looked at Concho expectantly. The Ranger told him what had happened, except he left off the part about the text message.

***

Answering questions, checking the crime scene, and wait-ing for the coroner took most of the afternoon. Concho later called John Gray-Dove, who was not only one of the best local mechanics but also maintained his own repair shop on the Rez. Gray-Dove came to tow the F-150. Concho rode along. Another good thing about Gray-Dove was that he didn't ask a lot of questions, such as "how come there are bullet holes in your truck?"

Once they reached Gray-Dove's shop, which wasn't far from tribal police headquarters, Gray-Dove gave the vehicle a good once-over and walked over to Concho.

"Holes in the body can be repaired," he said. "Nothing hit the gas tank. One tire shot out but the wheel is OK. The engine! Can't fix that. Can get you a rebuild nearly as good. Two or three days. Another day to put it in."

Concho nodded. "And the cost?"

"Not cheap. But it won't break you. Maybe the Rangers will pay for it?"

"I might get reimbursed eventually but it'll take more than two or three days."

Gray-Dove nodded. "Give me what you can. The rest later."

"Thanks," Concho said in Kickapoo. "Don't worry about it. Give me the price. I can cover it and get the money back from the Rangers later."

Gray-Dove nodded again. "I'll write it up. Give you a call. Need a loaner to get home?"

"I do," Concho said. "Is it something I can drive or do I have to ride it?"

Gray-Dove grinned. "Drive. But carefully."

"Thanks again."

"No bullet holes!" Gray-Dove said.

***

Early evening shadows had begun to gather around Con-cho's trailer by the time he got home. He pulled the vehicle Gray-Dove had loaned him, a 1997 green Chevy Silverado, up in front of his house and killed the engine. While the motor cooled and ticked, he sat and listened to the last cicadas of the day buzzing their love to the world.

He knew he needed to call Isaac Parkland, to tell him about the latest attack but also to give the man what he knew about Donnell Blackthorne. Thinking of the name took him right back to the day at Joint Base Lewis-McChord when he'd met Hamilton Blackthorne, who claimed to be Donnell's father...

"Though, of course, you are unaware of it," Hamilton Blackthorne had said as they left the base in Blackthorne's Bimmer, "I've been searching for you for a long time. It's quite amazing to meet in reality."

"I still don't know why," Concho had said.

"Let me treat you to a good meal and I'll explain everything."

Concho shrugged. "I could eat."

They drove into Tacoma, Washington, while Hamilton kept up a steady chatter about his status as a self-made man, a multi-millionaire who'd first earned his money organizing African American truck drivers, who'd then started his own insurance company and bought up real estate no one but a visionary such as himself could see the worth in. Concho figured there was much more to it, and probably a few things that at least skirted the edge of criminality if they didn't cross that border, but he didn't ask. He didn't really care.

After pulling into a covered parking garage in the bowels of a high-rise office building, Blackthorne and Abelard, with their bodyguard and Concho in tow, took a small private elevator to a penthouse restaurant with glass walls that looked out on a panoramic view over the city.

The restaurant had no signage. Concho couldn't even tell if it had a name. It was about half full of people who looked very rich. Yet, no one remarked on or even seemed to notice Concho's wrinkled fatigues. A maître d' in a black-tie led them to a table in a private, glassed-in alcove. Only Blackthorne and Concho went in. Abelard and the bodyguard waited outside; they'd both be able to see what happened in the room but wouldn't hear anything.

A waitress in a tasteful pencil skirt and a long-sleeved white shirt brought them menus and took their drink orders. Blackthorne ordered wine, some name and vintage Concho had never heard of. Concho told her the water on the table would be fine.

"I noticed you studying me as we drove," Blackthorne said when the waitress left. "You see it don't you?"

"See what?"

"The resemblance. These extra wide shoulders." Blackthorne shrugged. "Not easy to fit a suit over them without looking like a well-dressed savage. The skin color too. You're the same shade as I am."

"I've served with plenty of men who had the same skin tone," Concho said. "It doesn't mean anything."

"Hum," Blackthorne mused. "Maybe it doesn't always mean something," he said. "But in this case, there's a reason. I'm your grandfather."

***

Concho shook away the memories and climbed out of the loaned pickup. The closest cicadas fell silent. Evening's first cool breeze brushed over him, wrapping him in the smell of the drylands. A coyote yipped in the distance while a few late dining birds hopped around beneath the big mesquite tree where his firepit was located.

A light came on his trailer where no light should be.

CHAPTER 25

Concho drew his right-hand Colt and moved swiftly to-
ward his front steps. Ignoring the sound of the rattle under the
stairs, Concho turned the key in his door and eased it open, making
sure not to silhouette himself against the dying sun. He always kept
his door hinges oiled but, even so, there came a faint creak of sound.

Only silence met that noise.

Concho pushed the door open slowly with the barrel of his pistol and stepped inside. The light he'd seen was in the kitchen area
to his left. He could see the glow there but no movement. Nor was
there any sound. He became aware, though, of more lights on in
the back of the house that shouldn't be lit.

The living room in front of him brimmed full of shadows but
held nothing living. The door to the main bedroom on his right
was closed and he didn't remember closing it when he'd left this
morning. More than one person might be in the house—someone in the kitchen, someone in the bedroom. If so, he could be
caught in a cross fire.

Keeping his back against the front wall of the trailer, he eased
toward the kitchen. A lingering scent briefly brushed his nostrils,
too faint to identify. A toilet flushed in the bathroom behind the
kitchen. Concho brought up his gun as the bathroom door opened.

He heard footsteps, and a soft humming. He stepped forward where he could see the person coming into the kitchen. A gasp sounded as the person saw him in return. He sighed in relief and lowered his Colt. Now he recognized the scent too—perfume.

"Maria!"

Maria Morales slowly raised her hands over her head. "I don't think the gun will be necessary, Officer," she said, smiling.

Concho holstered his pistol and walked toward Maria. She met him and hugged him with her head on his shoulder. He returned the hug, forcing himself not to squeeze as hard as he wanted to.

"How did you get here?" Concho asked. "Where's your car?"

"Car's in the shop," Maria said. "Henry brought me."

"How *is* your brother?"

"Just as pompous and arrogant as he ever was. And he glared disapprovingly at me all the way over here. But he's my older brother and I love him."

Concho chuckled. He slid one big hand up Maria's arm over the sleeve of her black silk shirt. "I—" he started to say.

Maria gave another gasp as she saw his face more clearly in the light. "What happened to you? Are you OK?"

"Wrecked my truck," Concho explained. "Guess both our vehicles are kaput."

Maria shook her head. "Go sit by the table," she said. "I'll get your first aid kit and clean you up. I know where it's at. Looks like you've done nothing about these cuts."

"Maria."

She started to turn away. "You never take care of yourself."

"Maria!" He squeezed her arm, bringing her gaze back to his. "As much as I'm glad to see you, this isn't a good time for you to be here."

"Has there *ever* been a good time?" she asked, with just a hint of heat in the words.

"Better times at least. The wreck was no accident. Three men ran me off the road. Then tried to kill me. One of 'em was Aryan

Brotherhood. I'm sure they were looking for payback for what I did at the mall."

Saying nothing, Maria studied him with her gold-flecked brown eyes.

"The other two got away," Concho added, "but I don't know they won't come back. I don't want you caught in it."

"I've already been caught in it once," Maria said. "And you weren't anywhere around when that started. But you finished it. You saved me from it. And a lot of other people. The safest place in this world right now might be with Concho Ten-Wolves."

"The difference then was they didn't know I was coming. I surprised them. Now, I'm the one being hunted."

"Just means they aren't very smart."

"Most of them aren't," Concho agreed. "But Fallon is. If he's got a hand in this. I'd still feel better if you weren't around me at the moment."

Maria took a long breath. "I... I don't want to put you at greater risk having to watch over me," she said.

"That's not what I meant," Concho said.

She raised a hand to stop him. "I know. But it's still true. Look, let me treat those cuts before they get infected. After, you can take me back to town. Or I'll call Henry."

"All right," Concho agreed.

He sat at the kitchen table while Maria fetched his first aid kit from beneath the bathroom sink. While Concho toughed it out, she used cotton swabs and alcohol to clean the glass cuts on his face. Even the astringency of the alcohol couldn't hide the scent of her perfume from him.

"This one needed stitches," she said, swabbing carefully around an inch and a half long cut on his right cheek. "But it's already scabbing over so I best leave it alone. I'll put a band aid on it."

"Thanks, Nurse Morales."

They both grinned.

The sound of a vehicle driving into the yard erased the

grins. Concho rose to his feet. Maria stood at his side, her hands clenched. A gun case rested against the wall of the living room. It contained a shotgun and a couple of rifles, as well as two pistols. Concho strode quickly to it, took out a Smith & Wesson .38 with a four-inch barrel, which he handed to Maria.

"I want you to go into the bathroom and stay there until I call you," he said to Maria. "If there's any shooting, get in the tub. Will you do that?"

"No," Maria said. "But I'll be right here behind the wall as backup if you need me."

"Maria!"

She flipped open the cylinder of the revolver to check the loads, then snapped it closed again. "I'm a reasonable girl but sometimes you just have to give me my moments. You taught me how to shoot. If I have to, I will."

With no time to argue (and he wouldn't have won anyway), Concho nodded, left her there, and moved in a crouch to the front door. Standing to one side of the opening, he peered out the small rectangular window at the top of the door.

Night had almost taken over from the day. He could barely see the Silverado sitting where he'd parked it. Next to it stood another vehicle, a dimly glowing, white SUV with an emblem on the side. He recognized it—the same tribal police SUV he'd seen earlier today with Alvarado and Roberto Echabarri in it.

Echabarri's voice called out.

"Concho Ten-Wolves! We need to talk. Why don't you come out?"

CHAPTER 26

Concho glanced at Maria, who was peeking around the wall partition. She shook her head 'no,' and he put his finger over his lips to warn her to silence.

"You alone?" he called out to Echabarri.

"Yes. I left Alvarado at the casino."

"Move to where I can see you."

"This is ridiculous!" Echabarri protested.

"Means there's no reason why you'd mind."

Echabarri shrugged in the shadows, then stepped around his SUV and walked several feet toward Concho. Enough ambient light remained in the world for Concho to see the Kickapoo deputy's hands, which were nowhere near his holstered service pistol.

Concho glanced back at Maria and lifted his hand to indicate calm. He stepped out onto his front steps, leaving the door open. Not wanting to be silhouetted even by the dim light in the house behind him, Concho strode down into the yard. The rattle came from under his porch.

"What the…" Echabarri said, taking an involuntary step back.

"Don't worry," Concho said. "It's just Maggie. She only eats rats. You're not a rat, are you?"

"Alvarado was right about one thing," Echabarri said. "You

are an asshole."

Concho grinned. "Not as much as he is. So, what do we need to talk about?"

Echabarri reached up and scratched his high forehead. "If you tell Alvarado about this, losing my job is about the best outcome I can hope for."

"He won't hear anything from me."

Echabarri rubbed his nose and sighed. "I figured you needed to know. We found the black pickup. Parked near the back row of the casino lot. License plate was deliberately muddied but it didn't match that vehicle anyway. Stolen off a truck in Eagle Pass."

"Did you check the casino for the perps?"

"Alvarado did. But he said they'd probably just left the truck there and had another getaway vehicle waiting. I figured he was right."

"Probably," Concho agreed. "Any word on the dead guy?"

Echabarri shook his head. "Not yet. Not so I've heard anyway."

"You didn't need to drive all the way out here to tell me about the truck," Concho said. "What else?"

The deputy sighed again. "This could get me hurt."

"I may be an asshole," Concho said. "But not enough of one to betray someone who's given me good information."

Echabarri's gaze met Concho's. He nodded his head. "You were suspicious about how fast we got to the scene today. I guess I was too." He lifted his palms to preface what he said next: "I don't have *any* proof at all of it. You need to know that. But the whole thing was odd."

"I completed my training a couple of months back," the deputy continued. "But today Alvarado said he wanted to do a ride along. Make sure I was doing a good job. He told me what road to take. Just before the…incident, he had me pull over. He got out and was fiddling with his phone. At least I think he was. I wasn't paying much attention.

"Then I got the call about a 'shooting in progress.' And where.

Didn't occur to me that it sounded like a cop's wording. I don't see how it could have been Alvarado. But I can't rule it out.

"Anyway, I yelled for Alvarado and he jumped in the SUV. We were barely a mile from the site. I figured it was just... well...you know how Alvarado is lucky about such things. About...catching criminals."

"He's lucky because he's on the take, Echabarri. He's corrupt. The big fish throw him the small ones to keep him off their backs and make him look good."

Echabarri was nodding. "I can't know for sure. But I've had my suspicions. Can't just take your word for it, though. I don't really know you."

"You're a good man, Roberto," Concho said. "And I understand. You're in a hard place. Make sure you keep the stink off you."

"I think I'm going to have to resign. The line is getting too narrow to walk."

"You do what you have to do. But, there's no guarantee the Tribal Council will appoint Alvarado to follow Ben Deer-Run as chief of police. I know a council member who won't support him. And another who is waffling. Could be you instead."

"I'm not ready."

"You may have to be, and better start thinking about who you'll bring on as deputies. But what about the voice behind the phone call today? Recognize anything about it?"

Echabarri shook his head. "I've been racking my brain on that one. It was so quick. A few seconds. But I'm thinking it was disguised somehow. It sounded...echoey."

"Seems likely," Concho said. "Anything else you need to tell me?"

"I asked Alvarado about the Indian you said you saw. He told me you had to be mistaken. Said you'd just seen a white man with dark hair wearing a mask."

"You don't think I'd recognize an Indian?"

Echabarri shrugged. "I don't know I would in the middle of being shot at."

"Been shot at before."

Echabarri's eyes caught a little of the evening glow. "I guess so," he said.

"I'm betting the man involved is part of the resurgence of the NATV Bloods on the Rez. And I know a few young men came here recently from the Oklahoma Tribe. I met one of them, a Joseph Big-Pine. Another one is named Bull Knife but I haven't seen him yet."

"I know Big-Pine. Even did a ride along with him. Alvarado says he's training for the tribal police, too."

"What did you think of him?"

"A sullen sort of fellow. But he seemed OK to me. Didn't hear anything from him that sounded like he'd be in the Bloods. Alvarado says the resurgence thing is nonsense."

"He would. But he was hanging around the edge of that crowd when he and I were kids. Maybe he's still got those sympathies."

"Noted. But one thing you just said makes no sense. Why in any world would a NATV Blood be hanging out with white supremacists and trying to kill a Texas Ranger on the reservation? I can't see it happening."

Concho nodded. "You've got a point. There's definitely something I'm missing."

"I'll keep my ears open," Echabarri said. "I've been curious about this Bull Knife, too."

"Let me ask you another question," Concho said. "Have you seen a man named Jacob Drake around?"

"I know who he is. He's staying at the casino hotel. In a comped room from what I hear. Why?"

"I don't know how or what yet, but he and Alvarado are up to something shady. Pretty sure Big-Pine knows about it."

"I've seen Alvarado and Drake together several times," Echabarri said. "They do seem pretty chummy." He shook his head and expelled a long breath of air.

"You all right?" Concho asked.

"I don't know. But I better go. Alvarado will be wondering where I'm at."

"One last thing," Concho said. "Unrelated. Probably. Estrella Deer-Run's husband hasn't been home in nearly a week. Bearfoot. You know him?"

"I've met him," Echabarri said. "I'll uh…check up on him."

"Thanks." Concho took a few steps toward Echabarri and offered his hand. They shook, and the deputy climbed back into his SUV and drove off.

Concho returned to the house, to Maria. She put down her pistol and came into his arms to be kissed. Things escalated from there.

***

A few minutes after four in the morning, Concho awoke to the chime of his cell phone signaling a message. He lay in bed beside Maria. Her breathing came slow and steady and the heady mix of her perfume and the scent of their lovemaking hung in the air. He smiled and reached a big hand to lightly stroke her shoulder before rolling over on the king-size bed, which he'd bought right after buying this trailer.

A lot of Kickapoo slept in hammocks. Many considered it traditional. Concho hadn't done so since he was a kid. Not enough support for a fellow of his bulk, and he was glad of it now because of Maria.

His bedside table held his phone, a reading lamp, and a collection of N. Scott Momaday's stories and poems called *In the Presence of the Sun*. Picking up the phone, he swiped it on. One message showed. Frowning, he pulled it up and read it. A hot flush of anger drove everything else out of his awareness. The message read:

Blood will tell.

CHAPTER 27

Isaac Parkland answered the phone. He sounded like he'd been dragged out of sleep by a tractor. Maybe that wasn't far from the truth. It was barely 6 AM. Concho had waited as long as he could before calling the sheriff.

"Ten-Wolves," Parkland said. "What? What's going on?"

"Sorry to wake you, Sheriff, but I have news you need to hear. I was going to call you last evening but a lot of things happened."

Concho described the attempt on his life and his conversation with Roberto Echabarri. He then told Parkland about the two text messages he'd gotten.

Parkland sounded wide awake now. "From the same source, you think?"

"Pretty sure."

"And no idea who?"

It occurred to Concho that the same person who'd sent him the texts was likely the one who'd called Echabarri to report the attack on him along the road. That man had used the phrase "shooting in progress." If it were the same man, it might mean….

"Concho?" Parkland questioned as he waited for a response.

"Sorry," Concho said. "Was thinking. I don't know who sent the messages but it may either be a law officer or someone who knows the profession."

"Why do you say that?"

Concho explained.

Parkland sighed. "I hate to think it but your reasoning makes sense."

"I've got another name for you to check out. May be connected in some way."

"Hang on, let me get a pencil," Parkland replied. Concho heard the sheriff rustling around through the phone. A moment later came a "Shoot!"

"Jacob Drake," Concho said. "He's got something going on with Alvarado over at the casino. Not sure how it might tie in. Says he's from Germany originally but is a naturalized citizen. Don't know where he lives. He's staying at the casino hotel now. I'd like to know about his background."

"Gotcha. There's also…uhm, you said yesterday you thought you might know something about the second victim, Donnell Blackthorne."

"Yeah. The name knocked me for a bit of a loop. Had to call up some memories, but…well, I never met Donnell but I met a Hamilton Blackthorne nearly ten years back. Hamilton *claimed* he was my grandfather. And said Donnell was my biological father."

Parkland made no response for a moment. Finally, "OK, strange. Did you believe him?"

"He said he'd found some DNA match, or partial match, with my military records. He didn't show it to me and I didn't ask to see it."

"Can I ask why?"

"I didn't like the man and was skeptical about his motives. Or maybe I just didn't care. But the coincidence of the name Donnell Blackthorne popping up here, now, bears looking into."

"Agreed," Parkland said.

"What have you got on this Donnell locally?"

"Nothing. We can't even find out where he was staying. No local hotel has any records or recollections of him."

"Did you check the Lucky Eagle?"

"No, I was going to ask you to do it. Don't want to step on any toes."

"I'll check and let you know if I get a hit. Something else to keep in mind: Hamilton Blackthorne is very rich and didn't get that way legally. At least, not completely legally."

"Good to know. I'm gonna have to call him. Tell him his son is dead. Is he going to be a problem?"

"I don't know, but best keep my name out of it."

"Right," Parkland agreed.

Concho sighed. "I'll let you get back to sleep. I've got some things to do. Sorry again for waking you."

"It's OK. You watch yourself. And if you come by the department later today, I'll see you're issued a temporary vehicle to replace your truck."

"Thanks, I'll do that."

"Make it after ten, though," Parkland said, and disconnected.

Concho clicked off his phone. He stared out the kitchen window at the morning light rising in the world, and for the third time his memories took him back almost ten years to Washington state, to an exclusive restaurant and the man named Hamilton Blackthorne.

"I'm your grandfather," Hamilton Blackthorne had claimed. "My son, Donnell, is your father."

"Doesn't mean anything to me," Concho said. "My Kickapoo grandfather and grandmother raised me. They're my family."

"But you have another family. Don't you want to know about them?"

"I had the only one I needed growing up on the reservation. That time has passed."

"It hasn't for me," Blackthorne said. "I…my son and I…we don't speak really. I'd like to get to know my grandson. I'm seventy-one years old. I don't know how long I have left. I...need—"

"Not my concern," Concho interrupted.

He'd been suspicious of Blackthorne from the start. Now, suspicion blossomed into dislike. It had something to do with the arrogance and inability to talk about anything else but himself and his wants. It had to do with the casual but blatant display of wealth and power. It was partially the assumption that Concho would be honored to find himself related to a man he'd never seen before, a man who'd earned no place in his life. And perhaps, he admitted to himself, it had to do with this man's son taking his mother away from him when he was a child.

"You don't know what I can do for you," Blackthorne snapped. Clearly, he wasn't used to having his wishes thwarted. "I have wealth. Influence. If you want to stay in the army, I can make you an officer. Any posting you want. Or I can give you a job in my organization. More money than you've seen or *will* see in your life."

"I don't need to be made anything. Or given anything. I do for myself."

"Don't be a fool. You must have grown up dirt poor on that damn reservation. Not enough food. None of the finer things in life. I can give you those. And women if you want them."

Concho's dislike of the man turned to anger. The suave, controlled businessman of earlier was starting to show his hackles. They weren't pretty.

"My grandmother and I were wealthier in the important things than you'll ever be," Concho said. "I want nothing from you."

He rose to his feet and Blackthorne grabbed his arm in a still-powerful grip. "No one walks away from me!" the man snapped.

Concho closed his own hand over Blackthorne's wrist. He began to exert pressure. The older man's eyes registered Concho's immense strength as the bones in his wrist ground together. He let go. Concho let go.

It might have ended there but the bodyguard outside the alcove saw what was happening. He rushed in. The big guard's hand dipped inside his suit jacket and came out holding a lead-filled sap. He swung it toward Concho's head but the Army Ranger's trained reflexes were blindingly fast. He sidestepped, caught the guard's shoulder with one hand and the back of his head with the other, and smashed him face-first into the table.

The table was of real wood, dense and sturdy. It didn't break but the guard's nose did. Dishes also rattled. One glass fell over and shattered while another flipped into the air and crashed down in Blackthorne's lap, drenching him with water. Concho pulled the guard's head up by the hair.

The man was dazed, nearly unconscious. Blood dribbled down his face and fell in splotches on the table. The fellow must have weighed at least two-forty but Concho was angry. He picked the man up like a bale of hay and threw him across the table into the wall. The whole restaurant shook.

Turning toward the door to the alcove, Concho saw Cyrus Abelard coming through. The man had a gun in his hand and was lifting it to shoot.

"No!" Blackthorne shouted.

Concho was already in motion. He caught Abelard's wrist in his hand, forced the gun high. The lawyer cried out with pain; the small revolver dropped from his nerveless fingers and Concho caught it before it could hit the floor. He twisted Abelard around and shoved him down into the chair where he himself had been sitting.

Blackthorne was standing, the front of his expensive suit stained with mineral water and a spray of his hired man's blood. His eyes were slitted, his face gray.

"You're an animal!" the rich man snapped.

Concho met the man's gaze. He popped open the cylinder on Abelard's revolver and dumped the shells onto the floor, then tossed the weapon onto the table with a clatter.

"You leave me alone!" Concho said.

"You'll regret this!" Blackthorne said through gritted teeth.

"You…leave…me…alone!"

Concho turned and walked out. The entire restaurant was silent. People stared. At this point, the management just wanted him out of the building before he disrupted any more rich folks' meals. The maître d' rushed to work the elevator for him and Concho stepped in and rode it to the first floor, where he exited the building and hailed a cab to take him back to base.

The ride was long enough to give Concho time to think. Something had changed in him tonight. He'd been away from the reservation, away from home long enough. It was time for a return.

His army CO was disappointed when Concho decided not to re-up, but he didn't argue. He was also from Texas and had a brother in the Texas Rangers. Pretty soon, Concho had an application, and within a year was back in Maverick County patrolling as a police officer for the Texas Department of Public Safety. After serving an apprenticeship there, he'd transitioned to the Texas Rangers. It all felt right to him.

The sound of movement from the bedroom brought Concho's thoughts back to the present. He peeked in the door. Maria had gone through his closet and found one of his newer t-shirts. She'd pulled this on over the jeans she'd worn yesterday. The shirt was as big as a maternity dress on her but somehow she still looked cute.

"I'm stealing one of your shirts," she said. "You ripped half the buttons off the one I wore over here."

"Sorry."

"No, you're not. And neither am I." She came and gave him a kiss, then made a face. "We both need to brush our teeth, I think."

Concho smiled. "Your old toothbrush is still in the bathroom," he told her. "I think there are still a couple of your barrettes, too."

She shook her head at him. "Do you ever get rid of anything?"

His next words spilled out before he had time to think about what he was saying. "Not even old girlfriends apparently," he replied.

Maria's eyes widened and she punched him on the shoulder, then laughed. "Get dressed and drive me into town for breakfast before I decide to take that comment personally."

Concho smiled again and went to grab some clothes. Despite the fact someone had tried to kill him yesterday, he felt pretty good this morning.

CHAPTER 28

Concho and Maria stopped at Skillet's Restaurant off of Highway 277 for breakfast. Maria had an omelet with various green and red specks in it that Concho wasn't sure he could name. Concho had one of his favorites, biscuits with white gravy and sausage. Later, he dropped Maria off at her mother's.

After kissing him lightly on the side of the mouth, Maria gave him a long look. "I guess I won't see you tonight. It's Henry's birthday tomorrow and mom is doing the cooking today. I promised to help."

"I understand," Concho said. "We should keep things low profile until this case is solved anyway."

Maria nodded, and sighed. "Be very careful with yourself. And call me when you can. I'll worry."

He kissed her on the forehead. "I will. Both. But you shouldn't worry. I'm pretty tough."

Maria smiled. "Yes, you are."

Concho hesitated.

"What?" Maria said, studying him.

"The thing I said earlier. About not getting rid of old girlfriends. I'm sorry. It was just a lame attempt at a joke."

Maria burst into high-pitched laughter. It took her several moments to regain her composure, and she had to wipe away tears. Concho just sat there with his face flushed with heat.

Finally calmed down, Maria reached out and stroked Concho's embarrassment- warmed cheek. "Dear, sweet Concho," she said. "You don't have to overthink everything you say to me. I knew it was a joke and thought it was funny. In fact, I loved it because it said you were comfortable with me again." She gave him a smirk, then added, "Doesn't mean I won't give you shit over it."

Concho nodded, still looking contrite.

She kissed him again, a little longer and with lingering heat. "Just relax," she said. "We moved way too fast last time. We're going to take it a lot slower this time. Just let things happen. So stop worrying over every tiny little thing you say and do. I'm not that emotionally fragile."

"I'll try," Concho said.

Maria smiled and got out of the truck. "Just remember," she said, her voice suddenly serious.

"Remember what?"

"To get rid of all those other old girlfriends before I find them and have to murder them. And you!"

She grinned and twisted away down the sidewalk toward her mom's house. Concho smiled and drove on.

***

Just after ten in the morning, Concho pulled into a park-ing slot at the Maverick County Sheriff's office and went in to see Isaac Parkland. After waiting a few minutes for the sheriff to finish a phone call, Concho entered the man's office and was invited to sit. Parkland took a set of car keys out of his desk drawer and tossed them to the Ranger.

"There's a white 2016 Ram 1500 in the lot you can use," Parkland said. "It was Terrill Hoight's ride before he got his intercep-tor. Unmarked, but the lights and sirens work. You can leave the thing you're driving in the lot until the owner comes to get it."

"Appreciate it."

Parkland nodded. "Try to keep it out of the range of gunfire."

"No guarantees," Concho said.

Parkland flashed an eyebrow, then said, "By the way, the knife you brought in. From that Big-Pine fellow. The coroner said it's definitely *not* the blade used to kill Ben Deer-Run. Too straight of an edge. The murder weapon had a curve. Not sure how he knows but I guess I gotta trust him."

"Thanks for checking on it," Concho said. "Was a long shot anyway. If you've got it, I can take it back to the kid."

"Sure," Parkland said. He stood and went over to a row of half a dozen gray file cabinets against a wall. Reaching into one, he pulled out an evidence bag containing Big-Pine's knife and passed it across the desk to Concho.

"Thanks."

"In other news," Parkland said as he reseated himself, "we got a complaint on you."

"On me?"

Parkland scratched his head. "A claim by a father that you used excessive force against his son. Shot him with a bow and arrow, he said."

"Ah," Concho said. "Father of one of the terrorists. I shot two of them with arrows. It's a very quiet weapon. The other will probably be coming forward soon."

Parkland nodded. "I had him escorted out. He didn't take it well. Promised to get a lawyer so you may be looking at a civil suit."

"Been there."

"Also ran down some information on Jacob Drake for you."

"Now *that* I'm interested in."

Parkland picked up a sheet of paper off his cluttered desk and glanced it over before handing it across to Concho. The Ranger scanned it quickly while Parkland gave him a verbal rundown on it.

"Naturalized citizen," Parkland said. "Just like he claimed. Out of Dallas most recently. Officially, he runs a legitimate business called Drake Industries. They sell and service gambling equipment. Mostly slot machines. Reckon he's got some kind of contract with the casino. Looks like he's come under suspicion for a bunch of things but nothing ever stuck. Seems like he's pretty smart. And backed with a lot of money. I've got an officer looking into the possible source for the money but nothing yet."

"This 'gunrunning' thing mentioned here," Concho said, "says Drake was considered a person of interest in a case in Florida. The gun thing showed up with Donnell Blackthorne, too. And it's interesting considering how well supplied Darrel Fallon's pet army was."

"Yeah," Parkland said. "I didn't pick up on that."

Concho mentioned his conversation with Adrian Lastra, the SWAT Captain, about White-Tail Creek and the "target" shooting there. He added, "Lastra is hoping forensics can give him leads to a supplier. I'll work it from the other end. With Jacob Drake. At the moment, he's our only living suspect for running guns."

Parkland nodded and added something that knocked most other thoughts out of Concho's head.

"Something else I found out just this morning might interest you."

"What?" Concho asked.

"You remember Fallon's gang robbed the bank and jewelry store?"

"Yep."

"Well, they recovered the jewelry stuff and a bunch of money. They thought they had everything stolen but apparently not."

"Oh?"

"Yeah, the bank has reported a substantial sum still missing. Nearly a hundred thousand dollars! Not in cash, though. Bonds."

Concho blinked. "What was a small bank branch in a mall doing with that kind of inventory on hand?"

"The hundred-thousand-dollar question," Parkland said. "And apparently a lot of people are pretty upset about it. The bank's manager and at least one employee have been fired. Everyone has lawyered up so information flow has come to a stop. But looks like something underhanded was going on. Maybe some money laundering."

"Every time I think I'm getting a handle on this thing it grows a new layer," Concho said.

"I know what you mean. Oh, and I've got to call Daniel Alvarado with some of this. How much do I tell him? All of it?"

"I'd rather tell him nothing but we can't really do that. Is it possible to keep the Donnell Blackthorne name quiet a little longer? I might be able to use it as leverage in some questioning."

"All right," Parkland said, nodding. "I can give you twenty-four hours."

Concho pushed to his feet. "Appreciate it. And thanks for the loan of the vehicle," he hefted the keys. "I'm heading over to the casino. Maybe shake some trees."

"All right," Parkland said. "Stay in touch. And don't stand too close under the trees when you shake 'em. You might not like what falls out."

CHAPTER 29

Even in the middle of the day on a Friday, the Kickapoo casino boomed with visitors. Concho took a quick turn around the parking lot. Now that he was aware of Jacob Drake's official business, he noticed two panel trucks near the casino's loading dock with Drake Industries written on the side. One had just pulled in and its driver was disembarking. He pulled up beside the man.

"What are you carrying?" he asked.

The fellow studied the Ranger, noticing the badge. He seemed to be considering a sharp retort, then shrugged. "Some repaired slot machines," he said. "I've got a cargo manifest if you want to see it."

"Maybe later," Concho said. "Hang on to it."

The man nodded, strode on. Concho drove back around the casino and parked near the front entrance. He headed through the door into the gambling area. Walking past the slot machines and gaming tables, he took the stairs to the second floor. This time he bypassed the meeting rooms and went straight to the manager's office beyond.

"She's not in, sir," the male administrative assistant told Concho when he entered the office and asked to see the manager.

"Is she on the floor?"

"I'm not sure exactly *where* Ms. Nolan is," the man said smugly. "Perhaps *I* can help you?"

"When will she be back?"

"I couldn't say, sir."

"Seems like poor practice to have your manager out of touch," Concho said.

The administrative assistant, who looked as if he'd only started shaving yesterday, smiled condescendingly. "I am completely capable of dealing with most issues of importance in the casino, sir. What did you need to see Ms. Nolan about?"

"It's about the murder of Ben Deer-Run!" Concho said flatly, walking right up to the edge of the desk and leaning forward to make sure the man could see his badge up close. "I'm working it and I wanted to have a look at your surveillance recordings for the week before the killing."

The assistant blinked several times rapidly but quickly recovered. "I believe Chief Alvarado has already reviewed those recordings with Ms. Nolan, sir."

"You mean, Deputy Alvarado."

"Yes, of course," the man said, his smooth demeanor faltering again for an instant, "*Deputy* Alvarado."

"*Deputy* Alvarado reviewed the tapes for the tribal police. I'll be reviewing them for the Maverick County Sheriff's Office." Concho smiled. "So, if you can provide the recordings to me and a place to watch them, I won't have to bother your boss. That way, you'll prove you can handle just about any issue in the casino."

The assistant, clearly flustered now, still tried to maintain control of the situation. "I'm...I'm...well, I'm afraid that is one thing I can't help with. I don't have permission to share such material with *just* anyone."

Concho bent down and placed his hands on the administrative assistant's desk. He smiled his biggest smile, and it was quite impressive, although not one that particularly inspired friendliness.

"So, we're back where we started. Where's your manager and

how do I get in touch with her?"

"Perhaps…sir. Your cell phone number. I—"

"I only give my number to friends," Concho said. "And you and I don't seem to be hitting it off."

A new voice cut through the tableau. "Why are you harassing my assistant, Mr. Ten-Wolves?"

Concho turned his head to see Melissa Nolan standing in the outer office doorway. Rumor had it she was one-eighth Kickapoo but you couldn't tell by looking at her. She was in her early forties, tall and slender—or willowy as some had described her. Her skin showed no hint of melanin and her hair was platinum blonde, though it might have been dyed. Her eyes were hazel. The only remote sign of Indian ancestry Concho could detect was a certain aquiline thrust to the slender nose.

"Ms. Nolan," Concho said. "I bet your assistant is glad to have you back."

"What is it you want?"

Concho straightened, walked to the door to the inner office and opened it. He lifted a hand as if to invite Nolan inside. "Let's talk privately," he said.

Nolan hesitated for a bare fraction, then strode purposefully on her heels past Concho and into her own office. Concho followed and shut the door.

"I wanted to see your surveillance records from the week of Ben Deer-Run's murder. And," he held up his hand to forestall any protest, "I don't care if Alvarado already reviewed them."

Nolan watched him for a moment, then went around behind her desk and sat. She picked up a pen and tapped it on the back of her other hand.

"I'd be happy to indulge you," she finally said. "If I could. But the recordings have been erased."

Concho tsked. "People get arrested for that kind of thing. They call it tampering with evidence."

"It was an accident. No one's fault. During the storm the other night, the casino was struck by lightning. No serious damage for the most part, but one of our surge protectors blew. Several computers were wiped clean and had to be discarded."

"Including the one storing the surveillance footage!"

"Yes." Nolan looked away. "But it doesn't really matter. Deputy Alvarado reviewed the recordings fully before the data were destroyed. I'm sure he can provide you with whatever information you need."

"Convenient."

Nolan bristled, and she did it well. Concho almost believed it.

"I'm not sure what you're trying to imply, Officer. But I also watched much of that footage with the deputy. There was no sign of Ben Deer-Run in any of it."

"How *much* did you see?"

"Quite a bit!"

"Half maybe? More? Less?"

"I don't…. I'm not sure. Maybe half."

"Then there's a lot you missed. What about the skeletally thin black fellow who was killed with Ben?"

"You mean Donnell Blackthorne?"

"Interesting you know that name. How? Was he staying at the hotel?"

Nolan bit the swell of her lower lip before answering. "He wasn't staying here. Alvarado told me his name. I guess he must have gotten it from the Maverick County Sheriff's office. Didn't he?"

Concho ignored her question to ask one of his own. "You knew Donnell Blackthorne?"

"No! Never met him. But that name can't be common. I assumed he was the son of Hamilton Blackthorne."

"And how do you know Hamilton?"

"I don't know him either. Personally. But most people in my business would recognize his name."

"You mean the gambling business?"

"I *mean*," Nolan said, "the casino business. Blackthorne Enterprises owns controlling interests in a number of casinos, and partial interest in many others. I believe, though," she said rather proudly, "that our Lucky Eagle casino here is the first Native American casino Mr. Blackthorne has invested in."

"What kind of interest does he have in the Eagle?"

"Oh, it's rather a token at present." She waved her hand around. "But I'd assumed his son's visiting us in secret meant more interest down the line. It's such a shame the son was murdered." Nolan showed Concho her stricken face, which was about as calculated as her 'bristle.' "Has anyone informed Mr. Blackthorne of the death?"

"Not my job," Concho said, as he turned and walked out without shutting the door behind him. He had a lot to think about, and more questions than he'd had coming in.

Had lightning really erased the casino surveillance recordings? It seemed highly unlikely and he didn't believe it for a second. It probably meant Alvarado had found something on the recordings to cause trouble for him or those he worked for. That didn't mean it had anything to do with the murders of Ben Deer-Run and Donnell Blackthorne. Alvarado was surely involved in plenty of sketchy activity.

The craziest part was finding out Hamilton Blackthorne had a financial interest in the Lucky Eagle casino. That couldn't be a coincidence either. The man just happened to invest in *one* Indian casino, and it happened to be on the reservation where his supposed grandson lived.

For years after their confrontation in the Tacoma restaurant, Concho had expected to hear again from Hamilton Blackthorne. He'd been surprised when it hadn't happened. Why had Blackthorne reappeared now, after nearly ten years? And how had his son, Donnell, been involved? The last Concho had heard, Hamilton and his son were estranged. Had they patched things up? Had Donnell been here doing his father's bidding? Or perhaps working against him?

For certain, Nolan was either lying about knowing Donnell, or Alvarado had been dealing with him because neither of them could have gotten the name from Isaac Parkland yet.

And why did connections to a certain Concho Ten-Wolves keep appearing in the case? What did any of this have to do with him? He couldn't imagine it was anything good.

CHAPTER 30

Just as he reached the exit to the casino, it occurred to Concho that he'd allowed the word about Hamilton Blackthorne to distract him from some questions he'd wanted to ask Melissa Nolan—specifically about Jacob Drake. He was about to turn back to Nolan's office when a voice called his name:

"Concho? Concho Ten-Wolves!"

The man who'd called was just coming into the casino. He was strongly built, a little under six feet tall with dark hair clipped short. He looked familiar but the Ranger couldn't quite place him.

"It's Cole," the man said, offering his hand. "Cole Chase. We met at the press conference."

"Oh yeah," Concho said, shaking the fellow's hand as the memories flooded back. "Mall security."

"Yes. How you doin'?"

"I'm all right. How about you?"

"Really good." The man grinned widely. "Happy to be alive. Thanks to you."

"Glad I could help," Concho said, not quite sure what else to say.

"Say, say, running into you this way is sweet. How about you let me treat you to lunch. It's about that time of the day and I owe you that much at least."

"Not necessary," Concho said.

"Come on! It'd make me feel better. And I'd kinda like to talk to you anyway. About the Rangers and all."

Concho couldn't think of a reason to refuse so he said, "I guess it would be OK."

"Great. How about the Red Sky Grill?"

"Sure. Good barbecue."

The Red Sky Grill was one of six restaurants in the Lucky Eagle Casino/Hotel complex. It ran heavily toward Texas barbecue and offered jalapenos with just about everything. Cole Chase ordered a bacon-wrapped jalapeno appetizer to go with a rare sirloin. Concho had the pulled pork sandwich. A couple of drafts of Shiner Bock completed their meal.

"So, how's your case going?" Chase asked.

Concho frowned. "What case you talking about?"

Chase scratched his head. "Sorry, I know I don't have any right to ask that question. I was just wondering what was happening in the Ben Deer-Run investigation."

"I guess everyone has heard of Ben's murder," Concho said.

"Yeah, although a lot of folks are still talking about the mall attack. It's the biggest thing to hit Eagle Pass in a month of Sundays."

"Well, we don't have a suspect at present in the Deer-Run case. That's probably what everyone wants to know."

Cole Chase nodded as he took a bite of his steak. "I was lookin' more into the Texas Rangers," he said. "But I ran into a problem on the application."

"What?"

"It says you need eight years of experience with a law enforcement agency. And they don't consider security work. Or even military police. How did you get around that requirement?"

"I didn't. I worked with the Kansas state police when I was in college. They counted that, and after I got out of the military, I spent almost five years with the Texas Highway Patrol before I officially became a Ranger."

Chase looked surprised. "Oh. I thought...well..."

"That I got special consideration because I was an Indian?"

"No! Not at all. I thought...well, you're still pretty young. I thought maybe you knew someone who helped you."

"I knew someone who put me in contact with the right people. But I still had to meet their requirements."

Cole Chase's clean-shaven face showed a flush of embarrassment. "I didn't mean to imply anything under the table," he said.

"I understand," Concho said. "I didn't think you had." After taking a sip of his beer, he continued. "You're young yourself. Apply to the police, or the sheriff's office. Put in the time. Keep me up to date on how things go. And if you do a good job, I'll put in a word for you with the Rangers when it comes time."

Chase nodded. "Thanks. I...uh appreciate it. I'll probably take you up on that." The young man frowned. "Don't look now but some guy seems to be staring daggers in your back."

"What does he look like?"

"Big guy. Really big. Bigger than you. Shaved head."

Concho nodded. "That would likely be Jacob Drake's bodyguard. Name of Wayne. We had words the other day."

"Jacob Drake?"

"Rich guy. Appears to be staying at the casino."

"Why isn't his bodyguard with him?"

"Guess he's got more than one."

"Well, there's another guy at the table with him. Just about as big and with even less of a neck."

Concho turned and looked. Chase was right. Along with Wayne sat a slightly smaller and better dressed version cut from the same mold. As Wayne saw the Ranger looking, he held up his fist and pretended to crank up the middle finger.

Concho smiled, turned back to Cole Chase. He picked up his beer and finished it before saying, "Thanks for the lunch. Let me know how things go with the police job. I'm going to walk over and speak to Wayne for a moment. I'll have to catch you later."

Chase frowned. "Want me to tag along. I can watch your back."

"No need. I doubt he'll start anything here. I'm just going to talk to him."

"All right," Chase said. "But I'll be sitting over here if you need me."

Concho gave the young man a quick nod. "Thanks, but, like I said, nothing's going to happen."

The Ranger got up and walked straight toward the table of Wayne and his friend. Both men stood up as he approached and the two together made a pretty good slab of beef. Concho lifted his hands, palm open in a peace gesture.

"Gentlemen, gentlemen," he said. "Why don't we go outside where we won't disturb anyone's meal while I stomp your asses."

Wayne's friend seemed surprised. All Wayne said was, "Let's do it!" He started past Concho toward the door.

Concho moved to where he could keep an eye on both men as Wayne passed him. Across the restaurant, he glimpsed Jacob Drake walking toward them. Wayne stopped and straightened as he saw his boss, trying to erase the anger darkening his face.

Drake paused in front of the group. He eyed Wayne for a long moment, then glanced at Wayne's companion before looking at Concho.

"Officer Ten-Wolves," Drake said. "I apologize for Wayne here. He seems to be under the impression he can do whatever he wants without worrying about how it reflects on me as his employer. He is mistaken."

"But, sir—" Wayne started.

"Shut up!" Drake snapped, without looking at the man. "I trust you realize," Drake continued to speak to Concho, "it was not at my behest that Wayne has harassed you. It will not happen again."

"Sir, I—" Wayne started, and again Drake interrupted him, this time with the flat of his palm held up toward the bodyguard's face.

Drake turned toward Wayne. "You're fired. Leave my sight immediately. Your severance will be mailed to you."

"This—"

"If you say one more word," Drake interrupted a final time, "you're going to have an experience much worse than being fired." Drake glanced at the second bodyguard, "Tony, escort Wayne from the building and return."

The man called Tony stepped forward and took Wayne's elbow. Wayne shook it off, but turned to leave like a chastened puppy. Tony followed.

Drake returned his gaze to Concho. "Again, my apologies. Tony texted me that Wayne was behaving aggressively. I came right down. It isn't the first time the man has played fast and loose with my direct orders. It *was* the last. I hope you believe me."

"Considering you just fired him, I guess I'll have to," Concho said.

Drake smiled. Without looking around, he said, "We appear to have drawn the notice of everyone in the Red Sky Grill. I hate attention so I hope you'll forgive me if I return to my work."

"Just one question first," Concho said.

"That is?"

"Do you know a man named Hamilton Blackthorne?"

Drake's only apparent emotional response was a quick eye blink. "Not a name I expected to hear you mention," he said.

"So, you do know him. How?"

"Hamilton and I are…rivals, you might say."

"Business or personal?"

"Business."

"Gambling?"

"Casinos." He waved his hand around. "Like this one. As well as in other ventures such as real estate. Now, if you'll excuse me."

Concho watched Jacob Drake walk off. He glanced over toward where Coleman Chase was sitting. The young man lifted his Shiner Bock in salute. Concho gave him a trigger finger wave before heading out of the bar himself. As he crossed the parking lot toward his truck, a voice called his name.

"Ten-Wolves!" the man named Wayne shouted. "You and I ain't finished."

CHAPTER 31

Wayne stood alone. Tony, the other bodyguard, must have returned to his boss in the hotel.

"Imagine running into you here, Wayne," Concho said. "You're a little predictable."

"Keep talking, smart-ass. I'm gonna teach you respect for your betters."

"Guess we'll see," Concho replied. He lifted a hand. "Follow me to the truck. I'll take off my guns and badge. Don't want anything official getting in our way."

Wayne's eyes grew flat and cold, but he said nothing as he trailed Concho another fifty feet to the Ranger's truck. Concho opened the door, took off his gun belt and rolled it up on the driver's seat. He tossed his badge next to the guns. His back was to Wayne but his ears were attuned for what he knew was coming.

A flurry of footsteps sounded on asphalt as Wayne rushed Concho from behind. The Ranger slammed the Dodge Ram's door as he ducked and spun away from the attack. Wayne's fist swept past Concho's face by an inch and smacked into the closed window of the truck. The ex-bodyguard had put a lot of heat into that punch. Concho heard the knuckles crunch when the man's fist hit glass. Wayne gasped in pain.

As Concho straightened from his crouch, he slammed one fist into Wayne's belly and the other into the chin an instant later. Wayne staggered back, with Concho following. The man had training. With reflexes alone, he blocked a right-hand swing from the Ranger. He missed the left that blasted into his chest just over the heart.

Again, Wayne gasped. Concho stepped into him, crowding him back against the bed of the pickup. He threw lefts and rights to the bodyguard's face. Several battered their way through, smashing the nose askew, bloodying the lower lip.

Wayne's hands leaped upward to cover his face, and Concho whipped fresh punches into his belly. The man doubled over. Concho hammered an open hand down on the back of Wayne's head, driving his face down into the knee that came snapping up at the same time.

Wayne cried out at the blinding pain of his nose pulping. Concho stepped back. Wayne slid to his knees, his hands dropping uselessly to his sides. "Enough, enough," he moaned, the words garbled because of the damage to his nose.

"Damn, man," Concho said. "I thought we'd have more fun than this. Guess you're not as good as you thought you were."

Wayne looked up, his face smeared with blood. His lips and cheeks were swelling; his left eye was almost closed. Only the right eye seemed to focus and it ran red with burst blood vessels. One of the bodyguard's hands fluttered up, dropped again.

"Just stop. I'm done."

Concho offered Wayne his hand. The man stared at it with a frown, but then took it and let the Ranger pull him to his feet. Concho stepped in close to Wayne and the man flinched back with no fight left in him.

"Go tell your boss," Concho said, smiling, "his little ruse about firing you didn't work. Next time better bring Tony, too. Maybe a couple more. I'll give you another chance."

***

Concho was driving away from the casino toward home when his cell phone buzzed. The caller ID read Roberto Echabarri.

"Yes, Deputy?" Concho answered.

"Got an I.D. on the man you shot," Echabarri said. "Gary Anhalt."

"Anything else on him?"

"Not much. No prior convictions. But…word is he was a prospect for the Aryan Brotherhood. Not yet a member. But killing you might have been his ticket into the gang."

"Good to know I'm worth something."

"You better be careful."

"I've got news for you, too," Concho said. He told the deputy about his conversation with Melissa Nolan at the casino and about the "accidentally" erased surveillance recordings.

"That's convenient."

"More than a little."

"So, what does it mean?"

"Alvarado's got something to hide. But we already knew that. We need to know what."

"Maybe I can…get him to tell me something. I mean, if he's grooming me."

Concho remained silent for a long moment. "I'm not sure that's a good idea. He might be involved in Ben Deer-Run's murder. And if he is, and if he thinks you're fishing…."

"I understand the risks. I'm a police officer."

"All right. Just be careful."

"I'm not much for bravery. I'll let you know if I find out anything."

"Appreciate it," Concho said. "Hey, any luck finding Estrella's husband, Bearfoot?"

"Not a bit. No one has seen him. But at least his body hasn't turned up yet. Could be, he's just on a binge."

"Let's hope so," Concho said. He clicked off the call, but barely a second later got a chime to indicate a text coming through. He read it:

Liar, liar, house afire.

"What the hell?" he muttered to himself. Someone was taunting him and it was getting old. He thought back to the other two texts he'd gotten. The first had come right after the attempt on his life. Whoever had sent it had known about the failure of that attack so the two men who'd survived the attempt were the prime suspects in sending it.

Of course, they could have reported the failure very quickly to whoever was backing them. He figured Darrel Fallon and his associates were involved. Fallon was in custody, of course, but he had plenty of lickspittles who weren't.

The second text had been more cryptic, *Blood will tell.* He'd suspected it referred to his mixed-blood heritage but he couldn't know for sure. There was no way to tell if it had even been sent by the same person, but it seemed likely.

And now this, *Liar, liar, house afire.* What did that mean?

As per his usual, Concho was driving with his windows down. He became aware of a distant whining sound. The source came to him quickly. *Sirens!* Not far off.

He pulled his truck to the side of the road, leaned his head out the window to try and localize the sound. At the same time, his eyes scanned the sky. His eyes found the answer first. A spiral of dark smoke reached toward heaven through a cloudless blue.

Fire!

Coming from the direction of his house.

CHAPTER 32

By the time Concho reached home, even driving at high speed, his trailer was nothing but embers and memories. Two fire trucks were on the scene but had been reduced to wetting the trees and brush around to keep the flames from spreading in the dry climate.

Concho parked off to the side of the road behind the trucks and walked up. It wouldn't have done any good to run. The scents overwhelmed him, charred wiring, burnt leather, melted plastic and petroleum products, superheated iron—all the mineral and chemistry makings of a modern life cooked together in one great conflagration.

James Jeffrey, a Lieutenant in the Eagle Pass Fire Department, came to meet the Ranger. Concho had known him as a probationary firefighter, had seen him rise through the ranks. They got along well.

"There's ammunition in there," Concho said. "Better have your men be careful."

Jeffrey replied as they shook hands, "If it were going to cook off, it already has. We didn't hear it but the fire was pretty far along by the time we got here. I hope you have insurance."

Concho nodded. "It never covers everything, though."

"True. I'm very sorry."

"I'm gonna miss the books. Any idea yet what caused it?"

Jeffrey tipped his helmet back and wiped sweat off his forehead with a hand. He sighed. "Arson, I'm afraid."

Concho wasn't surprised, given the recent text he'd received about "house afire."

Lieutenant Jeffrey led Concho toward the right front corner of the burned trailer and pointed out a five-gallon gas can sitting turned upside down near the edge of the fire. The can's red paint, though bubbled and blackened in places, still shone through.

"They didn't even try to hide the accelerant they used," Jeffrey continued.

Concho felt fury building inside him and fought to control it. "Do you know who called it in?"

Jeffrey was studying the Ranger but made no comment on the anger that was surely clear to see. "Anonymous tip," he said.

"Of course."

"You didn't...have any pets, I hope."

"No. Unless you count the spiders and cockroaches."

Jeffrey smiled through the soot. "Yeah, we've got those too." He added, "The Fire Marshall will be out. But I doubt he'll find much useful. Looks like they wanted you to know it was deliberate. You likely have a better idea of who did it than we will."

"There's a line waiting to get at me," Concho replied.

Jeffrey slapped Concho lightly on the shoulder. "Hey, isn't making enemies your superhero skill?"

"Just one of my many talents," Concho said.

"You know you're welcome to stay with Donna and me for a bit if you want."

"I wouldn't put your wife through that. I'll stay at the casino hotel. I'm a stakeholder after all."

Jeffrey nodded. "I'll make sure the Fire Marshall calls you when he's done with his investigation. Or I will."

"Thanks," Concho said.

They shook hands again and Jeffrey returned to directing his crew. The hoses were shut off and everything loaded back onto the trucks. In twenty minutes, the firemen were gone and Concho was alone at the site of what had been his house for the past six years.

Of course, he'd lived at this site for a much longer time. He knew the trees and grass and dirt and rocks. He knew the smells and where in the nearby arroyo to dig for water if you needed it. He'd walked the low hills to the south and knew where all the animals lived. He'd grown up here in a trailer owned by his grandparents, but it had fallen apart and had to be replaced by the time he moved back after his stint in the military.

It occurred to him that whoever had tried to burn him out had only taken the shell where he slept. The land was still here. So was the juniper and mesquite and saltbush and desert willow. Some leaves were singed but would come back. Tonight, the coyotes would howl and the nightjars call. The quail and rabbits would run with the dawn. Life had not fled just because a dwelling had burned. This was his land and he would not be moved from it.

Concho walked over to his firepit, to have a sit-down in one of his lawn chairs. Someone had gotten those too. They'd hacked out the seats with a machete or hatchet. He shook his head and laughed. They wanted so badly to hurt him. They had no idea what hurt was; he intended to show them.

***

"Don't shoot this old man," a voice said from the scru-bland behind Concho. "I am not a rabbit."

"No guarantees," the Ranger said as Meskwaa came out from between two mesquite bushes and entered the yard. He carried an old Winchester lever-action .30-30 about the same age as the man holding it.

The old Kickapoo shrugged his thin shoulders and grinned at Concho's words. "Oh well, maybe it would be for the best if you did. I'm getting too old to keep worrying about you like this."

"How did you know about the trouble? Have another vision?"

Meskwaa waved his hand in the air. "Yes. I saw it painted like smoke in the sky."

Concho nodded. He nudged one of the hacked-up lawn chairs with his foot and said, "I'd offer you a seat but they're not what they once were either."

Meskwaa hocked up a little phlegm and spat. "I'm sure it was quite a battle. Great heroes fighting chairs. It should be sung about around the campfires. All the young women would swoon."

Concho nodded as he stared at his feet in thought. He could feel Meskwaa's gaze studying him.

"You can stay in my wickiup if you wish," the old man continued.

"You gonna protect me with that rifle?" Concho asked, gesturing toward the .30-30. "You sure it won't blow up if you shoot it?"

"This 'rifle' has taken more lives than even you, Ten-Wolves."

"Deer and squirrel don't count," Concho replied.

"They do to the deer and squirrel."

"I guess you're right."

"So, you will stay in my home?"

"Thanks, old man, but I have a plan."

Meskwaa gave a fake shudder. "I am, as your white men say, 'all ears'."

***

After Meskwaa left, Concho called Maria Morales. "How's the prep for the birthday party going?" he asked.

"Henry would be irritated to hear you call it a 'party'. He's too old for that at thirty-four. It's a fiesta."

"Aren't they pretty much the same thing?"

"Not if you're Henry."

"I guess so."

"I'm happy to hear from you, of course," Maria said. "But I'm guessing you have something more important to say than discussing Henry's fiesta."

"Yeah, I wanted you to know. In case you saw it on the news. Someone burned down my house."

"Burned your house! My God. Who…I mean, are you OK? What happened?"

"I'm fine. I wasn't here. Someone called the fire department but it was too late to save anything. They found a gas can used to help start the fire, though."

"Concho, I'm so sorry! Do they have any idea who did it?"

"I've got some ideas. I'll have better ones soon."

Maria said nothing for a moment. Then, "Do you have a place to stay? You're welcome to crash at my apartment. Maybe I should come to where you are. Do you need anything?"

"No, Maria. I'm fine. Really. And I'm not leaving the reservation. That's what they want me to do. To run away."

"But, they'll come after you again. They've tried twice already."

"They've been pushing me. It's time I pushed back."

"I'm worried."

"I know you are. And I thank you for it. But it'll end well for us. Not for them. I'm going to go dark for a few days at least. Then I'll be in touch. Whatever you hear, don't believe it until you hear it from me. OK?"

Maria sighed. "OK. I trust you. Please be…. Just take care of yourself."

"I will, Maria. Bye."

He ended the call, stood studying the evening redness growing in the west. Walking over to his loaner pickup, he opened the door to the extended cab. After he'd picked up the Dodge Ram from Isaac Parkland, he'd stopped by John Gray-Dove's shop and unloaded the contents of his Ford F-150 into the Dodge.

Now, he picked up the small yellow tin containing his warpaint and opened it. He smeared red ocher stripes beneath each eye before scrawling a circle on his forehead. He took up his bow and arrows and slung them over his back. Shutting the truck's door, he locked it. The sound had a finality to it. He liked that.

PART TWO
TEN-WOLVES

CHAPTER 33

Turning down the dirt road leading to Concho Ten-
Wolves' burned-out home, Roberto Echabarri pulled up beside
the Ranger's Ram 1500 pickup and parked the tribal police SUV.
The young deputy stepped out of his vehicle into the night, leaving
his vehicle lights on to help him see.

The trailer was a total loss. In the headlights, a few fingers of
gray smoke still rose lazily here and there to mate with the dark
sky. The frogs and crickets didn't seem bothered. Their voices
throbbed in the night.

Roberto called out. "Concho Ten-Wolves! You here?"

Hearing no answer, Roberto pulled the flashlight off his belt
and walked up to study the burn site. He wasn't quite sure what
he was looking for. Alvarado had gotten the courtesy call from
the fire department while Echabarri was with him. They'd said
it was arson. He didn't know how they knew but he guessed they
had their ways.

After a moment of fruitless study, he sighed and looked around
again. Where was Ten-Wolves? He needed to take the man's statement about the fire, but it was getting dark. He didn't particularly
like being out here at night. There were snakes. He remembered
the one he'd heard rattle under Ten-Wolves' front steps. Where

was it now? Not under those steps anymore. Snakes of the rattling variety were among his least favorite things.

"I just wanna finish my job and get back home," he murmured softly to himself.

"And what is your job, Echabarri?" a voice asked from directly behind him.

He jumped, twisted around and nearly fell. Concho Ten-Wolves stood within five feet of him. He would have recognized the man by his six-foot-four bulk even if the glow of his flashlight hadn't limned the expressionless face.

"God!" Roberto snapped, holding his chest with one hand. "You scared ten years out of me."

Concho said nothing.

"Where were you?" Roberto asked. "I was looking for you."

"I know. That's why I'm here. What did you want?"

Roberto sighed and shook his head. "Don't know how a man as big as you moves so quietly," he said.

"Practice," Concho said. "Now, are you going to tell me what you want?"

"I...uhm, I needed to take your statement. About the fire. Alvarado wants it by morning. The...fire department called him about it. To let him know."

Ten-Wolves took a couple of steps closer to Echabarri and Roberto found he didn't much like it. He forced himself not to step back. He noticed a smear of some dark pigment on the big Ranger's cheeks. And on his forehead.

What the hell? he thought. *Is that...warpaint?*

"I heard the sirens on the way home," Concho said. "Saw the smoke. Got here." He gestured toward the burned trailer.

"Right," Roberto said. "What did the firemen say? Was it arson?"

"The Fire Marshall hasn't been out yet but James Jeffrey with the Eagle Pass Fire Department showed me an emptied and half-burned five-gallon gas can used to accelerate the flames. It certainly wasn't mine."

Roberto nodded. "Any...suspects?"

"Too many."

"Well, you can discount Alvarado for starting it, at least. I was with him when this would have been happening."

"Doesn't matter. I'll take care of it."

"What's that supposed to mean?"

"A crime was committed. I'm an officer of the law."

"You don't have any jurisdiction on the Rez," Roberto said, forcing his voice deeper than usual. "You know we can't tolerate vigilante behavior."

"What do you tolerate, Echabarri?"

Roberto frowned. "You understand I'm trying to be fair about all this. I'm not against you. If I find out who is responsible for doing this to your house, I'll certainly arrest them and put them in jail."

"No matter who it is?"

"No matter," Roberto replied.

"Good. You've got your statement. You can take it to Alvarado in the morning." Concho turned as if to go.

Roberto gave his longest sigh yet. "Dammit, man! You don't make it easy on anyone."

Concho paused and turned back. "You're right," he said. A faint smile flickered across his lips. "By the way, you don't need to be afraid of snakes here. The one you thought you heard under my steps? It was just Maggie." Concho leaned a little toward the deputy and whispered, "She's not real. Maggie was motion activated. Just to discourage visitors."

Roberto threw his head back and burst out laughing. It verged on the hysterical and he knew it was from a release of the tension he'd been feeling in Concho Ten-Wolves' presence.

"Shoulda known," he said, then realized Ten-Wolves was gone.

"Where did you..." he started to mutter, before shaking his head and letting it go. He returned to his SUV and climbed inside. Only as he started the engine did another strange thing occur to him.

"Wait a minute," he murmured to himself. "How did he know I was thinking about snakes?"

***

After watching Echabarri leave, Concho returned to his truck to extract a few items. These included nylon feed sacks, heavy-duty gloves, a small flashlight, and a set of night vision goggles much like those he'd used with the Army Rangers in Afghanistan.

The dark was heavy and full now, with no moon yet, so he slipped the goggles on, and the world turned a strange shade of yellow-green. The night lost its satin smoothness and became textured, a breathing jewel through which he moved as a hunter. The remaining hot spots from the burned trailer were almost too bright to look at with the goggles on. He skirted the site and entered the desert behind his home.

Moonrise lay hours in the future but the goggles let Concho navigate easily through the rough terrain. He crossed the dried arroyo that just a few days earlier had run red with muddy water. It was bone dry again, though the dusty bed was littered with leaves and sticks dropped by the flood.

Stopping in a stand of mesquite, Concho sought his bearings. It had been years since he'd visited the place he sought. But it still burned brightly in his memory, and soon he had the direction in mind and began making his way generally west. Though he didn't expect anyone to be watching him, he stayed on the low side of hills and arroyos to avoid outlining himself against the sky.

An armadillo blundered past, seemingly unaware of his presence. He startled up a nightjar who was only *too* aware of the man who moved through its territory. Irritation swept him. He was better than that. He'd certainly been better in Afghanistan where startling up a bird would bring a bullet or rocket hurtling in your direction. He needed to be battle-good again, for it was clear his enemies did not intend for him to live.

After half an hour more, he reached his destination. Where two lines of low hills converged, there lay a small flat plain upon which saltbush and prickly pear and other arid-land plants grew. A stream ran down from the hills, soaking into the ground before it reached the plain, but the plants knew the water lay below and sought it with their roots.

Concho had hunted those hills for deer and fished the stream for catfish and perch when he was young, but his first memory of this area involved the plain, and his grandfather. A moment of scouting around revealed what he sought—the remnants of an old wickiup. Most of it had been reclaimed by the desert but he could still see the corner poles and a few piles of debris left over from the roof and walls.

Grandfather had built this wickiup some thirty years ago. Concho remembered it, though he could have been no more than about four-years-old. He'd even "helped" in its construction, though that mostly meant handing his grandfather tools or carrying an armload of sotol stalks.

And, of course, he remembered the storm—the sky a growing black, cracked with veins of lightning, the wind like a rushing stallion, the rain like stinging wasps where it hit you unprotected. But he'd not been unprotected. He'd sat on Grandfather's lap with the man's arms around him like a shield. He'd sat there on a bench on the ramada of this very wickiup.

That had been a long time ago when he'd needed to be protected. Now he could protect himself. He put on his gloves and began turning over rocks and piles of debris, gathering what treasures he found beneath.

CHAPTER 34

Joseph Big-Pine left the casino around 11:30 PM to fetch his bicycle from the rack in the parking lot. For the last few days he'd been talking back and forth with Selena Garcia, Daniel Alvarado's niece, who had just turned fifteen. She'd texted him a little earlier that she was home alone because her parents had gone across the Rio Grande to eat at a restaurant in Piedras Negras, in the state of Coahuila, Mexico, and were planning on spending the night with relatives.

Although sometimes considered a "sister" town to Eagle Pass, Texas, Piedras Negras was the much larger of the two, with more than 100,000 residents. The name meant "black rocks," in reference to the coal deposits in the area. The most important part was how delayed Selena's parents would be getting home, even in the morning with the traffic over the International Bridge.

Joseph badly wanted to see Selena. His mouth grew dry just thinking about it. At twenty years of age, Joseph knew he should not be messing around with Selena. But the voice in his head telling him that fact was a whisper while the voice of his body was a roar. He just had to make very, very sure Daniel Alvarado didn't find out.

As he reached the bike rack, he froze. Leaning against the

wall of the hotel next to the rack was a very large man with the dark skin of an African American but the features and straight black hair of a Kickapoo. Big-Pine knew only one man like that—Concho Ten-Wolves.

Concho was fiddling with his phone and did not look up at Joseph. Joseph took a few steps closer to his bike and stopped again. Concho still did not look at him but the young man was sure the Texas Ranger remained aware of his presence. Joseph cursed himself for the fear that was turning his legs to spaghetti. He took another step forward, and Concho spoke without looking up from his phone.

"Going somewhere?" the Ranger asked.

Joseph startled, and his voice stammered as he tried to respond calmly and failed. He cursed himself for that, too. "Just...just checking on my bike," he said.

Concho looked at him and smiled. Smears of red slashed the big man's cheeks. *Warpaint*, Joseph thought. His heart pounded faster. And for the first time he noticed a kind of light-colored ring, almost grey, around Ten-Wolves' brown irises. Strangely, that added to his discomfort as much as the warpaint.

"Besides, it's not your business," Joseph added in what, even to his own ears, sounded like adolescent bluster.

"Of course," Concho said. "Just making conversation before I give you the knife."

Joseph took a step back. "Wha...what?"

"The knife," Concho said, his voice deepening as he straightened and pushed away from the wall.

Joseph Big-Pine's mouth dried with sudden fear. His heart stuttered. The Texas Ranger reached behind his back, drew something glittering into his hand. Joseph was within a second of taking to his heels when he saw what Concho held—a clear plastic bag containing a big hunting knife. He recognized it.

"It's yours, isn't it?" Concho asked. He tossed the bag to Joseph, who fumbled it and let it drop to the sidewalk.

Joseph bent over to retrieve the bag, then thought better about it and straightened again. "I...I don't know what you're talking about. I was just checking my bike." He turned and hurried back toward the casino.

"It's clean," Concho called after him. "Not a murder weapon! At least, not for Ben Deer-Run!"

Each word the Ranger spoke seemed to hammer Joseph in his spine. Each word sent his steps flying faster, until he burst into the casino and onto the floor where the gambling took place. People glanced up at him but quickly returned to their own obsessions. He began to breathe again.

"He'll move on," Joseph murmured to himself. "He won't hang around my bike all night."

After texting Selena that he'd be there as soon as he could, he looked around for anything to distract him. He sat down at a one-arm bandit for some slot machine action. Though he wasn't actually of legal age to gamble, he had a fake ID listing him as twenty-one, and no one was going to question him given his acquaintance with Deputy—soon to be Chief—Alvarado.

Joseph began to calm. He won a small jackpot on his fifth pull. It was only thirty dollars but seemed a good omen. He looked up and around to see who might have noticed his win and saw Concho Ten-Wolves again.

The Ranger was playing a slot machine just one row back from Joseph. The warpaint was gone and he seemed completely oblivious of the young man's presence. Joseph didn't believe that. Every bad moment Joseph had had recently was due to Concho Ten-Wolves. The young man's smile faded, and the joy of his win turned to the taste of ashes—as so much else had done recently.

***

Daniel Alvarado, first deputy of the Kickapoo Tribal Police Force of Texas, who fully expected to be named the new chief of the department as soon as the Tribal Council met later this month, drove home slower than was his want. The fire-engine-red Mustang he'd purchased for himself just two weeks earlier had some 'get-up and go' and he liked to run it hard. But he'd been drinking with Jacob Drake and was still sober enough to be careful.

He was going to have to taper off on the drinking if he wanted to get everything he deserved out of life. Of course, Drake could supply much of what he wanted so it was important to stay on the man's good side. And Drake liked to drink, or at least ply others with drink of the expensive variety. They'd been at it since first dark and it was now after two in the morning.

As he turned into the driveway of the brick home he'd had built two years earlier, Alvarado reflected on one thing he hadn't gotten, or at least hadn't been able to hang onto. His wife and two kids had been the catalyst for building the new house in the first place, and for much else he'd done. Now they were gone.

He'd told everyone his family was on an extended visit to his wife's relatives in Oklahoma. Not true. His wife had discovered certain things he hadn't wanted her to know. She'd taken the kids and left him. He kept thinking they'd come back after Bella calmed down, but it was past a month and she showed no sign of giving in.

"Bitch!" he muttered to himself, as he pulled into the garage. "I did everything for you and the kids and you act like I'm some kind of criminal."

As he turned off the key on the Mustang and put the car in park, a small thump on the roof distracted him. He frowned. Pushing open the door, he swung one leg out and started to stand. The garage was dark but the car's interior light lit up the inside of the vehicle.

Something fell off the top of the car and landed with a plop on his leg. His frown deepened; then his pupils dilated and he huffed in sudden fear. A tarantula the size of a baby's fist was creeping up his black uniform pants.

Since a certain incident as a kid, during which he had come close to dying, Daniel Alvarado had developed an intense dislike for little scuttling things, particularly spiders and scorpions. He huffed again, louder, and slapped the tarantula off his leg before jerking the limb back inside the vehicle and slamming the door.

Another spider crawled down his side window, and a brawling mess of scorpions rolled down his windshield and broke into a dozen individuals who scurried for hiding places around the hood. He thought he could hear other tiny clawed feet scratching on his roof, as if he'd driven into a nest of vicious little insects, intent on getting at him.

In panic mode, Alvarado stabbed the key back in the Mustang's ignition and brought the car to life. He hit the windshield wipers, which sent scorpions flying. Barely looking behind him, he slapped the vehicle into reverse and punched the gas. The car roared backward out of the garage. The passenger side mirror caught on the edge of the garage and ripped off. He barely noticed.

Screeching to a halt in the driveway, Alvarado threw the car into park and bailed out, slapping at his arms and chest and legs in case any bugs had gotten on him. The Mustang's headlights were on. So were the interior lights. Alvarado could see a few spiders and scorpions clinging to the roof and hood of the car. Lying in front of the car was a small nylon feed sack that had fallen off his roof as he whipped out of the garage.

The sack must have contained the creatures. He'd not just driven through a natural nest of bugs. This had been done deliberately. The bag holding them must have been suspended from the garage rafters, perhaps held by a small thread like a fishing line that he hadn't seen when he'd pulled in. He'd snapped the line and the bag had dropped and spilled open.

It meant there were probably more of them. Everywhere. Maybe inside his house. And all over his Mustang. Who would mess with a police officer in such a way? Who would mess with *him*? The answer came: *Ten-Wolves*! Ten-Wolves knew about his fear.

Alvarado wiped his mouth on the back of his hand and spat on the ground. Unsnapping the strap holding his Glock 40 in his holster, he drew it and studied his surroundings. Where was Ten-Wolves? Was he still nearby? Was there more to his plan? Did the man figure to shoot him for their long history of conflict?

No one revealed themselves. But the night was not quiet. Alvarado didn't know if it were his imagination or not, but the whole world sounded as if it were filled with small crawling things.

He shuddered. He couldn't stay here, but he dared not get back into his car or go inside his house. Not in the dark. Not with spiders and scorpions everywhere. He tried to force himself to turn off the Mustang's engine and remove the keys. He couldn't do it. The things were watching him from the vehicle's roof; they were probably inside it by now. Let it run.

He drew his phone out of his pocket and activated the flashlight app. The light helped a little but darkness still lay too deep all around him. He backed down the driveway away from the Mustang.

He'd have to walk back to the hotel and casino, sleep there tonight and call an exterminator tomorrow to fumigate his house and car before he could enter either again. One last time, he turned his flashlight toward the house. The Mustang's missing mirror brought a wince. He shook his head at the bent frame of his garage door. Ten-Wolves had a lot to answer for.

On the concrete floor just inside the garage, a tarantula had squared off in battle against a scorpion. Each was big enough to stretch across his palm, and when they tangled it was easy to imagine two monsters locked in a titanic struggle. Alvarado wondered which of the two warring creatures represented Concho Ten-Wolves, and which represented him? Which one was going to win?

Alvarado didn't wait to find out. He turned and began walking rapidly toward the one place he might feel safe tonight. But even that was doubtful.

CHAPTER 35

Jacob Drake woke around 9:00 AM to a knock on his door.
His usual "wake up," he imagined, and a moment later a pretty voice called out, "Room service, sir."

He returned a response, "Just a minute."

Drake hadn't made it to his suite's bedroom last night but had fallen asleep on the couch, which was almost as comfortable as the bed. He rose and slipped a maroon satin robe on over his nakedness while screwing his feet into a set of moccasin-like house shoes provided by the hotel.

Tony, his bodyguard, stood beside the door and opened it once Drake nodded his head to do so. A lovely young lady with a wheeled cart stood outside his room on the top floor of the Lucky Eagle Casino Hotel. She smiled. Tony lifted the lids on the dishes and gave them a quick once-over, then jerked his head to indicate the woman was free to enter.

Jacob Drake smiled as well while the server pushed her cart past Tony and into the room. The woman was Latina, with perhaps some Kickapoo blood. Drake found it difficult to differentiate between Hispanics and Indians. Nor did he care much. Neither race made up his preferred companions, although he enjoyed the liaisons he occasionally had with darker skinned beauties.

This one was probably no more than twenty-four, with very long black hair and a skin tone that reminded him of a tawny port wine. He particularly enjoyed the way her skirt clung to her buttocks as she began unloading the cart onto the room's dining table. His mind began to consider certain possibilities and he moved closer to her.

The woman offered him a deferential smile as she lifted the lids on various dishes to show him the delights he'd ordered: steak tartar, mushrooms, and steamed vegetables. A small dish of dried pequin chilis had been included. He liked to crush these up and sprinkle them on his food whenever he ate in Texas or Mexico. A delicate red Malbec, which was almost a royal purple in the glass and went well with spicy foods, completed his order.

The woman turned toward him for a tip and he handed her a hundred while meeting her gaze directly and making sure to let his fingers linger on her hand. The contrast of his pale skin and her melanin rich flesh excited him, but he could tell the woman was uncomfortable and drew his hand back.

No matter. If he wanted her, he would have her. Few young women could resist the combination of power, money, and prestige he could bring to bear. He doubted this girl would be one, though he had other things on his mind for the present.

"Thank you," he said, still holding her gaze.

She smiled quickly and looked down, then slipped past him and left the room, leaving the cart behind for any empties he wanted to place there. He watched her walk out with faint sigh before turning back to his food. He was hungry. He'd imbibed a little more than usual last night as he consolidated his psychological hold on the local policeman—Daniel Alvarado.

A cloth napkin and several plates with dinner service remained on the cart. Taking a plate, he dished himself up a generous portion of steak, mushrooms, and vegetables. He sat and reached for the napkin, drew it toward him. Something large and striped in shades of brown clung to it.

The natural reaction at such a moment was to fling the thing away and he did so, recognizing as he did that the brown object was a very large scorpion. A blast of rage detonated in his chest. One hand pounded down next to his plate, the other clenched deathly white on the edge of the table.

Tony rushed to Drake's side, and he waved the man away as he swayed in his chair and fought for control. He won. The scorpion remained where it had landed on the carpeted floor. It lifted its menacing pincers in a threat and arched its vicious tail over its back.

Drake rose slowly from his chair, walked toward the scorpion. He studied it for just a moment from his position far above it, then stomped it brutally, leaving behind nothing but a paste.

Drawing a deep breath, he returned to his table. After examining the cart for any other surprises and finding none, he sat and resumed his meal. His thoughts were deliberate but not as calm as his outward demeanor.

Had the presence of the scorpion been an accident or an intent? If it were an accident, it provided him excellent leverage against the hotel if its management or employees caused him any future difficulty. He knew how to play the injured guest.

If the scorpion incident had happened by intent, could it be the server? He doubted it. This particular woman had not served him previously and so far he'd caused no harm to anyone in the hotel. It wasn't likely she had any relatives or loved ones here he could have damaged.

However, as with the hotel itself, the young woman *could be* blamed for the scorpion, which might work to his advantage. A combination of outrage and reasonableness on his part could do the trick of getting her to go along with any untoward requests he might make—whether sexual or otherwise. She probably needed this job. That gave him power over her. All he had to do was hint how he might report the scorpion, but that he surely did not want to get her into trouble. Maybe….

Grinning to himself, Drake finished chewing a bit of steak tartar and washed it down with a swallow of Malbec. He was considering other individuals who might be blamed for the scorpion when a fresh knock sounded on his door.

"Who is it?" he called.

"Alvarado!" a voice answered.

Frowning at this unexpected visit, Drake set down his wine glass and went to the door. "This is not a particularly good time, my friend," he said through the wall.

"I'm sorry to disturb you, Jacob. But it's something you'll want to know. It's about Concho Ten-Wolves."

"Ah," Drake said. He opened the door himself and Alvarado pushed inside at an entirely too familiar pace. The man was getting tiresome, but Drake still needed him for the moment, though that could change very quickly. He held back his anger, then noticed how disheveled the Kickapoo deputy looked.

"Did you sleep in your clothes, Daniel?" he asked.

"Yeah," Alvarado replied, as Drake closed the door and turned toward him. "And I walked all the way back here from my house at 3:00 in the damn morning."

"Why don't you tell me why," Drake said soothingly, although he really wanted to take this man and throw him out the window to see if he could fly.

"When I got home last night, that damn Concho had rigged a booby trap for me in my garage. He set it up so a big bag of scorpions and tarantulas got dumped out all over the place. They got in my car. They're in my house. No way I could stay there."

Interesting, Drake thought. What he said was, "Are you afraid of spiders and scorpions, Daniel?"

"Afraid? No! I mean, I'm not afraid. But I'm...allergic. I get stung by one of those and it'll kill me."

"Ah," Drake said again. "But what makes you say it was Concho Ten-Wolves?"

"I know how he thinks, how he works," Alvarado said, throwing up his hands. "This has his stink all over it. And I know he's suspicious of me already. He practically accused me of planning his assassination on the road."

"Imagine," Drake said.

Alvarado gave him a look that might have been a glare of anger but was softened by another emotion before it even reached the man's face. Alvarado was just a little bit afraid of him, Drake knew. It was something to savor.

"Well," Drake said, "looks like I have Ten-Wolves to thank for *my* little visitation this morning."

"What?" Alvarado asked.

Drake described his own scorpion experience.

Alvarado's face brightened. It was pathetic to see. "That's him, all right. Gotta be."

"Odd how he's taken such a strong dislike to me after only two brief meetings," Drake said. "He wouldn't happen to have discovered anything about the dealings between the two of us, would he?"

"Not through me," Alvarado said. "But he's always been the suspicious type. And," the chief deputy added somewhat slyly, "he doesn't like white men much."

Drake knew the last part was a lie. He didn't think Ten-Wolves was the type to like many people, but the man wouldn't judge them on something like skin color. It made Drake wonder what other lies Alvarado might have told him. But for now, it was best to go along.

"I see," he said, scratching his chin. He made a gesture toward his dining table, "Why don't you help yourself to some food, Daniel. I need to get dressed and make a phone call. Then we'll speak further."

Time to bring in professional help, Drake thought, as he headed for his closet and his cell phone.

CHAPTER 36

Concho opened his eyes in the late afternoon. He could hear water trickling in the stream nearby. A bird chirped in the juniper tree next to his truck. He pushed open his sleeping bag, which he'd spread in the truck's bed, and climbed stiffly down to the ground. The garish yellow light of afternoon was beginning to soften, and more delicate colors were beginning to show in the world—purple and mauve and deeper reds.

The place where he'd parked was a safe haven, far back on the Rez in an isolated canyon among low hills where no one journeyed. The small stream crossing it seldom ran dry, and there were even fish in the deeper pools. Trees grew along the banks, not just bushes. He counted oak and willow and pine and cedar.

Years ago, he'd found an old wagon road that allowed access to this area. He'd had to clear it in places to get his vehicle through, and he still always brought along an ax on his occasional visits to keep it up. One day he had built a wickiup here, for the isolation he craved. But for now, it was a safe campsite away from his enemies, where he could sleep and hope to wake up alive.

Even here, though, the world proved able to find him. His phone rang and he saw Sheriff Parkland's number pop up. "Yep," he said, answering.

"Sorry to bother you but you wouldn't happen to have a phone number on Hamilton Blackthorne would you? We can't find a listing. I've left messages with some of his business offices to call me back, but so far there's been nothing."

"I don't know it," Concho said. "But I can get it."

"Appreciate it," Parkland said. "How you doin', by the way?"

"Having the time of my life," Concho replied.

Parkland chuckled and hung up. Concho walked over to the stream and splashed tepid water on his face, making sure to wash off any remnants of his warpaint. He combed his fingers through his hair and tied the thick black mane back out of his eyes. In a few minutes, he had water boiling on a small camp stove and bacon frying.

It had been a busy night and morning. The people he most suspected of burning him out and trying to have him killed had been given a warning. They'd have no doubt he was watching them now. He didn't think it would scare them off; he was counting on it not to. In fact, his actions should bring the infection to a head. Everything should be over soon. One way or another.

The only thing surprising him was that he'd gotten no text messages from his secret adversary last night or today. Whoever was taunting him was either dealing with their own issues regarding what Concho had done, or it was someone other than the three men he'd targeted. He shrugged. All would be revealed soon enough.

Concho poured himself a cup of coffee and began to eat the bacon directly from the skillet. It was gone far too soon and he sopped up the dregs with a slice of bread and ate it with relish before licking the last drops of grease off his fingers.

After finishing his late afternoon breakfast, he dashed out the fire with the dregs of his coffee and washed his dishes in the stream. Within half an hour, his truck was reloaded and he was on his way back to the Lucky Eagle Casino.

Time to put more pressure on his enemies.

***

No sooner had Concho stepped through the doors into the casino than he saw Daniel Alvarado talking to the man named Tony, Jacob Drake's almost neckless bodyguard. Neither man noticed Ten-Wolves initially so he strode in their direction. Tony saw him and called Alvarado's attention to the Ranger's approach. Alvarado spun around in startlement.

The deputy did not look well. The whites of his eyes were bloodshot and dark bags hung underneath them. His hair was mussed and there were stains on his normally immaculate uniform.

"How's the investigation into Ben Deer-Run's death going?" Concho demanded before Alvarado could open the show.

The deputy ignored the question. "I can't believe you'd come here," he snapped. "Not after what you did last night?"

Concho grinned. "I did a lot of things last night. You'll need to be more specific."

"The spiders and the scorpions at my place," Alvarado snapped. "Does that refresh your memory? And you had to put one in Mr. Drake's room, too? Bad, bad mistake. You'll pay for that."

Concho neither denied nor confirmed Alvarado's statement. He merely shrugged, then repeated his question about Ben Deer-Run with embellishments.

"Ben wasn't scared by some harmless spiders and scorpions," he said. "He had his throat cut and was hung up on barbed wire like a sack of trash. Or don't you care about murder?"

Alvarado wouldn't be distracted from his outrage. He took a step toward Concho, lifted a hand, and poked a finger toward the Ranger's face. "Harmless! Those things are deadly. Especially if you have an allergy."

Concho shook his head. "Are you still telling everyone you're scared of scuttling things because of an…allergy? We both know why you don't like 'em. And it has nothing to do with them being deadly. The ones around here aren't going to hurt an adult even if they did bite or sting."

Alvarado's face paled, and he lowered his voice. "So, you admit it. I'm going to arrest you for criminal trespass!"

"Whenever you show me the proof," Concho said. "I'll go along peacefully."

Alvarado pushed his finger closer to Concho's face. "Your time is coming, Ten-Wolves!"

"Move the finger or lose it," Concho said softly.

Alvarado seemed to freeze at the implied threat. It was the bodyguard, Tony, who stepped forward and took Alvarado's shoulders, drawing him back and away from the Texas Ranger.

"Later," Tony said, and it wasn't clear if he was talking to Alvarado or Concho.

The two men walked away. Concho relaxed. Looking around, he saw quite a few people watching him. Word must have spread about his burned trailer, or maybe about what had happened to Alvarado.

Good, he thought. *Let it spread.*

He headed upstairs to Melissa Nolan's office. The same young administrative assistant that Concho had dealt with last time sat at his desk outside Nolan's office. The man waved an expansive and rather snide hand at the chairs in the waiting room.

"Please, Officer Ten-Wolves, have a seat. Ms. Nolan is quite busy but I'll inform her of your presence."

"It's all right, I'll inform her," Concho said, as he walked past the desk and opened the door to the manager's office.

The assistant rose from his chair as if he were about to do something about Concho's behavior. He squeaked out, "Hey, you can't barge in there!"

Concho glanced at him and smiled his shark smile. The man sat back down without a word. Concho stepped into the inner office and closed the door behind him. Melissa Nolan, Manager of the Lucky Eagle Casino and Hotel, was sitting behind her desk. She'd clearly been doing her long fingernails, which gleamed a fresh pink to go with her tan linen jacket and strict white shirt. The open nail polish container sat on the darkly grained wood desk in front of her and she made no attempt to hide it, only picked up the lid and screwed it on tightly before setting the small bottle aside.

"Keeping up appearances, I see," Concho said.

Nolan's hazel eyes did not flinch as they met Concho's gaze. "You are a most unpleasant man," she said. "If you knew anything about the casino and hotel business, you'd know appearances are a big part of what we do. They make the difference between breaking even and profit."

"You know, I believe you," Concho said.

Nolan gave a noncommittal, "Mmmh," and a "What is it you want?"

"I need a phone number on Hamilton Blackthorne."

"Oh really?" Nolan asked. She tapped her fingernails on her desk, then gave a small, irritated growl as she realized she'd cracked some of the fresh nail gloss she'd just applied.

"What makes you think I have it?"

"Appearances," Concho said. "He's an investor in the casino. You'll have his number."

"And what makes you think I'd give it to you if I did?"

"Because it's part of a police investigation. His son was killed on casino property and I need to speak to him about it. Of course, I can get a warrant if I have to, and any reluctance on your part will be seen as obstruction of justice."

Nolan stared at him for a moment, then sighed. "Give me a moment," she said, as she turned toward the laptop computer at the right side of her desk and began to click the mouse around on the screen.

Concho couldn't see what she was doing but decided to give her time. In about a minute, the wait paid off. Nolan took one of her own business cards out of a little silver holder on her desk and scribbled a number on the back of it. She offered it across the desk to Concho in between two fingers.

The Ranger took the card, read the number. A California area code, which he already knew had to be correct. "Thanks," he said, bringing the card up to his forehead as if giving her a salute. "Now you're no longer on the naughty list for Christmas. I'll let you get back to your nails."

Nolan's answering smile was a masterpiece of both relief and disdain. Concho wondered if she'd practiced it in the mirror or if it just came naturally. He gave her a genuine smile back and left, shutting the door behind him.

As he started past the administrative assistant's desk, the outer door opened and Jacob Drake stepped through, immaculate in a gray suit, white shirt, and yellow tie. Tony walked in right behind him. He also wore a suit, an ill-fitting one, and the faint bulge under one arm indicated a concealed carry. Something to remember.

Drake smiled broadly. "Officer Ten-Wolves. Fancy meeting you here."

"I'm everywhere," Concho said.

Drake's smile thinned slightly. "I remember you seem averse to shaking hands so I'll not offer you mine this time. Interesting to run into you considering how your name has been on many lips today."

"Oh? What have those lips been saying?"

"That you're quite the amateur arachnologist."

"Amateur? I'm insulted."

Drake actually grinned. He seemed to be enjoying himself. "I, myself, favor scorpions and spiders. They're so...elemental. But I think our dear Deputy Alvarado finds them discomfiting."

"I believe he does."

"He is allergic, I hear."

"You hear a lot of things around the Rez. Probably shouldn't believe *everything* you hear."

"Do tell?"

"Not my place to say. Ask him about his eleventh birthday party."

"Oh, and what present did you bring young Daniel for his eleventh?"

"I wasn't invited," Concho said. "I had to crash. But I'm pretty good at that."

He stepped around Drake, brushed shoulders with Tony and was out the door.

CHAPTER 37

As Concho stepped out through the frosted glass front door to Melissa Nolan's office, he considered what to do with Hamilton Blackthorne's phone number. He quickly texted it to Isaac Parkland, but wondered whether to keep it himself. He never wanted to speak to the man again, but it occurred to him that Blackthorne might be used as leverage against Jacob Drake, who'd admitted the two were "rivals," and not of the friendly sort.

As he considered his options and decided to keep the phone number close but unused, yet, a motion in the corner of his eye caught his attention. Nolan's office opened into a common space between several meeting rooms, but to the right was a corridor leading to a set of men's and women's bathrooms. Someone stood hidden in the opening of that corridor, studying Concho. Whoever it was must have moved a hand or shifted position, for that was what had caught his attention.

The Ranger turned toward the corridor, but the observer stepped quickly back out of sight. Concho got only an impression of a man with long dark hair whom he didn't know. An Indian! Who he didn't recognize? Maybe another of the Kickapoo visitors from Oklahoma?

Concho strode swiftly over to the corridor. No one was in

sight when he reached it. The man might have gone into one of the bathrooms, which were next to each other on the left-hand side of the corridor, but he'd heard no sound of a door opening and closing. He knew these bathrooms. They weren't much used except by employees of the casino, and the doors made noise when they were worked.

The corridor extended half a dozen steps beyond the bathrooms and featured a water fountain at the end. Now, Concho observed something else strange. A shadow lay across the fountain, as if someone standing off to the left of it in some concealed nook was being backlit by fluorescent lights.

A dozen fast strides took Concho to the end of the corridor, and he found something he'd never known. The corridor didn't end at the water fountain; it made a sharp left turn. Twenty or so steps beyond stood a closed door marked: Maintenance. Authorized Personnel Only. Alarm Will Sound.

No alarm had sounded but Concho felt certain the door must have just closed behind the mysterious Indian who'd been watching him. He rushed toward it, letting his right hand drop to the butt of his Colt semi-automatic.

The door opened as he pushed down on the latch, with no more alarm than a faint squeak of hinges. He didn't step instantly through, though. It could be a trap. Holding the door partially open, he extended his head cautiously forward to peer past it.

The area beyond was dank and smelled of oil and the musty stench of rust and mold. Somewhere, water dripped. The maintenance area needed maintaining. Lighting was dim, from a single overhead bulb covered with dust, but it pushed back the shadows enough for Concho to see cables and pipes and nothing alive.

Cautiously, he pushed the door the rest of the way back and stepped out onto a small concrete landing. Steps, also of concrete and painted gray, with a patinaed metal railing, extended both downward and upward. No one was in sight in either direction.

Whoever had come out here could have gone up or down. No

way for him to be sure. But, it was only one floor down and if the person had taken that route he'd already slipped out of the corridor and was mingling with the gambling crowd below. Concho would never find him.

The Ranger had a feeling, though, that his quarry had not taken the downward route. A hunch told him the man wanted Concho to follow, which meant it *was* likely a trap, just not an immediate one. Since the alarm system had clearly been deactivated on this door, and maybe on others in the maintenance area, the impression of a snare was strengthened. Concho would have to ask Nolan who had access to the alarm system and knew how to turn it off. Though, for all he knew, maybe anyone with a little engineering knowledge could do it.

Concho drew his pistol and started slowly up the steps, sideways so he could see above and also watch below in case of an ambush. His boots made little sound on the steps but every tiny shred of noise echoed in the hollow space.

He passed a door opening onto the third floor, then on the fourth. He didn't stop because he was sure neither had been used. Damp dust covered everything here, including the door latches, and it was undisturbed on those floors.

Then he did hear something. Very faint. The heavy doors in the maintenance area were difficult to manhandle even for a strong individual. He heard one close somewhere above him. The sound might have been deliberate, or an accident. He didn't care at this point. He wanted answers.

Moving faster and making more sound himself, Concho passed the portals to the fifth and sixth floors. He came to the roof access. The clinging dust on the latch had been smeared. Someone waited for him on the other side of the door. He doubted they wanted to shake his hand and shoot the breeze, though he was pretty sure "shoot" was in there somewhere.

***

In the aftermath of making love, Jacob Drake kissed Me-lissa Nolan between the shoulder blades and withdrew from her and stepped back. He pulled up his pants and zipped, tucked his shirt back in and straightened his tie, though it was scarcely askew.

From where she'd leaned forward over her desk, Melissa straightened too. She pulled her ivory-colored panties up and her ivory linen skirt down. Brushing her hair back from her face with her fingers, she rolled her shoulders to loosen the white shirt that clung to her skin from the faint sheen of sweat she'd worked up.

She turned toward Drake. "You were wonderful," she said with a dazzling smile.

Jacob Drake returned the smile. He took Melissa's hand and kissed the back of it. "Only beauty inspires me to such heights," he said.

"You're sweet," Melissa said. She took a deep breath before pulling her chair back into position behind her desk and seating herself.

Jacob walked around the front of the desk and seated himself there, crossing his legs and sharpening the crease in his trousers with the fingers of his left hand.

"So," he said, "what did our friend Concho Ten-Wolves want from you?"

CHAPTER 38

Holding his pistol ready, Concho pushed open the door onto the casino/hotel roof and stepped cautiously through. His boots crunched on gravel and tar. No one was in sight but plenty of big pipes and massive air conditioning units provided places to hide behind. Whoever was playing a game with him had to know he was following. No sense being quiet about it.

"Why don't you come out and we'll talk!" Concho shouted. "So far, you've done nothing wrong. I've got no reason to arrest you. I just want to know who you are and why you're watching me."

No answer came; he wasn't really expecting one. After making sure the door wouldn't lock behind him, Concho closed it and stepped farther out onto the roof.

"Look!" he called. "I'm putting away my gun. Come out and talk."

He stuck his Colt back into its holster and stood waiting. Scattered across the roof were leaves and twigs left over from the storm. He even saw a pinecone. It was hot, though the afternoon faded toward evening. The roof's tar felt tacky under his boots, and the gravel radiated the day's heat. Not even a fitful breeze cooled him. Sweat began to drip down his face and stick his shirt to his back.

Several minutes of silence passed. Time for a more active

search. But the roof area was large, with plenty of hiding places. On his right, as he'd come out the door, there was only forty feet or so to the building's edge. He turned in that direction; he'd search there and double back to cover the rest of the roof. It meant he'd only have to watch behind him for a little while.

Although he didn't draw his gun, his hand never strayed far from his Colt. He made no attempt to move with stealth but did watch carefully for an ambush as he passed each potential hiding place. He was about halfway to the roof's edge when a man stepped out from behind a screen of big pipes rising there.

At twenty feet, Concho got a good look at the fellow. He'd never see this Kickapoo before today. He was tall and well built, with long, straight black hair held back from the face by a leather band. Fringed, buckskin trousers encased his legs, and there were moccasins on his feet. He wore a red leather vest with no shirt beneath. The muscles in his arms and shoulders bulged. An eagle talon necklace encircled his neck. A bone-handled hunting knife at the man's belt appeared to be his only weapon, though he could have a gun tucked behind his back.

"Bull Knife, I imagine," Concho said to the man, who looked to be in his mid-twenties.

"Concho Ten-Wolves," the man said, without acknowledging his own identity.

"I've been wanting to ask you a few questions," Concho said.

"Concerning?"

"Ben Deer-Run."

"The past," Bull Knife replied.

"The murdered," Concho said. "Daniel Alvarado was supposed to question you about him. I take it he didn't."

"Deputy Alvarado is also the past."

"Does that mean you and others like you are the future?"

Bull Knife smiled a smile worthy of Melissa Nolan, brilliant and full of white teeth. "There is no past or future. Only the present. I am the present."

Concho shook his head. "What is it with you radicals and your philosophical bullshit? You sound like Darrel Fallon."

"Who?"

"Leader of a group of neo-Nazis," Concho said. "A fascist. A Hitlerite. But maybe all you gangbangers talk alike, whether you're white nationalists or red. Or maybe it's just the drugs."

Bull Knife smiled again, though not quite so expansively. "I actually know Darrel Fallon. I wanted to see if you did. And you don't. Sometimes, one finds friends among the enemies of your enemies." He shrugged. "Sometimes not."

"Whatever you have to tell yourself," Concho said. "But, you need to answer some questions about Ben Deer-Run. I don't give a crap about the rest. If you won't answer 'em here, I'll have to take you somewhere else."

"I don't think so," Bull Knife said, as he took two steps backward to the very edge of the roof.

Concho shook his head. "You're going to kill yourself rather than answer a few questions? Seems a little extreme."

"The present doesn't die. It is continually reborn."

"You practice that in the mirror?" Concho asked.

Bull Knife took a deep, satisfied breath. For just a bare instant, he threw a glance over Concho's shoulder to the roof behind the Ranger. Then he turned and stepped off the edge.

A thought flashed through Concho's head as he saw Bull Knife's look. *Now the trap!* He hurled himself sideways and down, his hand slapping for his Colt. A burst of sound withered the evening—a shotgun blast from behind the Ranger.

Concho felt the brutal sting of shotgun pellets ripping into his lower body as he struck the ground and slid on the graveled roof. The skin on his arms scraped away; his jeans tore at the knees. He grunted, but forced himself into a roll, his hand like a vise on his pistol.

A second gun opened fire, not a shotgun but a semi-automatic rifle. Bullets sent chips of rock and roof flying. Concho rolled into the lee of a big A/C unit. Another blast from the shotgun tore into the other side of the unit. The metal screeched as if in pain.

Blood ran down Concho's legs and along his arms but he couldn't tell how badly he'd been hurt. No time to worry about it. Thrusting the Colt around the side of the A/C, he double-actioned three shots. Someone yelled but he doubted he'd hit anyone.

A ricochet caromed off the ground near his boot and he jerked it back. He fired another shot before working his way into a crouch. Bullets and slugs kept hammering into the A/C unit providing his only shield. Fragments of metal abraded away.

Moment by moment, his enemies were tearing his protection apart, and the only other potential shelter between here and the edge of the roof was the stand of pipes Bull Knife had hidden behind. They wouldn't last long under this kind of fusillade, even if he could reach them.

Help would not be coming either. This ambush had been well planned. Alvarado had to be in on it. The deputy would have made sure no one from the tribal police or any other security guard who wasn't already aware of the attack was close enough to lend Concho a hand.

"Flank him," one of the attackers yelled. "We'll catch him in a cross fire and kill him!"

Concho was on his own.

***

Daniel Alvarado fidgeted. He glanced at his watch. Then he heard it. *Boom. Pop, pop, pop. Boom.* Distant gunfire on the roof of the hotel/casino. His breath caught. A strange combination of elation and dread swept over him. It was happening!

He stood in the open area outside the main door to Melissa Nolan's office on the second floor. Jacob Drake was still in there with her, just where he was supposed to be. Drake's bodyguard, Tony, suddenly rushed out of the office. Seeing Alvarado, he raced over.

"You hear that?" Tony demanded.

Alvarado cursed inwardly but nodded outwardly. The gunfire continued. He wished it would quit. He wished it was over.

"Fireworks, maybe," Alvarado said to Tony. "Is the casino having some kind of promotion?"

Tony froze for a moment, then frowned. "That's...not fireworks. It sounds like gunshots."

"I don't know...maybe. I'm not sure."

"Where's it coming from?" Tony asked. "The roof?"

He looked up, as if he could see through the ceiling to the source of the shots.

Both Melissa Nolan and Jacob Drake came through her doorway. Tony saw them and spun in that direction. He rushed to Drake, began urging him back into the office.

"What's going on?" Melissa Nolan demanded. "Is that shooting?"

"I think so," Tony said. "It's upstairs. Maybe on the roof. You two need to get back inside!"

Tony grasped Drake's shoulder; Drake grabbed Melissa's arm. Melissa resisted. Her face turned toward Alvarado.

"Aren't you going to do anything?" she nearly screamed.

"I'm...I'm going!" Alvarado shouted back.

He drew his Glock and rushed for the corridor that led to the roof. A last glance over his shoulder showed Tony pushing his charge and the casino's manager back into the woman's office.

Alvarado took the corridor to the end and threw open the door into the maintenance space beyond. He started up the steps. The guns above quieted for a moment, then sputtered to life again.

Why won't it end? Alvarado's thoughts screamed. *Why won't Ten-Wolves die?*

CHAPTER 39

Metal shrapnel flew off the A/C unit as a steady barrage of gunfire shredded it. Concho turned his back to protect his face. A slagged droplet of melted lead fell onto the back of the Ranger's hand. It burned; he flicked it away.

His attackers were coordinating their fire. He dared not show his face above the unit for even a second. Nor would it do any good to fire blindly back. He needed something, one momentary shock to bring a lull, to give him a chance. Then he saw it. Nearly at his feet lay a pinecone dropped by the recent storm.

Concho's mind flashed back to Afghanistan, to a terrifying moment when he and his fellow Army Rangers had been pinned down by machine-gun fire from a rocky bluff above them. Fortunately, they'd had more than guns with them. In a desperate act, Concho grabbed up the pinecone, lobbed it backward over his head, over the A/C unit toward the two men trying to kill him.

He screamed out, "Grenade!"

Like a miracle, the gunfire from the ambushers stalled. Drawing his second Colt, Concho rolled into the open, going flat on his belly with both pistols stabbed out in front of him. The men hunting him had to know logically that he didn't have a grenade. But a gunfight doesn't breed logic in most men.

The fellow with the shotgun instinctively shied away from where the pinecone landed. He knew it was the wrong move the instant he made it. But for that instant he'd left himself vulnerable.

Concho shot him three times with his two pistols. One shot went low into the man's leg. The other two punched him in the left shoulder and side. The shotgun dropped onto the graveled roof as the man cried out and fell sideways.

Concho twisted around on the ground, trying to see the second shooter to his left. This one had been trying to flank Concho. He probably hadn't even seen the pinecone and was still hidden from the Ranger's view. Only now he was alone, and he knew it. He lost his nerve and turned to run. As he stepped out of his sheltering nook into Concho's view, the Ranger shot him in the hip and sent him into a stumbling fall.

Concho rose. Blood dripped down his right leg as he stalked toward the ambushers. The shotgunner wasn't dead but was no longer a threat. He tried to crawl away from Concho, leaving his weapon and a trail of scarlet behind. The rifleman was Indian. He still had bite. He'd lost his main weapon but in desperation fumbled a huge nickel-plated revolver from his belt.

"Don't," Concho said.

Though not wearing a mask this time, this was the same man who'd tried with his cronies to kill Concho a few days earlier on the road.

"Don't!" Concho said again, louder, more forcefully.

Getting shot must have knocked all fear out of the man. He sat halfway up and eared back the hammer on the revolver. The barrel started to lift. Concho shot him once in the chest. He flopped back. The Ranger walked over and stood above him. The fellow's eyes were open but he didn't appear to be seeing much. The blood pulsing steadily from his chest began to falter as Concho went to one knee beside him.

"Who are you?" Concho asked.

The man's eyes closed and he was gone.

Concho came to his feet and walked over to the other shooter, who'd given up crawling and simply lay on his belly on the roof. His left arm, shoulder, and knee were mangled but Concho figured he'd live. The man turned his head toward the Ranger. No need to ask this one's name.

"Wayne!" Concho said. "My old friend. You shoulda stuck to fists."

"Go to Hell!"

"You're closer than I am," Concho replied.

Walking away from Wayne for a moment, Concho pulled out his cell phone to call 911. The phone had been on the receiving end of a buckshot pellet. Cursing, he stuffed it back in his pocket. Realizing he was only a few paces from the edge of the roof, he decided to check quickly on one other thing that made him curious. Where had Bull Knife gone when he stepped over the side of the building?

Looking over, he saw what he expected to see. A balcony jutted out from the hotel's sixth floor. It was empty of any Bull Knife now. He'd have to check on what room or rooms that balcony served.

Turning back toward Wayne, Concho heard the access door to the roof slam. He still had pistols in each hand and stepped to the side behind some pipes as he waited for who was coming.

Daniel Alvarado stepped almost tentatively into view, with his Glock in his hand. Concho moved into the open, lifted his pistols and took aim. Alvarado saw Concho with his guns. He threw his hands up in the air, still clutching the Glock.

"No, no! Don't shoot!" Alvarado begged.

"Put your gun on the ground," Concho yelled. "Now!"

Alvarado did as he was told, then slowly straightened again. "What's going on? What are you doing? Who are these men?"

"Shut up!" Concho ordered as he strode to Alvarado and used his boot to kick the Glock farther away from the deputy. "Don't move!" Holstering his own pistols, Concho patted Alvarado down from behind. He found a pocketknife and slipped it into his own pocket, but nothing else.

"You can't just—"

"I said, shut up!" Concho snapped, and enjoyed hearing the deputy's mouth snap closed on his retort. Concho grasped the deputy's shoulder and jerked him around to face him. "We're going to have a little talk," he said. "Was this ambush your idea or did someone put you up to it? Jacob Drake, perhaps?"

Alvarado sputtered. "I didn't... I don't..."

Concho took hold of the man's collar with both fists and leaned in close. But before he could say anything, he heard the sound of the roof's access door opening and closing again. Drawing one of his Colts, he pulled Alvarado around to face that direction and stepped behind him to use him as a shield.

Roberto Echabarri came into view, moving in a crouch with his face scared but determined. He had a pistol in his hand. He paused when he saw the dead and wounded ambushers on the ground, and the tableau between Concho and his boss.

Roberto lifted his gun into the air and slowly straightened. "OK," he said. "I don't know what's going on but let's all stay calm."

"Where did you come from?" Concho demanded.

"I was on patrol," Echabarri said. "Melissa Nolan called me. Said a shooting was going on. When I got here, everyone pointed toward the roof. Now, why are you holding a gun on Deputy Alvarado?"

"He's crazy!" Alvarado shouted. "He wants to kill me."

Concho released his hold on Alvarado and holstered his pistol. He spat on the ground. "If I wanted to kill you, you'd be dead," he said. To Echabarri, he added, "These two shooters came after me." He gestured to the dead Kickapoo. "That one tried it once already when he and two others attacked me on the road. This one," he pointed at the man named Wayne, "is one of Jacob Drake's bodyguards."

"Ex-bodyguard," Alvarado said. "Drake fired him. Publicly. Just a couple of days ago."

"I doubt it," Concho said.

"It was right downstairs in the Red Sky Grill," Alvarado argued, lowering his hands and stepping away from the Ranger. "There are twenty or thirty witnesses. And he was fired because of Ten-Wolves here. It's obvious he wanted revenge."

Echabarri frowned. He holstered his pistol and came walking toward Ten-Wolves and Alvarado. "Is that true?" he asked Concho.

"As far as it goes," Concho said. "But there's more to it. I just don't know what yet."

Alvarado started to bend down to pick up his Glock and Concho snapped, "Leave it!"

The deputy's face flushed with blood, but he left the gun alone.

"So what do we do?" Echabarri asked.

"My phone's dead," Concho said. "You call Isaac Parkland's office. It's obvious the Kickapoo nation is in no position to investigate. We'll have to let the sheriff in. And get an ambulance for Wayne here."

Alvarado started to protest and Concho stared him down. Echabarri glanced back and forth between the two for a moment, then reached for his cell phone.

"Looks like you need an ambulance, too," Echabarri said, gesturing toward the blood still dribbling down Concho's leg, darkening his jeans.

"Just get *one*," Concho said. "They've got an emergency clinic in the hotel. I'll have them look at me."

Echabarri nodded and made the call. Concho turned to Alvarado.

"Who is that?" the Ranger asked, pointing at the dead Kickapoo.

"I have no idea."

"You're lying."

"Prove it."

"I intend to. By the way, what does Bull Knife look like?"

Alvarado frowned. "That's not him," he said, nodding toward the dead man.

"I know," Concho replied. "But he was here. On the roof. I'm sure of it."

Alvarado merely shrugged tiredly. "He's got black hair. Fairly tall. Good looking fellow."

"Wears an eagle talon necklace?"

"Maybe."

Concho shook his head. "You always been useless, Alvarado?"

The expression in Alvarado's eyes went flat. He murmured so Echabarri couldn't hear. "Can't wait to laugh at your grave, Ten-Wolves."

"If you're in charge of putting me in it, I'm not worried," Concho said, as he walked away.

CHAPTER 40

Maverick County Sheriff Isaac Parkland arrived and took charge. They were able to skirt the jurisdiction issue because the tribal police force was in disarray, with the chief dead, the head deputy under suspicion, and the only other deputy left—Roberto Echabarri—having less than a year's experience on the job. Melissa Nolan, who was on the Tribal Council, and was the only member of the council actually on the reservation at the moment, agreed to the arrangement temporarily at the request of Echabarri. Concho knew enough to stay away from Nolan.

Wayne, whose last name turned out to be Quaite, was taken to the hospital under close guard. He'd talked, but not about Jacob Drake, only about how much he hated Concho Ten-Wolves, who—he said—had cost him a well-paying job. He claimed to have hired the dead Kickapoo to help him, although he gave no details about the supposed transaction.

The coroner arrived to look at the body of the dead Kickapoo, who no one seemed able to identify. It was dark by then and they had to string lights on the roof, which the casino's staff of electrical engineers handled admirably.

Concho's last second anticipation of the ambush and his dive to the side had saved him from being cut in half by Wayne Quaite's shotgun, which had been loaded with double-aught buckshot. He'd still caught three pellets. One had killed the phone in his pocket, another had lodged in the meat over the hip, and a third had cut through his jeans and across the back of his right thigh, leaving a deep groove that caused most of his bleeding.

The Ranger had himself sewn up in the hotel clinic by a young man named Sam Reyes, a Kickapoo tribesman in training to be a nurse practitioner. Reyes was smooth and efficient and very professional as he removed the pellet from the hip and stitched up both wounds. He also cleaned and disinfected various scrapes on Concho's hands and arms from where he dove into the gravels pebbling the roof.

As he was leaving the clinic, a voice called out to Concho. He turned to see the young man named Coleman Chase coming toward him with a look of concern on his face.

"Dang, man!" Chase said, "I was worried. I heard you were shot!"

Concho shook the hand Chase held out. "News doesn't waste any time spreading in *this* place," he said. "But it's not always accurate."

Chase flashed a grin. "Every fish gets bigger with the retelling," he said. "You OK?"

"Lost a little blood but I'll live."

Chase's grin turned to a frown. "What the heck happened?"

"Afraid I can't give you any details. We're still investigating."

"Right, right," Chase said, nodding. "I understand. Was surprised to see the Sheriff's Office here, though."

"They're assisting," Concho confirmed. "But look, I need to get back to it. Good to see you."

"You too," Chase said. "Glad you're OK. Let me know if you need anything."

"Will do," Concho said, as he headed toward the elevators and took one to the sixth floor. The first thing he wanted to do was check on the balcony which Bull Knife had jumped down to before the ambush.

As he got out of the elevator, a hallway to his left led straight down to a set of glass doors opening onto a balcony. He tried the doors, found them surprisingly unlocked, and stepped outside. It was a little after 10:00 PM, still very warm and humid. The night was quiet, with a few wispy clouds catching the early moonlight overhead.

Three balconies were here, this center one outside the hallway, and slightly smaller ones to the left and right outside of two suites that were generally reserved for the casino's highest rollers. Looking up to study the roof, Concho could see that Bull Knife had used the balcony outside the suite to his left.

That didn't mean much, though. Only a few feet of sky separated the balconies, and a brave jumper could easily leap from one to the other. Bull Knife might have jumped from the one balcony to this one and exited out into the hallway. They'd have to interview anyone who might have been on this floor at the time, to see if they'd seen anything.

Stepping back into the hotel, Concho went to the door of the big suite on the right and knocked. No one answered. He waited a moment and tried again. Still no response. He crossed to the other suite and knocked. Bull Knife had certainly jumped to the balcony outside *this* suite first, though whether he'd entered the room was unknown.

Movement came from inside the room. The door opened a crack to reveal Tony, Jacob Drake's bodyguard.

"What do you want?" Tony demanded.

"I'd like to come in and look around."

"Not without a warrant."

"Figured you'd say that. So, were you and Jacob Drake in your room when all the shooting happened?"

"You know where we were. You saw us downstairs in Melissa Nolan's office."

"I saw you there maybe twenty minutes *before* the shooting."

"We were still there when it started. Mr. Drake was in conference with Ms. Nolan. She can confirm it. And so can Deputy Alvarado. He was outside Ms. Nolan's office when I came out to see what was going on."

"Really! Interesting. Did Alvarado seem surprised by the shooting?"

Tony frowned. "I don't know what he was. Weird. He acted like he thought it was fireworks."

"Then what happened?"

"Ms. Nolan came out of her office with Mr. Drake. She yelled at Alvarado to do something. He took off with his gun in hand. I imagine for the roof. I was busy doing my job."

"Which was?"

"Getting my charge back in the office where he'd be safe. And Ms. Nolan too."

"Would there have been anyone up here in the suite when this was all going down?"

"Shouldn't have been."

"I guess you know your friend Wayne was involved in the shooting?"

"I heard it. But he wasn't my friend. We worked together. Until we didn't. That's all."

"You don't expect me to believe Drake really fired Wayne!"

"You heard him do it."

"I heard him say the words."

Tony shrugged. "You'll have to take that up with Mr. Drake."

"Is he here?"

"He's having a nice long bath. As he always does before bed. I'm sure he'd be willing to talk to you tomorrow."

"And you knew nothing about Wayne's plans?"

"I don't like you," Tony said. "Doesn't mean I want you dead."

"Comforting," Concho said. "Who told you Wayne was involved?"

Tony made an amused face. "Surely you don't think it's a secret.

Everyone knows that Wayne and some Indian fellow ambushed you on the roof. More than one person has mentioned it to me."

"Alvarado was one of them, I guess," Concho said.

Tony shrugged and closed the door.

Concho decided not to push it for now. He found the stairs leading up to the roof and rejoined Isaac Parkland there. Parkland looked wilted from a long day's work but was still at it.

"You OK?" asked Parkland.

"I've had worse. Anything new here?"

"A little bit. Roberto Echabarri swung by. He says the body of the Kickapoo belonged to a man who called himself Tall Horse. Although it might not be his real name. Another of those fellows out of Oklahoma. Echabarri seems like a level-headed sort. I sent him off to look for Joseph Big-Pine. Maybe ask some questions about Tall Horse. Maybe he'll get something."

"Good idea," Concho said. "What about the coroner?"

"He's gone. Took the body. The chest wound killed this Tall Horse. As you know. That Wayne guy is going to be all right. I've got Terrill Hoight with him. I doubt we'll get anything out of him, though. Turns out he's already had a stint in prison. For robbery. He didn't inform on any accomplices last time."

Concho nodded, then gave Parkland the information he'd gotten from Tony downstairs, and what he could deduce about the balcony Bull Knife used to escape.

"What the hell is going on, Ten-Wolves?" Parkland asked. "You got any theory at all on this thing? Other than Alvarado? I just don't see him alone in this thing."

"I don't believe he is. Though I'm pretty sure he's the man who hired Wayne and the dead guy to kill me. At least, he knew it was going down. According to what Tony told me, Alvarado was weirded out by the firefight and tried to cover it by saying he thought it was fireworks. I expect he thought it would be over quick. One shot, which could easily have gone unnoticed or been mistaken for a car backfiring."

"It almost was one shot, wasn't it?"

"If I hadn't moved when I did."

"So who's pulling Alvarado's strings?"

"I'm thinking it's Jacob Drake, but he's too smart to give himself away. I need to think on it. Maybe a good night's sleep."

"Yeah, we're about to close up here. You should get on home."

Concho said nothing, and after a moment Parkland realized his error. "Damn, sorry. Where you gonna sleep?"

"I'm thinking right here in the hotel," Concho replied.

"What?" Parkland said, sputtering. "Surely you're kidding."

"Keep your friends close," Concho said. "And your enemies closer."

CHAPTER 41

Once Parkland closed down the shooting investigation for the night, Concho got a room at the hotel and stripped down to sponge away as much as he could of the day's sweat and dirt. With all the bandages on him, he couldn't have a proper shower or bath, but he'd made do in worse situations.

At least this time he had plenty of soap and running water. Not like in Afghanistan. Since it was beginning to look like he was growing a beard, he even managed a shave using one of the razors supplied by the hotel.

The contrast between the stark white of the bandages and his dark skin made him think of the new scars he'd picked up today. Plenty of old ones showed up in the mirror. Each one had its own unpleasant story. A puckered old bullet wound in his left shoulder reminded him of events he didn't want to relive tonight. He forced them away.

His hotel room, the one he'd requested, was the VIP suite across the hallway from Jacob Drake's. Concho's was 601, Drake's 600. Concho figured the two rooms had similar setups. This one had a full bathroom, a lounging area, and a separate bedroom. The furniture and walls were decorated with various Native American imagery, including wooden and ceramics masks, framed sand paintings, and beautiful woven rugs.

It came with modern American amenities as well, and one of those was a man's maroon satin lounging robe big enough to fit him—albeit tightly. He felt completely ridiculous but it was gentler on his injuries than clothes.

No doubt, Maria would tell him it went with the delicate lavender scent of the room's potpourri. He thought about calling her but decided against it. The Morales family was probably celebrating brother Henry's birthday right about now.

As he tried to decide whether to just go to sleep or maybe read a little bit of the newspaper he'd been left while snacking from the complimentary cheese tray, a soft knock sounded. His .45 never strayed far from his hand these days so he picked it up and padded to the door.

Making sure to stand well to the side of any shot that might come through the door, he called out, "Who's there?"

"A visionary," a man's voice answered.

Concho opened up, and Meskwaa strolled through. The elder Kickapoo went straight to the cheese plate and began helping himself. Concho grinned and locked the door, then joined his friend at the tray and began helping himself as well.

"Guess I better get in a few bites before it's all gone," Concho said.

"Yes," Meskwaa said. "And to keep this old one from having enough to eat."

"Mmph. I suppose I could order one of each kind from room service, so you won't die of hunger."

"Yes," Meskwaa said again. "Do so and I'll take it with me when I leave. Charge it to your cop army."

"You mean the police force?"

"Yes," Meskwaa replied.

"Maybe first you'll tell me why you came to see me."

Meskwaa stuffed two squares of cheese in his mouth, chewed carefully for a minute and swallowed. He looked around and pointed toward the door leading onto the balcony.

"Need a smoke," he said.

Concho understood. The elder had something to tell him and didn't want to risk this suite being bugged. As it quite likely was. Nolan was the type to seek every advantage she could in dealing with her customers.

Still carrying his pistol, Concho led the way onto the balcony and shut the door behind them. He left the light off but the crescent moon made enough glow to see by. The night air felt good.

Meskwaa fired up one of his filterless cigarettes and waved the smoke over the side of the concrete rail. "I have a message for you," he said softly.

"From?"

"A woman you know."

"Hum," Concho said. "And what does she want to tell me?"

"Someone wishes to meet with you."

"Who?"

"If you attend the meeting, you'll find out."

Concho understood. Whoever wanted to talk to him, and he had a pretty good idea who it might be, was being very cautious about anyone finding out. That meant he, or she, was afraid of the people in this hotel. Maybe they had good reason to be.

"I'll have to know when and where."

"You know when and where the sun sets, do you not?"

Concho wanted to arch an eyebrow but had never been successful doing just one at a time. He could only do both, which just looked goofy. Meskwaa's comment told him everything he needed to know, though.

"All right," Concho said.

"There is another thing. A true seeing, I believe."

"Tell me."

Meskwaa drew on his cigarette, let the smoke purl from his nostrils. "Light upon a ridge," he said. "And a bad feeling about it. I know it's not much."

"Your visions are usually enough to help," Concho replied.

"Let us hope so," Meskwaa added. He was quiet then, before gesturing at Concho's bathrobe. "By the way, do you feel this is a good look for you?"

Concho felt his face flush but tried to joke it off. "Can't be shooting people all day. I needed some downtime."

"Glad I arrived before you applied your pink mud mask and retired for the evening. Now," Meskwaa pinched out the nub of his cigarette and tucked it into his shirt pocket, "why don't you call up this room service you spoke of. I am close to death from starvation."

***

After Meskwaa left with his arms full of goodie bags, Concho lay down to sleep. It was just after 10:00. He found it difficult to relax. His wounds hurt; his mind roiled. He finally drifted off only to have the hotel phone by his bedside jangle him into wakefulness. Instinctively grabbing the pistol beneath the pillow beside him, he sat up. The radio clock read 11:11.

Four sticks! he thought.

Picking up the phone, he said, "Yes."

"Third time's a charm," a muffled voice said, and hung up.

"Not unexpected," Concho murmured. His "secret adversary," as the Ranger had taken to calling him, was certainly dialed in to the gossip line about Concho. He knew what room the Ranger was in. He must have also heard that Concho's cell phone had been damaged in the gunfight on the roof. Unable to text, but not wanting to pass up a chance at a dig, he'd risked calling on the hotel phone to promise another attempt on Concho's life.

Two failures! Third time's a charm.

The threat wasn't needed but the texter probably got his jollies from the psychological violence of the act. The risk of it was that, unlike with texting on a cell phone, the call on the hotel phone had to either be passed through the local switchboard, or it came from another phone inside the hotel.

Concho would check the switchboard but he doubted the caller had been so stupid. Nor would he have likely called from another room, which could also be traced through the switchboard. He'd probably used one of the courtesy phones located around the casino. Most of those were on the second floor and Concho considered heading down to check them out. Then he shrugged. The caller would be long gone.

Strangely, Concho felt more relaxed after the call. It had been like waiting for a pot to boil and it finally had. He slid the pistol back under its pillow and lay down. Soon he was asleep. His dreams took him back to when he was nine years old, to the day of Daniel Alvarado's eleventh birthday.

A broiling Saturday in July along the Rio Grande. Concho floated the morning away in a pool that the kids on the reservation often used for swimming. After, he hunted the rocks along the banks for insects to fish with. He was alone; he liked it that way.

Under one rock he found a big brown and white striped scorpion, an evil looking thing that he much admired. Using the blade of his pocketknife, he scraped the scorpion into a Prince Albert chewing tobacco can he kept in his tacklebox. He was carrying the can when the birthday party arrived in the back of a beat-up old pickup.

Concho was big at age nine but Daniel Alvarado was bigger at eleven. The two had fought several times, and Daniel had won. Daniel didn't like Concho, for reasons the boy didn't understand at that age.

Concho wasn't exactly afraid of the other youth, but he was cautious. He walked away from the birthday celebrants, climbed up on a slab of rock that swimmers sometimes used as a diving platform. His cane fishing pole lay there. But Daniel came after him, with two other boys in tow.

"Don't want you here, Ten-Wolves," Daniel said. "It's my birthday. Don't want you ruining it."

"Not gonna ruin it," Concho said sullenly. "Ain't gonna bother you."

"You ruin stuff just by bein' places. Go on now!"

Concho looked around. Daniel's mother and father had driven the birthday group here, but they were arguing in the truck and not paying any attention. Concho felt his face flush hot. His fists clenched.

"Oh, ha ha," Daniel said. "You gonna fight again? What happened last time? I whipped you is what happened."

"That's right," one of the other boys said with a taunting laugh.

Concho shook his head. He took a deep breath to calm down. Saying nothing, he picked up his pole and started to leave. Daniel snatched the pole from his hand, and when Concho spun around, the older boy snapped the cane down across his knee and broke it.

Concho lunged toward Daniel but the boy to Daniel's left kicked out a foot and tripped him. Concho fell to his bare knees on the rock, and the Prince Albert can dropped from his hand.

Daniel kicked Concho in the face; he fell back. The bigger boy stepped in to kick him again but trod on the can and the lid popped open. Daniel looked down. His eyes bulged as the big scorpion came boiling angrily out of the can and ran up his bare foot.

Daniel gurgled in fear. The scorpion arched its tail and struck, the stinger burying itself in the muscle just beneath Alvarado's ankle bone. Daniel shrieked. He did a mad dance, shaking his foot wildly. The scorpion clung, it's stinger still buried.

Daniel kicked harder. The scorpion went flying, but the older boy lost his balance and fell backward off the rock toward the water below. The side of Daniel's head struck the edge of the rock as he went over. He was unconscious when he splashed into the pool. Concho lunged to his feet and rushed to the edge of the rock. The other two boys broke and ran, shouting loudly for Daniel's parents in the truck.

As Concho looked over the side of the rock, he saw Daniel surface in the pool. He floated face down. Concho leaped into the water, splashed in next to Daniel and quickly grabbed the other boy. He twisted Daniel onto his back and tugged him toward the bank, only to be shoved aside as Alvarado's father arrived and grabbed his son.

Within a few moments, Daniel Alvarado was sitting up, alternately crying, gagging up water, and screaming about scorpions. Concho picked up his little tin tacklebox, his broken cane pole, and his crushed Prince Albert can and walked home.

CHAPTER 42

Daniel Alvarado's shoulders quaked; his hands twitched.
A near constant tic twisted his cheek. He sat in the casino parking lot, in a white panel van he'd commandeered temporarily from among the casino's fleet of vehicles. It had not been possible for him to get back in his Mustang. Not possible at all.

Nor could he go to his house. Not until it was fumigated. And no company he'd called would do it until Monday. It was Sunday morning now, sometime after midnight. He felt exhausted. He'd slept no more than a couple of hours last night, crashing on a sofa in one of the meeting rooms outside Melissa Nolan's office. He'd have to sleep in the van tonight. If he could.

Though he'd done it often enough, he didn't want to ask Melissa Nolan to comp a room for him at the hotel. He didn't want to see the same look in her eyes she'd shown him when the shooting broke out and he'd hesitated to respond—the look that named him "coward."

"Damn you, Ten-Wolves," he murmured. "This is all your fault! I ought to…" His hand fumbled at the handle of his Glock. He drew the pistol into his lap. "I ought to walk in there right now and shoot you in the face."

He knew he was too afraid to try. Ten-Wolves was in a

comped room himself tonight. Probably sleeping the sleep of the righteous. It was like the man was charmed, as if he were some kind of sorcerer. How else to explain his escape from two well-planned ambushes?

The Oklahoma Kickapoo named Tall Horse had claimed the Texas Ranger's spirit was filled with strong magic. Daniel remembered sneering to himself when Tall Horse and Joseph Big-Pine decided to curse the man by leaving a decapitated deer head outside his trailer. Twice now, Concho's luck, or his magic, had been stronger than anything thrown against him, stronger than bullets.

And, Daniel knew, *he* would be blamed for those failures. They weren't his fault. He'd considered everything. The attempts shouldn't have failed.

The passenger side door of the van wrenched opened; a man slid inside. Alvarado jumped and nearly pulled the trigger on his Glock.

"Dammit!" he said. "You startled me. I could have shot you."

"Don't worry about it, man. I know you're going through a rough patch. I'm here to help."

***

Concho slept late. He rolled out of bed a little after 7:00 in the morning. Because of the need to change his bandages, it took him a while to get dressed. He then headed into Eagle Pass. Skillet's Restaurant provided him a breakfast of sausage and biscuits. Verizon was next on his list, to pick up a new cell phone. They weren't able to save anything from his old one, but by accessing his email he managed to restore most of his contacts.

The first person he called was Maria Morales, who was at work. The mall had yet to reopen but management was on the job putting everything right. They chatted for a few minutes, mostly about mundania. She'd heard about the shooting at the casino but had no details and didn't know of his involvement. He left it at that.

After getting off the phone with Maria and talking himself out of driving over to see her, the Ranger's next stop was Isaac Parkland's office. The sheriff was in and didn't keep him waiting. Concho fell into a seat that made a tight fit for him and studied Parkland's gray face and red-rimmed eyes.

"You look like Hell," Concho said.

"Feel like it too. Getting too old for this kind of stuff. But if you think you look better than me, you've got another think coming."

Concho flashed a tired grin. "Point taken. I slept but I don't feel much rested today. Bad dreams."

"At least we both made it to dawn. I wasn't sure you would, lying down in the lion's den as you did."

Concho shrugged. "The lions offer good room service," he said.

"I reckon." Parkland scratched his head, a sure sign he was thinking. "Been trying to figure this thing out," he said. "I keep imagining it's one of those Gordian knot type things. You know, if you cut the right thread it'll all fall apart and you can see it. But, if so, I haven't found the right thread yet."

"Maybe a recap," Concho said.

"Right," Parkland said. "You start."

"OK." Concho took a deep breath. "Darrel Fallon leads a bunch of Neo-Nazis to take over a mall. We think it's terrorism but find out the mall bank was robbed and a lot of financial bonds are still missing. Maybe some other stuff. Blackmail stuff. Illegal stuff for sure."

"Right," Parkland said. "And then we have two murders. Right on the border of the Rez. Ben Deer-Run, the tribal police chief, and a druggie and criminal who just happens to be the son of a Croesus-rich businessman and crime lord."

"Croesus, even. And Gordian Knot before that," Concho said, grinning. "Tossing out the mythological references today, aren't you?"

Parkland shrugged. "I do that when I get tired. But I'm having a hard time connecting those two. Ben and this Donnell Blackthorne. And figuring out why the bodies were 'displayed' rather than just made to disappear."

"We know Ben was looking into a possible resurgence of the NATV Bloods," Concho said. "Could give the gang a reason to get rid of him. And if Blackthorne was pushing into their territory with something illegal, they could have…well, decided to kill two birds with one stone. The displaying was some kind of message to someone."

"From what you found out about the surveillance videos at the casino," Parkland added, "Daniel Alvarado is covering up something. Either a connection between Ben and Blackthorne. Or some other illegal activity. But we don't know what."

"Alvarado is in way over his head," Concho said. "The mere fact he didn't protest having you come into investigate the shooting last night is proof. In fact, I think he's pretty close to cracking up."

"Can you have another go at him? See if you can *make* him crack?"

"I can try," Concho said. "But there might be another possibility."

"Who?"

"Melissa Nolan. I'll talk to her. She doesn't like me but I don't see her willingly getting involved in murder. Maybe with a little pressure she'll tell me what she knows."

Parkland nodded. "Good idea. What about this Jacob Drake? We're pretty sure he's dirty but not how. Is he involved with the murders? Or just shady stuff? He certainly seems to have a hold on Alvarado."

"He's got a hold on Melissa Nolan, too," Concho said. "I don't know how strong. But it's there in how she responds around him. I'll have to feel her out on that, too. And, Drake is rich enough to be another Croesus."

"What else are we missing?"

"Hamilton Blackthorne his own self," Concho said. "How did he react when you told him his son was dead?"

"He gave a long sigh. Asked if it were drug related. I told him it was murder and we were looking into it. He asked if we had any suspects. I told him, none at this time. But promised to call him if we made an arrest. Overall, he seemed very…calm about it."

"Interesting. He's not a very calm guy when he's stymied."

"Shock, of course."

"Maybe," Concho agreed. "But that's another mystery here. He and Drake are rivals and Drake seems to be horning in on Blackthorne's interest in the Lucky Eagle Casino. It means Blackthorne would have an agent here seeing after his interests. Who?"

"Wasn't it his son?"

"I doubt it. Or, maybe Donnell was *one* agent, but Blackthorne would have had someone else keeping an eye on his son's actions. That's how he operates."

Parkland nodded. "All right. Any idea who?"

Concho shook his head. "None."

"So," Parkland said, "you're gonna talk to Melissa Nolan. What do you want me to do?"

"It would be great if we could get a list of the bank's customers. Find out who's missing something. And if any names show up on both their list and ours."

"The FBI is handling that investigation," the sheriff said. "But…uh, I have a friend at the agency. She might be able to get me something. I'll see. It'll likely take a while."

"We may not have a while," Concho said. "Feels like this thing is picking up speed toward the end of the line."

"Yeah, it does."

Concho climbed to his feet. "One bit of good news. At least I hope it is. I've got a meeting this evening with an unknown someone who I think is going to give me a clue."

Parkland arched an eyebrow and Concho tried not to feel jealous of the man's god-given ability.

"They've tried to kill you twice already," the sheriff said. "You don't think this could be a trap?"

"Don't think so, but I'll be careful. I'll keep you in the loop. Who knows, this may just cut that Gordian Knot of yours and bring down Croesus. Whoever he is."

CHAPTER 43

Once again, Concho found himself at Melissa Nolan's office in the Lucky Eagle. The same young male assistant sat behind the secretary's desk when Concho came in and walked right past him.

"The door is *locked!*" the man said. "Unless you decide to smash it down with a *boot!*"

Concho turned toward the fellow and smiled. "Depends on how quickly you alert Ms. Nolan on the intercom and get me in to see her."

The assistant blanched a trifle at Concho's sharky smile and immediately keyed the intercom to announce him.

"*He* is here," the man said into the machine.

A garbled response came back but the assistant understood. "She'll be right with you. If you'll wait *just* a minute."

"All right," Concho said.

"You…can have a seat," the assistant said.

"I'll stand," Concho said, stepping closer to the desk.

The man practically flinched and did not look happy until the inner office door opened and Melissa Nolan stuck her head out to beckon Concho inside. The Ranger followed the casino manager and sat down in the visitor's chair while she walked around behind her desk and seated herself. Today, she wore a black pencil skirt and a prim yellow blouse with a bow tie.

"I wish you'd stop scaring my assistant," Nolan said as soon as she was seated. "He's very good at what he does but he's not comfortable with physical confrontation."

"Then he shouldn't have been a dick the first day I met him," Concho replied.

Nolan's mouth twisted into a look of distaste but she let Concho's words pass without a retort. "So, what do you want from me today? I hope you're not going to shoot up my casino again."

"I thought it was the tribe's casino."

"Now who's being a dick?"

Concho relaxed in his chair and offered her a less threatening smile than he'd given her assistant. "You're right. I apologize. But as for the shooting, it happened on the roof. Technically, that's outside the casino. Pretty considerate of me if you think about it."

"Yes, I imagine you *do* think of it as considerate. But, again, why are you here?"

"For the same reason I was here before. Surveillance footage for the week before Ben Deer-Run's death."

"I told you it was destroyed."

"You *told* me a load of bull. If it was destroyed, it was done by human means, not from a storm surge targeting just the right computers."

Melissa Nolan stared at him. Her mouth worked but no words came out.

"Look," Concho continued. "There have been two murders already. Another man was killed on the road a few days ago. A fourth one on the roof yesterday. They all died on the reservation. Two were Kickapoo, people who you—as a member of the Tribal Council—have a responsibility for. I'm trying to save lives. What's your motivation?"

"Two of those four died under your guns," Nolan snapped. "Your 'saving lives' doesn't seem to be working."

"You might prefer it if I'd been one of the dead, but I did what I had to do to protect myself. And I'm also a member of this tribe. If you're trying to shelter Alvarado, that's not your job. Whatever is going on here, he's up to his armpits in the filth of it."

"I know Daniel Alvarado better than I know you," Nolan said.

"So you know I'm speaking true," Concho continued. "But you're not covered with dirt yet. You've only done what *Deputy* Alvarado asked you to do as part of a criminal investigation. Nothing so bad it won't wash off. Why don't you tell me what you know?"

Nolan wasn't quite ready for that yet, but she squirmed in her chair for comfort and didn't seem to find any. "With Ben's death, Alvarado is head of the tribal police," she said finally. "He has authority here and you don't."

"For how much longer?" Concho demanded. "The other two members of the Council will be back from Mexico in a month. There'll be a meeting then. With everything going on, Alvarado may be on his way out. I'm going to recommend Echabarri to replace Ben."

Nolan snorted. "Echabarri's a good man but he's inexperienced."

"He's not crooked, which is what's important. As for Alvarado, you've seen the cracks yourself. He's starting a downward slide. I doubt he'll even last until the Council meets. When are you going to jump off the ride before he takes you with him?"

"You don't understand!"

"Make me understand."

The woman huffed a breath. Her shoulders slumped just a bit. "The data is gone but it wasn't lightning." She cleared her throat. "Alvarado took the computer it was on. Probably destroyed it. He came up with the idea to blame the storm."

"Was it to protect himself from something on the recordings?"

Nolan shook her head. "Not...specifically. I mean, maybe there were things I didn't see. But...well, he said *you* would use the surveillance data if you got ahold of it."

"Use it for what?

"To become chief of the tribal police."

Concho was caught by surprise. He blinked. "Why would I want that?"

"You don't?"

"I like being a Texas Ranger. I have zero interest in replacing Ben. What did Alvarado give you to support his claim?"

"He said you were in trouble with the Rangers. Said you'd had a big fight with your boss and were looking to transition."

Again, Concho blinked. He recalled the press conference for the mall attack. Plenty of people had seen the tension between him and Max Keller and noted Keller's anger. But Alvarado hadn't been there. Who would have told him about the incident?

"I don't get along with my boss," Concho said to Nolan. "Doesn't mean I want to leave my job. And how could I use the security footage to take over the tribal police anyway? What was on there?"

Nolan abruptly pushed to her feet. She began to pace, rubbing her hands down her skirt to wipe away a nervous sweat. Concho let her work up to what she wanted to say.

"I…when I said I hadn't seen Ben in any of the recordings, that wasn't quite true."

"Oh? Why did you lie?"

A flash of indignation crossed Nolan's features, then dissipated. She turned to face Concho. "Ben was gambling," she said. "I'd never seen him do that. I mean, a nickel here or there at the slot machines. But he was playing poker at a table. And losing. I saw it in person, not just on the recordings. I…mentioned it to Alvarado. He said Ben had a problem and it was getting worse. Daniel… Alvarado said he'd been helping Ben. And when he noticed it on the tape, he said you shouldn't be allowed to see it. That you'd use it to make trouble for Ben. To get him replaced. With you."

"You believed him?"

"I did."

"Why? Gambling isn't illegal. The Council wouldn't vote out Ben for me just because Ben was playing poker and losing. You certainly wouldn't do that and you're on the Council yourself."

"They…we…might vote him out if he had a gambling addiction."

"You only have Alvarado's word that Ben had a problem. You said yourself, you'd never seen him do it before."

"No."

"Look, I know you don't like me very much. Can't say I like you all that much either. But I liked Ben. If he were gambling, he had a *reason*, not a problem. What about Donnell Blackthorne? Was he around? Did you see him? Did you lie about that too?"

"I didn't lie about it," Nolan said. "I said I didn't know him. And I didn't. I certainly had no idea he was related to Hamilton Blackthorne. But I did see him on the recordings. You just didn't ask the question directly. And I wasn't going to volunteer any information."

Concho shook his head. "Who knows what that cost us. Was Donnell anywhere around Ben?"

"Yes. I only saw him a few times. One was the night Ben was gambling. Blackthorne was playing at the same table."

It felt like a strobe light had just gone off in Concho's face. "Ben was losing to Donnell on purpose," he said. "And he had some reason. Maybe just to make contact. Maybe to get on his good side. Blackthorne was involved in something underhanded, too. Possibly with Alvarado but I don't know. Ben must have been investigating it."

Nolan frowned. "I don't…. I didn't see…. But maybe you're right! Donnell and Ben talked afterward. Just a couple of minutes. No idea what they were saying. It didn't look suspicious to me then. Gamblers share their tips and strategies and wins all the time."

"It sure would be nice to have those recordings."

"They're gone."

"And Alvarado got his way."

"You have to understand," Nolan continued. "I had little choice but to believe him."

"No, I don't understand."

Nolan started pacing again. "I don't really know you!" she said. "What you're capable of. Only by reputation. They say you're a hard case. I've certainly seen it. Alvarado said you were so 'by the book' you'd turn in your own brother for breaking the rules."

Concho snorted at the "by the book" comment but let it pass. "Was Blackthorne gambling a lot?"

"Pretty constantly. Mostly slots. He appeared in several places on the recordings actually. And I saw him a few times on the floor. The only thing I saw him do...well, suspicious, was coming out of the bathroom once wiping his nose. Like maybe he'd snorted coke. No way to be sure but it's not unheard of here anyway."

"You didn't see either Ben or Blackthorne coming in or leaving?"

"No, but there was plenty of data I didn't review."

"What else did you see? On the recordings, or in person?"

Nolan forgot herself enough to shrug, which made her seem more human than Concho had given her credit for. "I don't... know what you're looking for," she said. "How do I know what's important and what's not?"

"Anything suspicious. Anything that didn't belong."

"I...I don't think so."

"What about with Alvarado himself? Did you see him doing anything unusual?"

Nolan bit her lower lip and sighed. "I only saw Alvarado doing one thing...odd. Not suspicious necessarily. But...."

"What?"

"After this I'm going to need my own bodyguard to protect me from Alvarado."

"I'm not going to tell him where I got any of this information."

"He'll figure it out. He's not stupid."

"No, he isn't, but he's soon going to have bigger things to worry about than you. In fact, I bet he's already got 'em. It's pretty clear he orchestrated the attack on me yesterday. And probably the one on the road a couple of days back. Both failed, and whoever his bosses are, they aren't going to appreciate that."

"That's ridiculous!" Nolan said, but Concho could tell her mind was working over the evidence and not finding a way to dismiss it.

"Think about it," Concho said. "Think about how he's acted lately. The things he's said, what he asked you to do. Decide for yourself if it makes sense. But in the meantime, tell me what odd thing you saw Alvarado involved with."

Nolan chewed her lower lip some more, then sighed. "Well, I didn't see anything illegal. But it was right around the time Ben got killed. And it was on the surveillance videos. Alvarado was at the bar talking to a woman who turned out to be a prostitute. We had to…ask her to leave."

"She have a name?"

"She called herself Melody. I doubt that's her real name. A white girl. She was in a few times before we figured out what she was doing. When I saw Daniel talking to her on the recordings, he told me he was just rousting her. I'm pretty sure that's not true."

"Don't suppose you'd know where I might find this Melody?"

"No idea," Nolan said, "but I'll ask my security folks. I'll call if I get any information."

Concho stood up. "Thanks," he said.

Nolan paused and Concho paused.

"Am I in trouble?" Nolan asked.

"Not with me. I can't guarantee down the line you won't be called to testify in court. But it's unlikely. You don't really have any hard information except about Alvarado taking the recordings. Where is our deputy, anyway?"

"I don't know. Haven't seen him today."

"All for the best," Concho said, as he turned and left.

CHAPTER 44

As soon as he left Melissa Nolan's office, Concho called Roberto Echabarri.

Echabarri answered with "Who's shooting at you now?"

"No one at the moment, but there are still plenty of hours in the day."

Echabarri chuckled. "What can I do for you?"

"I'm looking for Alvarado."

"You try the casino?"

"I'm there."

"Then I don't know. I haven't seen him. But I'll swing by his house and see if he's at home."

"Thanks. Let me know."

"Will do," Echabarri replied as he hung up.

Concho's stomach growled and he realized it was lunchtime. He had a long wait until his secret evening meeting and plenty of food could be had at the casino. He stepped into Azul's restaurant for a burger and fries. The place was packed. There was a wait. He was only a few bites into an Angus burger before Echabarri called back.

"Yep?" Concho answered.

"Something a little weird," Echabarri said. "Alvarado's car is in the garage but there's no lights on inside and no answer to a knock at either door. Everything's locked up."

"Maybe he's having a walk."

"Maybe. But I called his cell phone. I can hear it ringing inside the house but it just goes to voice mail. I can't see any sign of him through any of the windows."

"I'm on my way," Concho said, as he hung up and signaled the waiter for a to-go box.

***

While he drove, Concho stuffed fries in his mouth and wolfed down the rest of his burger. He finished the last crumbs of french fries in the bottom of the bag as he pulled into Daniel Alvarado's driveway and parked beside Echabarri's white SUV.

As he climbed out, his eyes were drawn to a ridge about a hundred yards south of Alvarado's house. It was covered in saltbushes and a few low bunches of mesquites. He'd hidden behind the same ridge the other night, watching through his night vision goggles while Alvarado dealt with the trap box of scorpions and spiders. Something seemed different about it today, though.

He frowned in thought, but Echabarri was standing by Alvarado's front door and waved him over. He joined the deputy, wiping greasy fingers on his jeans.

"No hide-out key, I'm guessing?" Concho asked.

"No. Not that I know of."

"Anyone else have a key?"

"His wife, I guess. But she's in Oklahoma visiting relatives."

"Yeah," Concho said. "Did you try the windows?"

"All locked."

"He could be dead or hurt in there," Concho said.

"Do you think we should break in? I don't know if that's a good idea."

"I'm going to check the garage."

"The door there is locked, too."

"I'll just make sure. You stay here."

Echabarri looked puzzled but Concho walked away without further explanation. Alvarado's two-car garage held only the chief deputy's red Stanger, with the passenger side mirror torn off. The mirror had been tossed onto a long table at the front of the garage amid a pile of various other junk.

Something was wrong with this whole picture. Just the night before last, Concho had watched Alvarado scurry away from his house and down the road toward the casino. He'd left his Mustang running in the driveway, with the broken mirror lying on the floor just inside the garage.

Though the tarantulas and scorpions didn't like people any more than people liked them and had dispersed back into the wild, Concho couldn't imagine Daniel Alvarado trusting to that. The man had a serious dislike of scuttling things. He wouldn't have gotten back into his Mustang so soon. Or his house. So who had moved the car?

"I hate mysteries," Concho murmured to himself as he tried the garage door. As Echabarri had said, it was locked. Concho took a good hold on the knob anyway. He took a breath, then twisted.

The lock resisted; he exerted more strength. The muscles corded across his big shoulders. A crack sounded from within the door and the knob came apart under his hand. The inner part clattered to the floor inside the house. The lock popped loose and the door opened.

Concho stepped through with his hand resting on the butt of his pistol. No lights were on. The place was quiet. It smelled faintly musty, as dwellings often do when men live in them alone. He sniffed another odor too, very faint, but recognizable. The Ranger went through the house to the front door, unlocked it and opened it for Echabarri.

"How did you…? Never mind, I don't want to know."

"Come in," Concho said. "We need to search. There's something dead in here."

***

"They've arrived," a man's voice whispered into a cell phone. "Ten-Wolves and Echabarri."

A muffled voice on the other end said, "Good! You have your instructions." The line clicked dead.

The first voice spoke again, whispering into nothingness. "Thy will be done."

***

The death smell wasn't strong. It might even have been something as small as a dead mouse in the wall, but Concho doubted it. The house was big, probably over three thousand square feet. Concho and Echabarri split up to cover it all quickly.

A few minutes later, Concho found the source of the smell in the den. He leaned out into the hallway to call Echabarri, then turned back to examine the scene. It was dark in the room. Thick curtains were pulled over the picture window. But he didn't turn on the lights at first.

It was a TV room, with a big flat screen against one wall and all the furniture arranged to face it. The numerous bookshelves were enough to make Concho jealous but almost none of them held books. Most carried DVDs, the cheap two or three dollar copies people bought at Walmart. The collection seemed to run heavily toward kid's movies and older crime flicks.

Alvarado had two kids, Concho knew. A boy and a girl, somewhere between five and eight. They apparently enjoyed such fare as *Ratatouille*, *Zootopia*, and *Moana*. The Ranger figured the crime films were Alvarado's: *Scarface*, *Goodfellas*, *Once Upon a Time in America*, *No Country for Old Men*.

Alvarado sat in an easy chair facing the TV, but he wasn't watching it. He would never watch it again. The chair had been tilted back, and Alvarado looked almost like he was resting, but coagulated blood stuck to the right side of his head and had dripped down, leaving a Rorschach wine stain on the chair's cushion. The deputy's Glock .40 lay in his lap, with his hand lying loose across the handle. He'd been dead several hours.

Echabarri stepped into the room, gave a gasp, and gagged.

"Don't throw up in here," Concho warned.

Echabarri gagged again and stepped back out of the room to get control of himself. Concho walked over and flipped on the lights before returning to stand over Alvarado's corpse. After a moment, Echabarri joined him, holding a white handkerchief to his mouth.

"He…he shot himself?" Echabarri asked.

"Looks like it," Concho said.

"You don't sound sure."

Concho glanced over at the young deputy. "Are you?"

Echabarri shook his head. "Maybe the coroner will be able to tell."

"Possibly," Concho said. "But it's either real or whoever faked it did a good job."

"Who would want to fake it?"

"The kind of people who don't tolerate failure. Alvarado had to be involved in both the recent attempts on my life. He couldn't get it done. And it became clear yesterday he was starting to crack under the strain. I wanted to talk to him today because I could see the cracks and thought he might be ready to break. Maybe somebody with a lot to lose saw the same thing and figured it was a danger."

"So, who are we looking at?"

"You tell me."

Echabarri considered. "Jacob Drake," he said after a moment.

"What makes you choose him?"

Echabarri shrugged. "I don't know. There's something about him. Since you brought him up to me, I've been paying attention. He's not a nice guy."

"My suspicion, too. But we don't have any proof and can't arrest him for not being nice. Wayne Quaite, his supposed ex-body-guard, is the only route to him I can think of. But I'm sure Quaite is being well compensated for his silence. He's unlikely to break. Though," Concho offered a grim smile, "maybe he should be put on suicide watch anyway."

"All right," Echabarri said. He glanced over at Alvarado's body and away again. "I've got to get out of here. I'll call it in. And call Parkland."

"I'll go with you," Concho said.

The two lawmen went back through the house and out the front door. Echabarri reached for the cell phone holstered at his left hip. A glint of light from the nearby ridge caught Concho's eye.

Meskwaa's vision!

The Ranger tackled Echabarri, who cried out in shock. The boom of a rifle shattered the afternoon heat.

CHAPTER 45

Concho hit the ground with Echabarri on top of him as a bullet passed through the air where they'd stood and smashed into the brick front of Daniel Alvarado's house. Concho rolled, bringing Echabarri with him, and practically threw the lighter man toward the garage.

"Get inside!" Concho shouted, as he rolled up into a crouch, drew his right-hand Colt and unleashed a hail of shots toward the ridge where the light had flashed.

Knowing he couldn't hold this position, Concho threw himself sideways just as a second bullet from the sniper whipped like a hornet past his face. He crashed to the ground next to the front bumper of Echabarri's SUV and squirmed into the vehicle's shadow.

A bullet clanged into the other side of the SUV but Concho was safe for the moment. Having emptied his pistol, he pressed the button to release the useless magazine and grabbed another from his belt to shove up the well.

Glancing around, the Ranger saw that Echabarri was unharmed and had drawn his own service revolver. The young man stood just at the corner of Alvarado's garage, searching for the shooter on the ridge. He didn't realize he was partially exposed to the sniper.

"Get back!" Concho shouted, waving his hand desperately.

Too late. Concho heard the sound of the shot but had already seen Echabarri stagger backward as he was struck. The young deputy cried out, dropping his pistol. He swayed.

Concho lunged from cover and crossed the gap to the garage in four swift strides. He caught Echabarri around the waist with one arm and yanked him to safety. Another shot from the sniper snarled past, as if angry at being thwarted of its prey.

Concho held Echabarri upright while he examined the young man's wound. The bullet had struck the meat of the deputy's left shoulder and passed all the way through. The hole in the deputy's back was big enough to stick two fingers in and showed torn muscle and fragments of slick white bone mixed with fibers from the man's uniform. It was bleeding but the flow was more of an ooze than a gush, indicating no artery was cut.

"You'll live!" Concho said. "Get back in the house. Call Parkland."

"I...I dropped my phone."

"Use mine," Concho said, pushing his own cell into the younger man's hands. "And get some towels to press against the wound. To stop the bleeding."

"What about you?"

"I've got a plan," he said.

Echabarri nodded and staggered toward the door into the house while Concho waited for the sniper's next shot. From the rate of fire so far, he was pretty sure the shooter was using a bolt action rifle. No matter how trained and how fast you were with such a weapon, you still had to take your hand off the trigger for an instant to chamber another shell. That was the moment Concho needed.

A bullet clanged into the wall of the house half a foot away from Concho; the hollow boom of the shot followed. Concho was already moving as he lunged out of the garage and dove behind his truck. The wounds he'd taken in from the last ambush were far from healed. One of the stitches at his hip popped loose. Blood began to trickle down his leg but he had no time to worry about it if he and Echabarri were going to survive the next few minutes.

The Dodge Ram pickup he'd got as a loaner from Isaac Parkland sat on the opposite side of Echabarri's SUV from the shooter, at least partially hidden from the sniper's direct line of sight. Remaining in a crouch just in case, Concho unlocked the passenger side door and slid into the vehicle.

The engine started smoothly, with a low rumble that Concho knew the sniper would hear. He'd probably think Concho was about to flee, though. It was almost certain Echabarri had just been in the wrong place at the wrong time. He wasn't the target. Concho was who the shooter wanted.

Let the man have what he wanted, Concho thought.

Throwing the truck into reverse, Concho punched the gas. The Dodge screeched backward down Alvarado's driveway. A bullet smashed through the driver's side window, sleeting glass across Concho, who was driving bent over with his head as far down behind the dash as he could get it and still see.

Concho slammed on the breaks, shifted the truck into Drive. He stomped the gas again and wheeled around the SUV. The front tires dropped off the slightly raised side of the driveway and plunged into dirt. Concho hit the button to engage the four-wheel drive and pushed the gas pedal *into* the floor.

The big engine roared; the truck launched itself up the hill toward the sniper's position. A bullet crashed through the front windshield. Another slug slammed into the truck's grill. Steam burst upward but couldn't stop this steel juggernaut.

Dirt spun into the air from under the truck's big tires. Small bushes tore away as the vehicle crashed over them. They climbed the hill in seconds. Concho saw the sniper rise to his feet and draw a bead on the small portion of the Ranger's head showing above the dash.

Concho didn't wait to be shot. He aimed the truck and ducked.

The bullet whipped over his head through the shattered windshield and thudded into the seat behind him.

Concho lifted his head again. His aim with the vehicle was true, straight for the shooter. The engine's roar sounded like a crashing plane. The sniper tried to work the bolt of his rifle but jammed it in his panic. He tossed the gun, dove to the side. The bumper of the pickup clipped the man's foot, sent him spinning hard to earth.

Concho heard the fellow cry out even over the sound of the engine. The Ranger hit the brakes, shifted the truck into park and bailed out, drawing both his Colts as he did so.

Rushing to the tail end of the pickup, he peered around the side. The sniper's rifle, which appeared to be the scoped weapon of a professional assassin, lay in the dirt like a sleeping predator. It didn't mean the man was unarmed. He probably had a sidearm. But there was no sign of him anywhere.

"You're no ghost," Concho murmured to himself. "You're here somewhere. Waiting."

CHAPTER 46

"You might as well give up!" Concho shouted to the would-be assassin. "The officer you shot is alive and has already called the sheriff's department. They'll be here soon."

No answer but the breeze. Concho moved to the front of the pickup, peered around it. He couldn't see any sign of the sniper here either, and there weren't many places on this hillside to hide. The man must be lying just over the lip of the hill, on the downslope. Perhaps he'd found a little hollow to nestle into.

"The only two ways out of here are dead or in handcuffs!" Concho called.

Still no answer.

"All right," Concho said. "We wait. If you're hurt, it's going to seem like a long one."

"My leg's broken," a voice shouted from just over the hilltop.

"A Dodge makes a helluva 'Ram,'" Concho called back.

"Not really funny," the man replied. "Look, I'm going to give myself up. I've got a pistol. I'm throwing it out!"

Concho saw a semi-automatic come arching into the air from over the hill's rise to smack down in the dust a few feet from him.

"That's good," the Ranger said. "Stand up. Show yourself."

"Can't. My leg. It's busted. And there's something wrong with my hip. Maybe dislocated."

Concho holstered one pistol and centered the other on the point where the voice was coming from. He eased around the truck, whose engine still chugged along. He didn't tell the man he was coming. Let him wonder. And he didn't come at him straight on but worked in from the side.

After a few more seconds, Concho reached a place on the hill where he could see the guy lying almost face down on the ground. The leg indeed looked twisted, though the Ranger couldn't tell if it was broken. The fellow's jeans weren't torn but that didn't mean much. Both the man's hands were empty and in plain sight where they rested in the dirt. Concho still didn't relax. The sniper could have a second hide-out gun.

"Keep your hands where I can watch them," Concho ordered.

"Sure," the man said, turning his face to where he could see Concho. "Haven't got anything else to do with them."

The Ranger moved closer. The sniper was black, at least in his early forties. He had the look of ex-military. Tall and lean, the accent suggested east coast—Baltimore area maybe. Sweat and dust covered him.

"I take it, I was your target," Concho said.

"I don't even know who you are."

"A Texas Ranger."

The man offered a faint shrug. "Say, can you help me roll onto my side? This position is really painful for my leg and hip. I'm not going to resist. I'm done."

"Your day is just beginning," Concho said. "All those interviews when you get to jail."

Again, the man shrugged. "If it'll get me out of this heat. How do people down here stand it?"

"Helps to be born to it," Concho said, as he stepped closer to stand over the sniper.

The man struck like a panther, twisting himself toward Concho and lashing out with a clawed left hand. The hand closed around the back of Concho's boot and jerked the leg out from under the Ranger.

Concho fell backward, slamming into the ground. His gun hand banged down hard on a rock. The pistol spun away. The sniper surged up to his knees, raising a long stiletto blade he'd kept hidden under his body. The blade flashed as he stabbed at Concho's leg, trying for the femoral artery. A cut there would bleed a man out in seconds.

The Ranger kicked out. The knife scraped across his boot but the man's aim was deflected. Concho rolled and came to his own knees. The sniper was there, slashing down with the knife. Concho threw himself to the side; the blade cut dirt.

The two men rose simultaneously and faced each other, barely three feet apart.

"You're a liar," Concho said. "The leg looks pretty good."

"It hurts but it works."

"And," Concho added, "you're quick!"

"So are you," the sniper replied. "Quick that is. And here I thought this job was going to be boring."

"You may wish it had been before it's finished."

The man hefted his knife, sidled a little closer to Concho. "You've still got a gun on your hip," he said. "Think you can draw it fast enough to beat me at this distance?"

"I don't think I'll have to," Concho replied.

"Oh, ho," the man said. "Aren't you tough!"

As he uttered the word "tough," the man lunged with his knife out, snake quick. The steel blade glittered in the sun as it slashed toward the Ranger's stomach. Concho wasn't surprised, and was even faster. His hand struck downward, locked around the sniper's wrist behind the knife.

The man grunted, tried to force the blade forward into Concho's flesh. It didn't move, and then he felt the power in Concho's grip as the Ranger exerted himself and the bones in the sniper's wrist ground together. The sniper struck with his left hand, trying for an open-handed blow into the collarbone to numb Concho's shoulder. The Ranger caught that hand, too, and head butted the hired killer in the face, pulping both the man's lips against his own teeth.

The assassin cried out, his legs buckled, his right hand spasmed open and dropped the knife. Concho twisted the man around and slammed him down on his back on the ground. Before the gun-man could recover, he found himself forced onto his belly with his hands ricked up behind him. He groaned in pain.

Concho snapped on the cuffs and stood. He took a few deep breaths. "Now," he said, "who hired you?"

The man's answer was distorted by his smashed lips but easy enough to understand. "Somebody else will be coming. As many as it takes."

"Fine," Concho said. "Just like playing whack-a-mole."

CHAPTER 47

Concho picked up the pistol he'd dropped and stuffed it in its holster. He pulled the handcuffed assassin to his feet and pushed him the dozen yards over the hill to the Dodge pickup. The truck was still running. The engine was beginning to smoke. One of the assassin's shots had pierced the radiator.

"Looks like you killed the truck at least," the Ranger said.

The sniper only smirked.

Concho held the fellow against the side of the pickup while he reached in, turned off the motor, and removed the key. He looked around for the shooter's ride. The man must have had an escape route planned.

On this side of the hill, the ground sloped down to a line of taller than average mesquite. A dirt road in the distance made a winding scar through the landscape. Nosed in among the trees, Concho glimpsed something unnatural.

"A four-wheeler?" he said, glancing at the shooter. "You don't look like the off-road type."

"And you don't look like a comedian. But here we are."

Concho grinned. The faint sound of sirens tickled his ears. "Your new ride is on the way," he said to the shooter.

Pulling the man down the hill toward Alvarado's place, Concho kept a tight grip on one of the fellow's elbows. He drew the sniper into Alvarado's garage and called through the open door to Echabarri.

"Roberto! You OK? I've got the assassin."

"I'm...I'm all right," Echabarri replied. "I'm coming out."

"No need!" Concho shouted hastily. "Just rest. I hear the sirens coming. The ambulance should be here soon."

Despite Concho's words, Echabarri appeared at the door and came into the garage. His face was pasty and covered with sweat. His hands shook. One of Alvarado's big bath towels had been wrapped around his shoulder and duct taped down.

"Sit, man!" Concho said. "There's no need."

"I'm all right," Echabarri protested. "I want my phone." He walked slowly past the Ranger and his prisoner, offering a weak smile to Concho but giving no glance to the sniper.

Concho shook his head but pushed the assassin back out of the garage and over toward Echabarri's SUV. The sirens were getting closer. Blue lights flashed at the end of Alvarado's road and turned on to it.

Carrying his phone, Echabarri walked slowly over to lean against the SUV. Concho took the deputy's handcuffs from the man's belt and used them to secure the prisoner to the vehicle's door handle.

Terrill Hoight, Isaac Parkland's chief deputy, came racing down the road in his Dodge Charger and whipped into Alvarado's driveway. He lunged out of his vehicle, tossing his sunglasses onto the seat behind him as he drew his service revolver.

"It's all right!" Concho called, lifting his hands. "We got him."

Hoight slowed, then straightened to his full height and holstered his gun. "Glad to see it," he said. He noticed Echabarri with blood silently dripping from his left hand to the ground, and quickly pressed the transmitter on the microphone attached at his collar.

"Calling the ambulance," Hoight said to the others. "Getting them up here right away."

Concho nodded. Echabarri sighed and slid down the SUV to a seated position against one of the tires. Concho bent over him concernedly.

"I'll be all right," Echabarri said. "But you've gotta get Melissa Nolan to swear you in as a temporary tribal policeman."

"Me? No!"

"You're the only one that can do it," Echabarri said. "The only one left with experience. Promise me or I can't go to the hospital."

"Now you're being stupid."

Echabarri fumbled at his chest, awkwardly unpinned his badge, and thrust it toward Concho. "Show her this. So she'll know I approve."

"Listen——" Concho started.

"Promise me!"

Concho sighed but took the badge. "OK. All right, all right."

The ambulance arrived; two paramedics rushed up to Echabarri, and Concho stepped back out of the way. Hoight had uncuffed the sniper from the SUV and was leading him toward the back of his police car.

"Watch him close," Concho called. "He's already proven to be a tricky one."

Hoight gave a nod but said nothing.

Parkland walked up as the paramedics got Echabarri onto a stretcher and hurried him toward the ambulance. The sheriff nodded to Echabarri and spoke a quick word in passing, then turned and came over to Concho.

"Is he going to be all right?" Parkland asked.

"I don't know for sure but I think so. The bullet went clean through his shoulder but it did some damage. I hope he'll be able to use it again."

The sheriff nodded as the ambulance turned on its sirens and tore out for the hospital with Echabarri on board. As soon as the sound died away, Parkland asked, "And this sniper just opened fire as the two of you came out of Alvarado's place?"

"Yep. He didn't get Echabarri right away, though. It was later. When the deputy was being brave."

"You think the guy's a pro?"

"Absolutely."

"But he missed his first shot?"

Concho shrugged. "I saw something on the hill just before the shot," he said. "I knocked Echabarri down. Got me out of the way, too."

"Saw what?"

"I thought it was a glint of light off his scope." He didn't tell Parkland about Meskwaa's vision. "But it seems weird a pro wouldn't be more careful."

"Yeah," Parkland said. He lifted his palm to shade his face and squinted up the hill to where the assassin had been hiding. "Is that my truck?" he asked.

"Afraid so," Concho replied. "It died a hero's death, though. Shot through the radiator while charging into enemy fire."

"I seem to remember telling you not to get bullet holes in it."

"Circumstances intervened," Concho said.

Parkland scratched his chin. "Maybe we better take a look at Alvarado," he said. "Before other circumstances intervene."

***

After a largely silent examination of Alvarado's corpse, Concho and Parkland headed back outside to wait for the coroner. Concho fetched his first aid kit and used surgical tape to cover the place on his hip where the stitch had popped. The bleeding had largely stopped but his damp jeans clung on that side. Fortunately, he always carried some spare clothing in his truck. Since the fire at his trailer, it was all he had.

"So, what do you think about Alvarado's death?" Parkland asked Concho after he finished changing.

"I thought it might be possible it was suicide. With his wife leaving him and the other things lately that have gone wrong for him. But the presence of our assassin makes it seem less likely."

"Right," Parkland said. "But that raises its own question. Why stage a suicide for Alvarado if he was going to hang around and shoot you down as an obvious murder? Doesn't one of those negate the other?"

"I don't have an answer."

"Maybe he'll talk," Parkland said.

"I wouldn't count on it. His kind stay alive by not talking."

"You think whoever hired him might try to…uhm, hit *him*?"

"Hit him?" Concho asked. "You been watching Mafia movies again?"

Parkland snorted, which was his equivalent of an eye roll. "You know what I mean."

"I do," Concho said. "I wouldn't rule it out but I don't think it likely. Course, weirder things have happened around here in the last few days."

"Fellow don't sound like he's from around here."

"East Coast, I think," Concho said. "He crossed state lines to knock me off. That means the FBI will probably want in and we'll be cut out anyway."

Parkland shook his head, then said, "I agree it's odd for this shooter to be around right when Alvarado 'commits suicide,' but why would he have killed Alvarado anyway?"

"Because Alvarado was close to breaking. And when he did, he would definitely have talked."

Parkland considered. "And I guess you're saying Jacob Drake couldn't allow it?"

"Drake is my inside bet to be behind it," Concho said.

"If he is, he's a slippery SOB."

"Agreed. By the way, when the coroner gets here, can you give me a ride over to John Gray-Dove's? He's got my F-150 and may be done with it by now. I need another vehicle. I can have John come pull our Dodge Ram hero down off the hill, too. His prices are reasonable."

"Sure. We've got insurance to cover the repairs. I can give Gray-Dove the details when we get there."

"There you go," Concho replied. "No harm, no foul."

"This whole thing's pretty foul," Parkland said.

"Good to see you haven't lost your sense of humor, though."

"It's the company keeps me laughing," Parkland replied dryly.

Concho grinned.

CHAPTER 48

By the time the coroner arrived at Daniel Alvarado's place and went over some details with Parkland, the afternoon shadows were starting to get long. Concho began to chafe. He had to meet a potential informant at sunset, and if it was who he suspected, the man would not wait around if Concho showed up late. Finally, Parkland motioned to the Ranger and they headed for the sheriff's blue Tahoe. A moment later they were on their way to John Gray-Dove's auto repair shop.

"You gonna be able to make your rendezvous?" Parkland asked.

"Got to," Concho said.

Fortunately, Gray-Dove had finished with Concho's F-150 just that morning and it was ready to go. Thinking ahead, Concho had loaded all his gear from the Dodge at Alvarado's into Parkland's Tahoe while the sheriff talked to the coroner. Now, he transferred the stuff back into its original home in the Ford and raced off to his meeting, leaving Parkland and Gray-Dove to work out the details of payments and such.

Meskwaa had said the meeting would take place "when and where the sun sets." Concho knew exactly where that was. It came from a story written by Estrella Deer-Run in high school. It had won a contest and been published in the local Eagle Pass paper.

The entire Reservation had been proud.

The story involved a Kickapoo maiden who found the exact spot where all sacred deer were born, at sunset, on the grounds of the Texas Rez. The spot lay back in the southwest corner of the reservation, well off the main roads, in a sheltered little hollow where the wind never seemed to blow. Concho drove swiftly to reach it.

With the sun still ten minutes above the horizon, Concho pulled his Ford down a bumpy old hunting road to the edge of a thin meadow of native grasses and wildflowers. He parked and got out, stood in plain view beneath a sky that was nearly black but still streaked with yellows and reds in the west.

Mars was the evening star now. It already shone brightly in the lower quadrant of the eastern sky. Concho remembered when he was fourteen, just after he had read *A Princess of Mars* by Edgar Rice Burroughs, standing outside his grandparent's trailer and holding his arms up to Mars just like John Carter had done when he transitioned to "Barsoom." The trick hadn't worked for him, and he'd had to remain on earth. But at least there weren't any fifteen feet tall, four-armed green men to deal with.

About fifty yards from Concho stood a big oak tree, so close to an old arroyo that some of its roots stabbed through the side of the arroyo wall and poked out into thin air. The oak had played a part in Estrella's story. According to the tale, the base of the oak looked like an upside-down deer head, with the roots representing the branching antlers of a great buck. It did, in truth, resemble such, especially if the viewer had been primed by the words of the story.

Concho walked over and leaned against the textured bark of the tree. The day's last cicada droned on somewhere behind him. He listened until it stuttered to silence. A distant coyote momentarily took up the challenge of the quiet. In the deep stillness that followed, darkness began to sweep down.

The Ranger heard something moving along the bottom of the arroyo. Whoever or whatever it was, it was trying to be stealthy and failing. Identifying the sounds told Concho his visitor was human. A boot scraped against dirt. The heel slid across a rock. Jeans creaked as they stretched with the person's movements.

"Bearfoot," Concho said softly. "I'm here."

The movement stopped but Concho could still hear the sound of breathing. He turned and glanced into the arroyo. A shadowy shape, indistinct, stood against one wall of the ravine. A sigh came from the shape as it moved closer, showing itself to be a man.

The Kickapoo known as Bearfoot, the husband of Estrella Deer-Run, grabbed hold of one of the oak's exposed roots and started to pull himself up the side of the arroyo. Concho reached down and grasped one of the man's hands to lift and deposit the fellow alongside him by the oak.

Bearfoot wasn't very heavy; he stood no more than five feet seven and weighed less than a hundred and fifty pounds. Enough of the day's light remained for Concho to see the older-looking thirty-year-old up close. The man's dark hair was long and stringy. His eyes were sunken, his lips too red against the pallor of his face.

"How did you know it was me?" Bearfoot asked.

"Estrella's story," Concho said. "It wouldn't have been anyone else."

Bearfoot nodded. He was breathing harder than he should have from the exertion of being pulled up the side of the arroyo.

"You look worn out," Concho said.

"I've been better," Bearfoot replied. "I didn't think you'd hear me so easily. I guess I'm not a very good Indian."

Concho didn't like Bearfoot. He wasn't a good husband to Estrella. Not that he beat her or anything. He probably didn't dare. But he'd always run around on her and had seldom done his share to support the family. Nor was he a good father in the sense of being there for his children when they were sick, or wanted fed, or needed a diaper change, although he could play with kids almost as if he were one himself. But, despite the young man's faults, Concho felt sorry for Bearfoot in this moment.

"Being quiet in the wild doesn't make you a good Indian. It just means you've been taught how to move."

Bearfoot nodded, though it didn't seem sincere. "Thank you for coming," he said.

"You had to know I would. Meskwaa wouldn't have delivered an unimportant message."

"I figured."

"And since Estrella was in on it, I take it you've talked to your wife? She's been worried about you."

"I listened to *her* talk," Bearfoot said. "I didn't get to say many words."

"Would they have been worth hearing?"

The small man shrugged. "Probably not."

"Where have you been?"

"That's part of what I have to tell you."

"Then tell it," Concho said.

Bearfoot seldom got directly to a point, but he did now. "About a month ago, a new supply of ice began to appear in the area. Both in Eagle Pass and on the Rez."

"By 'ice,' you mean crystal meth, right?"

"Yes. You know I used to use. But I've quit. I didn't try any of this stuff but from what I hear it was good. Strong, you know."

Concho didn't believe for a minute that Bearfoot hadn't sampled the drug but he needed to keep the man talking so he merely said, "OK."

"The distributors. Well, they were a surprise," Bearfoot continued.

"The NATV Bloods," Concho said. "Particularly, these three new ones out of Oklahoma."

Bearfoot seemed surprised. "Yes. How did you know?"

"Estrella said her father was investigating a resurgence among the Bloods. And I've met the Oklahoma contingent. It all fits together."

"Well, it was them on the distribution end. But you're probably more interested in the supplier."

"Who is?"

"It *was* Donnell Blackthorne."

"Ah," Concho said. "Things begin to fall into place."

"From what I understand, Donnell may have met the Bloods in Oklahoma. May be, *he* encouraged them to come to Texas."

"How is it you 'understand' this?"

Bearfoot stumbled over his response. "Well, uhm, I…I guess Donnell and I kinda…got to know each other. I mean, we talked. Sometimes. He…well, he wasn't a bad guy."

Concho could feel his back starting to stiffen and forced himself to relax. "So, you two talked. Told each other your troubles. That sort of thing?"

Bearfoot stared at Concho for a moment. His face registered doubt. Maybe he'd heard something judgmental in the Ranger's voice, and Concho didn't want that right now. He couldn't afford to have Bearfoot clam up.

Taking a breath, the Ranger said in a friendlier tone, "We all do things we aren't proud of."

"Yes," Bearfoot said. "Exactly."

"I appreciate you telling me all this," Concho said. "It's important. But I'm more interested in murder than meth."

Bearfoot nodded. "I'm coming to that. I liked Estrella's father. He didn't like me. I know why. But he was a good dad to my wife and I want to see his killers get justice."

"Then name names."

"I intend to."

CHAPTER 49

Jacob Drake had just placed a bite of prawn in his mouth when Tony stepped into the room and started toward him. The man did not look happy. Drake sat at his dining room table in the best suite in the Lucky Eagle hotel. He did not like to be disturbed while eating so Tony surely had something important to tell him. Still, Drake held up one finger to silence his employee for a moment while he finished chewing the prawn and swallowing. Only after taking a sip of wine to wash down his food did he gesture for Tony to approach.

"What is it?" Drake demanded.

"Just got a call. Alvarado is dead but an attempt on Concho Ten-Wolves' life failed. The shooter has been arrested."

Drake nodded slowly and took a deep breath. "All right," he said.

Tony's wince was barely noticeable as he turned to leave. Drake ate another prawn, had another sip of wine. He dabbed his lips with a white cloth napkin and rose slowly to his feet. A low grunt came from his mouth as, with one smooth motion, he grabbed the rim of the table and flipped it. Plates and bottles and glasses flew, then crashed down onto the floor a second later, leaving a mess.

Tony rushed back into the room. Drake brushed his hands

together as if ridding them of dust, then turned and walked past Tony toward his bedroom.

"Don't speak," he told the bodyguard as the man's mouth opened. "Not until I tell you to."

He shut the bedroom door behind him.

***

"Then name names," Concho had told Bearfoot.

The skinny Kickapoo hesitated for a bit, as if working up his courage, but finally started: "Donnell was using the NATV Bloods to move meth onto the Rez. Alvarado found out and demanded his cut. The money was good for everyone. Too good, maybe. Someone moved in on the deal."

"Jacob Drake," Concho said.

Bearfoot nodded. "Yes. I have a feeling Alvarado took the idea to him. To Drake. Don't know for sure. But Drake and Donnell. Well, seemed like something personal lay between them. Like it wasn't just about money."

"It wasn't," Concho said.

Bearfoot nodded, and when Concho didn't elaborate, he went on. "Anyway, Drake and Alvarado, they lured the others away from Donnell. He was…gambling. And maybe not keeping as close an eye on his business as he should."

"He was using, too, wasn't he?"

Bearfoot's gaze skittered away from Concho's. "Yeah, I think so. Donnell knows some powerful people. He threatened to make trouble for Drake. And Alvarado. That's when they killed him. Or first planned to kill him anyway."

"What about Ben Deer-Run?"

"I knew Ben was investigating Donnell already. He'd talked to me about it. Trying to get information." Bearfoot sounded bitter as he added, "Anytime something happened with drugs on the Rez, my father-in-law suspected me of being involved. He was never gonna forget my history."

"Forgetting is hard work," Concho said. "Not easy to do."

Bearfoot let out a deep breath. "Yeah. The night Ben died, the night he was killed, he was looking for Donnell. I think he was going to arrest him. Could be he was just in the wrong place at the wrong time. Or maybe he came upon Donnell being grabbed and tried to intervene. I don't know. All I heard was that Ben 'poked his nose in.'"

Concho chewed at his lower lip and tried to keep his anger at bay. He wanted to grab Bearfoot and shake him till he bled. But the truth was coming out. He couldn't do anything to dam it up again.

"Who did the actual killing?" Concho asked.

"A fellow named Wayne. Worked for Drake and the Kickapoo Blood known as Tall Horse. I think Joseph Big-Pine was there but too scared to do anything."

"What about the guard named Tony?"

Bearfoot shook his head. "No. Tony is pretty much a straight arrow. He knows his boss is a criminal but he generally tries to keep his own nose clean."

"Why the hell didn't Ben have backup?"

"He did. Alvarado. Who made it a point not to be anywhere around that night."

Again, Concho's anger threatened to break free. "He should never have trusted that...."

"Ben was pretty smart," Bearfoot said into the quiet pause that followed. "But sometimes he couldn't see what was right in front of him. He saw all the bad in me but very little of it in Alvarado."

Concho knew Bearfoot was correct. The only real argument he'd ever had with Ben was about Alvarado, when Concho had suggested the man wasn't fit for the police.

"Why'd they cut Ben's throat? Why not just make the bodies disappear?"

"I'd...seen Donnell earlier that night. He was dosing. Not meth but heroin. I guess they figured the easiest thing would be to give him a little more push. But Ben? No one would have believed he'd ever taken drugs. I think…somehow, they'd convinced Ben they'd let 'em live. That it was a demonstration. To throw a scare into them. And Wayne and the others were wearing ski-masks so they couldn't be identified. But the way they killed Ben…" Bearfoot stopped for a moment to swallow heavily. "It had to be a message."

"For who?"

"For Alvarado. To keep him in line."

Concho nodded. "Almost seems like you were there. How is it you know all this?"

"I wasn't there. Tall Horse liked to get messed up. On liquor mostly. And when he did, he bragged about how badass he was. He started talking one night, giving details of what he called a 'story.' And he made a joke about killing an old 'Injun,' and a… well, a black man. He started laughing and said Big-Pine wasn't man enough to cut a throat. 'Ceptin, none of it was a joke. I could see it on Tall Horse's face.

"Big-Pine was there and got furious. I laughed it off, made out I believed it was a joke. Then I disappeared. I've been hiding. If they killed Donnell and Ben, they'll kill me to keep their secret."

"Wise of you," Concho said. "You know Wayne has been arrested and Tall Horse is dead, don't you?"

"I know you took 'em out. Estrella told me. That's…one of the reasons I'm here. I think Big-Pine has disappeared, too. Not sure if he's still alive. Guess he's got bigger problems than to come after me, anyway."

"But none of those folks gave the orders to kill," Concho said.

"No. Jacob Drake gave the orders."

"You don't have any proof? This Tall Horse didn't claim it was Drake, did he?"

Bearfoot shook his head. "No, they never mentioned Drake in that regard. But his shadow loomed over them all the time. But even if you can't pin murder on him, there's something else you might be able to get him for."

"What?"

"You know, folks discount me. Even when I'm around, people act like I'm not. They let things slip. Like I'm a servant or something. Not worthy of consideration. I met Drake one night." The young man shook his head. "He's cold. He wouldn't ever let anything slip. But some of the others working for him are not so perfect.

"Drake didn't come to the Rez to sell drugs," the man continued. "That just fell into his lap. He came to sell guns. You've seen his trucks around. He uses 'em to haul slot machines and such. But you pull the inside panels on those things and there are spaces for weapons behind them. Guns and all kinds of military stuff."

"You saw this?"

"I made a few bucks a couple of times helping 'em unload some slot machines. Like I say, people talk around me as if I'm not there. I figured some things out."

Concho nodded. "I imagine his best customers were the local Aryan Brotherhood members."

"Them. And other gangbangers. But that's all I know."

Concho pushed away from the oak where he'd been leaning. "It's enough for now. I appreciate it."

"I'm not...surfacing until Drake is in jail," Bearfoot said. "And he may be more than even you can handle, Ten-Wolves."

Concho smiled, although Bearfoot wouldn't have seen it in the darkness that was now complete. "Guess, we'll see," he said.

***

As soon as Concho left Bearfoot, he called Isaac Parkland and told him what he'd found out.

Parkland's anger hummed in his voice as he replied, "You were right about Drake. But this doesn't give him to us. The prosecutors would never be able to make it stick in court."

"Especially not with an addict as a star witness," Concho agreed. "Even if we could get him to testify, which I doubt."

"So what do we do?"

"First, I do what Echabarri suggested."

"What's that?"

"I go see Melissa Nolan. Get her to appoint me temporarily to the tribal police force. It'll take care of the jurisdiction issues. Then I can get a warrant to search Drake's trucks. If we find weapons, or anything else illegal, we're back in business."

"You want me to come support you with Nolan?"

"No. Absolutely no. She doesn't like me much but has to acknowledge I'm Kickapoo. If we have—excuse me—white cops behind me, she'll get her back up for sure."

"All right. Keep me in the loop."

"Will do," Concho said. "And be ready to move in an instant if I need you."

"Right," Parkland said.

Concho ended the call. It was a long way till dawn.

CHAPTER 50

Concho drove straight to the casino and parked around back just behind a Drake Industries truck. He made his way inside. The casino floor was its usual busy self, and unpleasantly loud after the quiet of the country night. Concho glimpsed Cole Chase working a one-armed bandit but went the long way around to avoid the young man; he didn't feel like spending time right now explaining why he looked like Hell, or talking about Chase's hopes of joining the Texas Rangers.

Other people stared though. The Ranger's face and hands were dirty, his hair tangled and matted with sweat. He limped. Stopping by a bathroom, he managed to clean himself up a little. He drew enough attention as it was.

Since it was after hours, Melissa Nolan's office was closed. Concho knew she had a personal room on the fourth floor, however. His first knocks on her door were ignored, but he kept at it until an exasperated voice from the other side demanded,

"What is it now, Ten-Wolves?"

"Something important enough to bother you after work. Open up."

No response came at first, but finally Concho heard the chain lock disengaging inside. The door opened three-quarters of the way. Melissa Nolan stood framed in it. The casino manager looked like a movie version of a woman who was ready for bed. She wore a long silver satin robe tied tightly around her waist. It dangled almost to the floor but didn't quite hide her boudoir heels. Her blonde hair hung loose around her face, falling to her shoulders. She still had on her day's makeup, or had applied fresh. Concho wondered who she was expecting to visit, and knew it wasn't him.

"As you can see," Nolan said. "I'm getting ready for bed. Make this quick."

Concho fished Echabarri's badge out of the pocket of his blue work shirt. He held it up to show Nolan.

"Echabarri was taken to the hospital. Gunshot wound."

Nolan gasped. One hand flew to her face. If it was an acting job, it was well done. But Concho thought she was genuinely shocked.

"Is he… What happened?"

"We went to Alvarado's. To find out why he disappeared after the shooting on the roof. He was dead. It looked like suicide at first but then someone tried to shoot me as we left. Got Echabarri in the process. He'll be OK but he's going to be out of commission for a while."

"My God!" Nolan said. "That's awful. What…what are we gonna do?"

Concho could almost see the wild and fearful thoughts darting through the woman's hazel irises. And when she began to gnaw on a fingernail despite how it smeared her lipstick, he knew she was genuinely disturbed.

"The reason I'm here," Concho continued, "is the Rez has *no* remaining officers on the tribal police force. Echabarri suggested a short-term solution. He demanded it, actually, and gave me his badge to prove it to you. I resisted at first. But he's right. As a member of the Council, you can appoint me as a temporary officer of the tribe."

Nolan's face whitened. Her lips thinned and tightened. "No! That's! No! It sounds like Alvarado was right about you wanting to take over the tribal police!"

"Figured you might think that. It's why I said 'temporary'. We can put it in writing if you want. In fact, I'd prefer it. I'm not quitting the Texas Rangers."

"That's *exactly* what you would say."

"So who are you going to get? In case you haven't noticed, we're in the middle of a crisis. With the other members of the Council out of the country, you're left to decide. Maybe you'd better get dressed and start making a list of who can do it and who is willing. I see a long night of phone calls ahead of you. And a very short list at the end of it. Most of those will say no."

Nolan was trapped, and she knew it. "How long will Echabarri be out?"

"I don't know. Call the hospital if you want."

Nolan stared at him; her breathing raced too fast.

"What would you do? As a member of the tribal police?"

"Do my best to protect the Kickapoo."

Nolan blinked. She took a deeper breath than those she'd been drawing. "Wait here," she said.

Concho waited. Nolan returned to the door a few minutes later holding a pad of hotel stationery. She handed it to Concho. The time and date were printed at the top of the first sheet. He read the words below out loud.

"Concho Ten-Wolves will serve as a temporary deputy of the Kickapoo Tribal Police of Texas for ten days from today's date. This appointment is nonrenewable."

Nolan's signature was below that. "I'll find someone else in ten days," she said, "if Echabarri isn't back." She handed Concho a pen.

"Good!" Concho said, signing his name below hers.

Nolan straightened her back, lifted her hand with the palm out flat. "OK," she said. "Repeat after me."

CHAPTER 51

After being sworn in as an officer of the tribal police, Concho returned to his pickup. He pinned Echabarri's badge to his shirt just under his Ranger badge, then pulled a crowbar out of the toolbox in the bed of his Ford.

He considered the Drake Industries truck parked in front of his pickup. A moving vehicle was subject to search if an officer had a reasonable suspicion it was stolen or contained contraband. The law seemed to grant police officers close to the border with Mexico even greater leeway in this because of concerns over drug smuggling.

The Drake truck wasn't moving, but he'd seen it when it pulled in and had even declared to the driver that he might want a look inside later. He figured this gave him the right to search it. Such would certainly be disputed in court if things went to trial, but Concho needed to know if what Bearfoot had told him was true about Drake smuggling weapons.

Checking his surroundings for onlookers and finding none, Concho used the crowbar for leverage and broke the lock holding the truck's cargo area closed. The sound echoed loud as a gunshot across the parking lot and he waited for almost five minutes to see if anyone came to investigate. When nothing happened, Concho grabbed a flashlight and a set of screwdrivers from behind the seat of his Ford and climbed into the big panel truck. His head almost brushed the ceiling.

After sliding the rear door closed, Concho flipped on his light. The vehicle was empty, swept clean, and almost spotless. He could detect no odors other than a faint and not unpleasant scent of oil. Each sidewall of the truck was covered by a single large metal panel with wooden two-by-fours stretched across them for cushioning. The panels themselves were bolted like armor into the truck's primary wall all the way around.

Concho started with the top, front screw on the left panel. It must have been bolted in with a drill because it resisted moving until he exerted nearly his full strength. Finally, it began to turn. He took out three screws and pulled the panel out from the wall to peer behind it with his flashlight.

The gap between the truck's inner and outer walls was not as wide as he had imagined, and nothing rested in the gap as far back as he could see. He shone the light up and down. Again, nothing.

Although the outer skin of the vehicle felt solid, tapping it with his knuckles returned a faint echo. You'd have to be listening closely to hear it. He frowned as he studied the wall. A thin seam of beaded material indicating a weld ran along the edge of the truck's roof. Concho tapped this with the handle of the screwdriver. It shifted slightly and Concho froze.

Reaching up, he squeezed the seam between his fingers and tugged. It should have been slick and unmovable, but it shifted. He walked his hand along the seam to where it ended. Pinching it there hard with his thumb and forefinger, he gave a jerk.

The seam split, almost like a zipper, and as he peeled it back another compartment appeared right next to the actual outer wall of the truck. This one was filled with pink insulation.

As Concho pushed his fingers into the insulation, he discovered pockets of empty space behind it. Then his fingers poked into unemptied space. He pulled back the pink foam and drew out a rectangular package about the length of his lower arm. It was wrapped thickly in duct tape.

The Ranger pulled his Bowie knife and sat down on the floor. After positioning the flash for the best light, he cut open the tape and unwrapped the bundle. It was a disassembled machine pistol, looking like a smaller version of the old Israeli Uzi.

"Gotcha!" Concho muttered to himself.

Working by flashlight, Concho reassembled the gun and placed it on the floor. It was a fully automatic MAC-10, chambered for .45 caliber, the same caliber his Colt Double Eagles fired. Several of these weapons had been found at the site of the Mall de las Aguilas attack.

A thirty-round magazine was included in the bundle, but there were no bullets. Well, he wasn't planning on shooting it, but if he had to, he could use some of his own extra cartridges.

Replacing the empty packaging inside the wall, he pushed the insulation in around it and resealed the seam. He screwed the panel bolts of the inner wall back in, leaving no apparent sign of his explorations.

Slipping out of the back of the truck, he returned his tools and flashlight to his Ford and placed the MAC-10 in a duffle bag. Re-entering the hotel, he rode the elevator to the sixth floor.

Tony the bodyguard answered Concho's knock on the door to Jacob Drake's room. He seemed to be dressed in the same slightly rumpled blue suit he had worn every time Concho had seen him. And, as before, the bulge of a shoulder holster bulked under the suit.

"Mr. Drake has already retired for the evening," Tony said. "Can you come back tomorrow?"

"Afraid not," Concho said. "And it's official tribal business." He tapped the new badge pinned to his shirt. "Get him!"

Tony looked shocked to see the two badges Concho was wearing. Shock turned to a frown, which gave way to an irritated sigh. "Wait here!" he said, as he turned and started across the room toward a closed door leading to the suite's bedroom.

Concho followed.

Tony stopped and turned. "I asked you to wait," he said.

"This will save time."

It looked like Tony wanted to argue but he must have figured it would do no good. He continued on and knocked on the bedroom door. When no one answered, he knocked again, louder, and said, "Mr. Drake! I'm very sorry to disturb you but that Texas Ranger is here."

Still no response. Tony frowned and tried the knob. The door opened and Tony peered inside. Concho looked over his shoulder. The big room beyond was dark. The only light showing shone through the glass doors at the far end of the room where they opened onto the balcony.

Tony flipped on the overhead lights. The room lay empty.

"Where is he?" Concho demanded.

Tony looked genuinely surprised. "I…I don't know. He came in here about half an hour ago."

"So how did he slip out again and get past you without you seeing him?"

Tony chewed his lower lip. "I don't know that either. Maybe…I went to the bathroom. Or something."

"Or something," Concho repeated, and he was looking over Tony's shoulder toward the balcony.

"I'm sure he'll return soon. By morning certainly. If you want to come back."

"Call him," Concho said.

Tony sighed but took the cell phone out of his pocket and punched in a contact. Concho could hear the other end of the call. The phone rang once and went to voice mail. Tony could see Concho listening. He shrugged.

"Be back in the morning," Concho said, turning to leave.

As soon as Tony shut the door behind him, Concho headed for the stairs that would take him to the roof.

CHAPTER 52

The stars hung in the sky like glitter dust spread across moiré silk. Concho stopped to appreciate them a moment. He wished he had time to camp out under the stars, to cook over an open flame, to sleep with the sounds of crickets and frogs in his ears—to maybe kiss Maria Morales beneath the moon. He was tired. His leg hurt where two shotgun pellets had hit him right here on this roof. Bruises tattooed him. His limbs felt heavy.

He was tired. But there could be no rest yet. He stalked past yellow crime tape left from yesterday's shooting and stepped to the edge of the roof. The balcony to Drake's suite lay just below. Bull Knife had simply stepped off the roof, but if he did that he'd make a lot of noise when he landed on the balcony. Such might attract Tony's attention.

Slinging the duffle bag containing the MAC-10 over a shoulder, he sat on the edge of the roof, then grasped the edge and eased himself down. When he was stretched to his full, considerable length, he let go and dropped the remaining couple of feet to the balcony. His wounded leg spasmed and almost gave way; he bit his lip. But the sound of his drop was barely discernable

After waiting several minutes to make sure no one came to investigate, he tried the latch on the balcony door. As he'd expected, it was unlocked. This had to be the way Jacob Drake had slipped out of the apartment without attracting Tony's attention.

The lights were off inside as he stepped within, but enough ambient starlight bled through the wide glass doors to show Concho the room. A bed, a table, a couch, a TV. It was almost identical to the other VIP room where Concho had spent the previous night.

Finding the darkest corner of the room, Concho seated himself. He kneaded the muscles of his injured leg to keep them loose, and waited for Drake to return.

***

Just after one in the morning, Concho heard movement on the balcony. A moment later, the door slid back and a shadowy figure stepped into the room. The figure flipped on the lights. Jacob Drake still looked natty but a bit more disheveled than Concho had previously seen him. His hair was mussed. He wore no jacket or tie. His white shirt wasn't tucked in evenly all around.

An image flashed into Concho's mind of Melissa Nolan dressed bedroom-ready. He suddenly had an idea of just why Jacob Drake might have snuck out of his room, and where he'd spent the last few hours. It might have been funny if the two had been teenagers.

Concho cleared his throat. Drake spun around, eyes widening. Concho held up a hand. "Easy, I'm not here to *assassinate* you."

The businessman recovered quickly. His shoulders relaxed as he moved farther into the room.

"Ten-Wolves," he said. "How did you get in here? Am I going to have to fire Tony?"

"Tony knows nothing about it," Concho said, rising to his feet.

"Then how—" Drake started to ask, before stopping himself. He glanced back at the balcony through which he'd just entered. "I see. You came via airmail."

"Seems to be the trend tonight."

"You have a great talent for being irritating."

"It's no talent," Concho said. "I've had to work at it."

Drake shrugged. "What do you want?"

Concho walked over to the room's dining table. Slinging the duffle bag off his shoulder, he removed the MAC-10 taken from a Drake Industries truck and set it gently down on the wood.

Drake watched him. "That looks like some kind of gun but I don't know why you're showing it to me. I don't care much for guns."

"Guess where I found it?"

"I'm also not good at games."

"I think you probably are. But in the interests of finishing this long night's work, I'll tell you. It was hidden in the side panel of one of your trucks. No bullets in it but it'll make good evidence."

Drake didn't even blink. "I doubt you found it where you claim. But...*if* it were true, it would mean you obtained it through an illegal search and it would not be admissible in court. Providing, of course, you were trying to pin some ridiculous charge of gun-running on me."

"It's not illegal to search a moving vehicle for contraband if an officer is suspicious," Concho said. "And I saw this particular truck moving just the other day. What it tells me is that you're the one who armed Darrel Fallon's fanatics so they could take over the Eagle Pass Mall. I figure you also provided the sniper rifle to the hitman you hired to kill me yesterday. I guess neither the terrorists nor the assassin were as good as you expected them to be. You had better luck with the men you sent to kill Ben Deer-Run and Donnell Blackthorne. They only had to surprise an old man and murder a meth-head."

"You must have worked on your imagination along with your people skills," Drake said. "Both are quite extraordinary."

Concho smiled. "I'm going to arrest you now. We'll go down to the jail here on the Rez and have a talk about imagination. Don't worry, you can call your lawyer."

"I don't think so."

Concho nodded. "I was hoping you'd resist."

"You have no authority here. Deputy Alvarado—"

"You probably already know Alvarado is dead," Concho interrupted. "Maybe you tossed away that card too early. And this," he tapped Echabarri's badge on his chest, "gives me authority here. Or didn't Melissa Nolan tell you everything when you visited her tonight?"

Drake blinked. His throat worked but he said nothing. A knock sounded on the bedroom door. A voice called through it, "Sir! Are you OK? I hear voices."

Drake cleared his throat. "Tony!" he called out. "Please come in here a minute."

Concho shook his head as Tony entered the room. He took a step back from the table where he could keep both men in view. The bodyguard saw the Ranger and went still. His hand started to move, to slide across his chest toward the pistol holstered under his arm.

"Nope!" Concho said, with his right hand resting on the butt of his Colt.

Tony stopped moving. He glanced over at his boss, who was too busy staring holes in Concho to pay attention.

"I'm about to arrest your boss, Tony," Concho continued. "If you intervene, I'll take you in too."

"Tony," Drake said. "You see the gun on the table? Have you ever seen me with such a weapon?"

Tony took a few steps toward the table for a better look. His gaze met his boss's. Concho frowned, wondering what the two were up to. To discourage any nonsense, he drew his right-hand Colt and pointed it generally between the two men.

"I think it's what they call a machine pistol," Tony said of the MAC-10. "I've never seen you handle *any* gun. Much less one of those."

"Wow!" Concho said. "There's some convincing evidence of Mr. Drake's innocence." The Ranger still carried the duffle bag that had held the MAC-10. He tossed it on the table next to Tony.

"Why don't you put the weapon in the bag," he said. "I'm taking it with me. Keep in mind, it's not loaded. And while you're at it, put your own pistol in there, too. But move very slowly when you do."

Again, Tony glanced at Jacob Drake. "Go ahead," Drake said.

Tony stepped up next to the table, picked up the machine pistol and stuck it in the satchel. Moving very slowly, as ordered, he reached under the jacket of his suit and used two fingers to remove a semi-automatic pistol from its shoulder holster. He placed this in the bag as well and zipped it closed.

"Now—" Concho started to say.

Drake interrupted. "I borrowed the little document you signed with Melissa Nolan. Tore it up." He took a step toward Concho and the Ranger shifted his Colt to cover him. "She's such an innocent, though she prides herself on being a woman of the world. When I'm…finished with her, she'll testify to anything I want. No one will believe you're not just a rogue cop. Hell, you are! Your boss in the Texas Rangers knows it. You're about to be sued by a father for the wrongful death of his son. You've killed," Drake threw up his hands as if in exasperation, "who knows how many people in the last few days."

Drake smiled a shark smile to match any Concho had ever flashed. He thrust out his hands. "So arrest me!" he said. "Let's see how long it holds."

Concho was tired and hurting, perhaps a little slower and less attentive than he would have been otherwise. Tony swung the bag holding the MAC-10. It slammed into the Ranger's Colt, sent it flying. Tony followed with a lunge.

CHAPTER 53

Tony's lunge hit Concho squarely in the chest. Maybe the bodyguard had played football; he wrapped the Ranger in his arms like a linebacker meeting a running back in the hole, picked him up, and drove him ten steps to smash into the wall. The room rattled; pictures fell; statuettes toppled.

Concho had only one arm free. He hammered an elbow down into the other man's shoulder. Tony grunted as his muscles knotted, but he held on. The bodyguard had large ears. Concho grabbed one, tried to tear it off.

Tony twisted his head, snapped his teeth at Concho's arm. The Ranger jerked that arm away and managed to pull his other arm free too. He cupped his hands, smashed them across Tony's ears. The man cried out and let go.

As Concho landed on his feet, he smashed two heavy blows into Tony's face, rocking the man's skull on his shoulders. Tony shook his head, stunned. Concho shoved him away; he tripped and fell.

Jacob Drake hadn't moved. Now, he shook his arms loose at his sides and came up on his toes. "I thought Tony could handle you," he said. "Guess I'll have to do it myself. I've wondered since we met if you could take me. Time to find out."

Concho felt no need to prove himself. He reached for his

second Colt, only to find that being slammed into the wall had jarred it out of its holster. He snarled and took a step toward the businessman.

Drake launched a kick. Concho blocked with a forearm. The man dropped to a squat and spun, sweeping out with a leg. Concho had seen such before and skipped backward out of the way.

Tony was starting to get up. Concho spared him a glance. Drake lunged in a blaze of speed. The man was obviously trained but Concho hadn't expected him to be so fast. The Ranger blocked two open-handed blows as he backpedaled, but his right foot came down on his own pistol and it slid beneath him.

Concho staggered, dropped to one knee. Drake swung his leg up, tried to stomp the Ranger in the face. Concho caught the foot, twisted and shoved, but came away with only a shoe as Drake pulled back.

Tony was on his feet again. He rushed Concho, who was still on one knee. No time for finesse; the Ranger punched Tony in the groin. The bodyguard uttered a strangled scream and dropped to his knees.

Concho powered to his feet, coming up with a knee as he did so into the underside of Tony's chin. The bodyguard's teeth clacked loudly as they smashed together. The man's head snapped back and his lights went out.

Concho glanced toward Drake. The businessman kicked his other shoe at him. Concho merely swayed to the side, letting the shoe hit the wall. He clenched and unclenched his fists.

"Just you and me," he said.

"How it should be," Drake replied, smiling. He bounced on the balls of his feet.

Concho charged, with his arms up. Drake hit him with two opened-handed blows but they couldn't get past the shield of Concho's forearms. Concho shoved the smaller man hard and sent him reeling away into the table, which toppled on its side.

The Ranger came after him. Drake dodged. Concho grabbed

the overturned table by a leg and slung it. Drake blocked with one arm but was forced backward. He grunted as the table broke in half.

For an instant, the fight paused. Drake plucked a splinter from his cheek. He studied his fingers, saw his own blood speckling them. His demeanor changed. He no longer looked like the cool, calm businessman he'd always resembled. His face grew dark with murderous hate.

"I'm going to tear you up," he snarled.

Concho's leg wound was bleeding again. A wave of weakness battered him, but he didn't show it. He smiled as he stepped toward Drake. "You know what they say. Don't bring a little man to a big man's fight."

Drake growled an inarticulate response. He launched a blazing attack. The man's fighting style was much like Darrel Fallon's when he and Concho had tangled outside the Eagle Pass Mall. Only, Drake was faster, better. His raging movements drove the Ranger back against the wall.

But Concho Ten-Wolves was at least four inches taller than Drake; he outweighed the man by forty pounds; he had speed of his own, like a young lion; he was stronger. And, he had his own rage.

The two men fenced with hands and feet snapping, impacting, blocking. Concho stopped moving backward; he pushed forward. His punches began to get through. Not fully, but enough to sap Jacob Drake's strength.

One of Drake's kicks got through, hammering into Concho's wounded leg just below the hip. Concho's teeth ground together in pain. His leg almost gave out, but he was still fast. His hands darted, caught Drake's ankle and slung him. The businessman had good balance but couldn't quite maintain it. He stumbled and fell.

A chill slipped down Concho's back. Drake had fallen next to the duffle bag containing the MAC-10 and Tony's pistol. Drake realized it at the same moment. He grabbed the bag, his hand finding the zipper.

With his injured leg, Concho had no chance to reach Drake in time. A ceramic Indian mask hung on the wall next to him. He plucked it up. As Drake's hand dipped into the bag and came out with Tony's pistol, Concho side armed the mask like the discus he'd occasionally thrown in track and field. The heavy object hit Drake in the face, knocking him backward and down. The pistol dropped from his hand.

Concho limped over to where one of his Colts lay on the rug and scooped it up. He cocked the hammer. Tony had rolled over and gotten onto his hands and knees. He froze at the metallic sound. Jacob Drake was also trying to rise, moaning as his hands cupped his face where blood poured from his smashed nose and lips.

"Now we've got *that* nonsense out of the way," Concho said. "You're both under arrest. Lie down flat on your bellies and don't move!"

***

Concho had only one pair of handcuffs. He slapped these on Jacob Drake, who was defeated enough to actually hold his wrists out for them. For Tony, the Ranger ripped an electrical cord off a lamp and used it to bind the bodyguard's hands behind him and tether him to the metal frame of the king-sized bed, which was too heavy for anyone to drag around.

"Someone will be along in a bit," Concho told Tony. To Drake, he added, "I figured your only connection to Darrel Fallon was the weapons you sold him. But you fight alike. I'm gonna have to look into whoever trained the two of you."

Maybe Drake's rage made him forget who he was talking to. Or maybe he just didn't care anymore. "I trained Fallon!" he said. "For over a year."

"Really!" Concho said. "Humph. Guess he needed a better teacher."

Drake glared. Concho shrugged, then called Isaac Parkland,

who answered after five rings in a sleep-heavy voice.

"I seem to be making a habit of waking you up, Sheriff," Concho said. "Sorry. But I've just arrested Jacob Drake and his bodyguard and I need backup. Can you send Hoight to take custody of the bodyguard? His name's Tony and he's tied up in Suite 600 in the casino hotel. I'll leave the door wedged open so he can get in. Also, we've got probable cause to get a warrant to search all the Drake Industries trucks in the casino parking lot. I'm pretty sure we'll find guns in their walls."

"So, your informant was right about Drake running weapons."

"Yep. Drake's the one supplied Darrel Fallon and his so-called Aryan Brothers. Apparently, they have an older connection too. Drake may have taught Fallon martial arts for a while."

"Interesting," Parkland said. "I'll look into it. And call the judge about that warrant. You putting in the request as the only currently active member of the Kickapoo Tribal Police?"

"I am. Melissa Nolan swore me in."

"Good. Where's Drake?"

"I'm taking him down to the tribal jail," Concho replied. "I'll make sure he's read his rights and has a chance to call a lawyer."

"All right if I come over?"

"You're welcome," Concho said. "But you don't have to. Drake will still be in a cell come morning."

Drake snorted at those words. Concho ignored him. He got off the line with Parkland, walked over and jerked the businessman to his feet. "Let's get you over to your new quarters," he said.

"You're a dead man," Drake replied. "I promise you."

"Plenty tried," Concho said, shoving Drake ahead of him. "Even you. And I'm still here."

CHAPTER 54

As they exited Drake's suite, Concho held onto the busi-nessman's elbow while he leaned down to block the door open for Deputy Hoight. As he straightened again, a voice called his name.

"Concho!"

There were other VIP suites at this end of the Lucky Eagle Hotel. None were as nice as 600 or 601 but they contained high rollers and their paramours of the evening. Cole Chase stood outside one of those rooms talking to a young woman. He raised his hand and called Concho's name again. After saying something to the woman, he started down the hallway toward the Ranger and his prisoner. The woman went back into her room and closed the door.

"Crap!" Concho muttered to himself as Chase approached.

The young man wore jeans and an open blue windbreaker with "Security" written on it. Concho wondered if he'd left his mall job and gotten a hotel security position here. He certainly seemed to be around enough.

Chase's eyes shone with surprise when he saw the handcuffs on Jacob Drake.

"What?" Chase said. "You've arrested Mr. Drake? What's going on?"

"I can't share that information with you, I'm afraid, Cole," Concho said. "I'm taking Drake downstairs now, though."

Cole nodded. "OK. Of course." He turned to walk alongside the two men as Concho headed for the elevator, still holding tight to Drake's elbow.

"I'll get the elevator for you," Chase said.

"Thanks," Concho replied.

Drake tugged against the Ranger's grip and Concho tightened his hold, jerking the man against him. The jerk turned his body slightly to the left and something punched him low down in the back on the right side. He twisted his upper body in surprise. His legs went numb as he tried to turn completely; they wouldn't support him. He collapsed hard, landing on his left arm as Jacob Drake jerked free with a triumphant shout.

Cole Chase stood over Concho with a crimson stained hand. "Darrel Fallon sends his regards," Chase said. "That's his personal huntin' knife in your spine. And now," the man reached beneath the back of his windbreaker and drew out a snub-nosed .38 revolver, "I have one more of those texts I've been sending you. Reckon I'll just have to say it to your face: One riot, one dead Ranger!"

Chase lifted the pistol, cocked the hammer. Concho tried to move his legs. They twitched but were still sluggish. The blow of the knife must have shocked his spine but not severed the nerves. The numbness was going. But it was too late. Concho snarled.

Chase said, "By the way, I burned your house down, too." He took aim.

A gunshot banged.

Concho flinched, thinking he'd been shot. Then he saw Chase blink his eyes, saw his mouth open. A small blue hole had appeared in the left side of Chase's neck, and when the man turned his head to look for the source of the shot, Concho saw the exit wound on the other side of the throat. The jugular vein and right carotid were gone. Blood pumped into the air like an open hose.

The revolver fell from Chase's hand, discharged as it hit the carpet. The bullet whined away down the hallway. Concho swung his head to look for the shooter. A face shadowed by long dark hair ducked back into Drake's suite. It looked like Bull Knife, the Kickapoo Blood, though the Ranger caught only a glimpse.

Jacob Drake screamed, not a sound of pain but of pure rage. He might have had a chance to get away, but instead of running he dropped to a squat by Chase's still form. His handcuffed hands scrabbled for the fallen .38. They found it, scooped it up. He twisted toward Concho.

"Kill you! Kill you!" Drake shouted as he brought up the pistol.

With blood pooling beneath him, Concho grabbed at the knife sticking out of his back. His hand closed on the hilt and jerked the blade free. A sharp shock of agony swept his whole body but that didn't stop him.

Drake shoved the pistol out in front of him to take aim. Concho swung the heavy knife blade across with all his considerable strength. Razor-sharp steel met the flesh of Drake's left wrist and sheared through, met bone and sheared through. One of Drake's hands dropped away like a falling bird wing. The knife still had momentum; it sliced into Drake's right hand, cutting deep. The gun tumbled free and bounced on the carpet.

Now, the strength came flowing back into Concho's lower body. He swung his legs around, clipped Drake's legs and took them from under him. The man fell on his back, his eyes wide as he stared at the stump of his left arm spouting blood.

Concho came to his knees and brought up the knife. Drake screamed again as he saw the blade rise. This time it was fear. He threw up what was left of his remaining hand. Concho brought the knife down hard, but at the last minute reversed it to hammer Drake in the forehead with the heavy pommel of the blade. Drake's scream broke as unconsciousness took him.

Concho became aware of his own loud gasps for breath, and of how the hotel carpet rapidly began to saturate with the blood of himself, Drake, and Coleman Chase. He lifted his head. Spots danced in his vision. He'd never felt so weak.

Down the hallway, he saw the woman who'd been talking to Cole Chase. She'd stuck her head back out of her room at the commotion. Her mouth hung open on a scream that hadn't surfaced yet.

"Call 911!" Concho tried to shout. It came out a croak.

Awareness left him as he collapsed on top of Jacob Drake.

CHAPTER 55

Concho opened his eyes on a dim room. Something beeped at him. He turned his head. It hurt. He was in the hospital. Beneath a window with the curtains pulled shut, someone sat slumped in a chair. He realized who it was after a moment—Maria Morales, sleeping. He smiled.

Lifting each arm, he found they both worked. His lower body still felt numb but when he moved his feet slightly underneath the bedclothes, they did what he told them to do. He sighed in relief.

Maria must have heard the sigh, though he'd not intended to wake her. She sat up in the chair, glimpsed him looking at her. Pushing quickly to her feet, she stepped to the side of the bed. She grasped his left hand in both of hers. Her skin was warm, so warm.

"How are you feeling?" she asked, then shook her head. "I know it's a dumb question. You can't be feeling good."

"I'm OK," he said. "Or I will be. I hope the doctors agree."

Maria smiled and wiped a tear away from one eye with a finger. "Yes," she said. "They told me that if you stop getting shot and stabbed for a little while you'll heal just fine."

"I'm going to start attending SGH anonymous," Concho said.

"SGH?"

"Stop getting hurt. I hear they're only a ten-step program."

Maria laughed. She wiped her eyes again. "I'm just glad you're OK."

"So...what happened?"

"A woman from the hotel called 911. She had some medical training. She slowed your bleeding. Jacob Drake's, too. Probably saved both your lives. The other guy was already dead."

"Coleman Chase," Concho said. "He had me fooled. I thought he was just an irritatingly friendly young man."

"He cut you deep. The doctor said he nicked your spine. But only got bone. It didn't sever any nerves. You were very lucky."

"I feel like it."

Maria squeezed his hand.

"Where's Drake now?" he asked.

"Here," Maria said. "Fort Duncan Regional. Heavily sedated, I'm told. I asked because...well, you know, he tried to kill my man."

"Your *man*?"

"Sure. As long as you've gotten rid of all those other old girl-friends you talked about the other day."

Concho started to chuckle and stopped with a wince. Maria squeezed his hand again sympathetically.

"No one around can compete with Maria Morales," Concho said.

She grinned. "Guess your brain is still OK. Or as OK as it ever was."

"You'll pay for that," Concho said, smiling.

"Not for a good long while."

A light knock sounded on the door to the room.

"Come in," Concho called.

A nurse entered, followed by Isaac Parkland, who stepped against the wall out of the way. The nurse busied herself checking things and gave Concho a cup of water with ice and a plastic straw in it. He drank greedily until she pulled it away.

"Slow," she said. "You can't restore all your fluids in an instant."

Concho nodded as she turned and left. Maria squeezed Concho's hand one more time before letting it go. "I'm going to get some coffee," she said. "Maybe a bite to eat. I'll let you talk to the sheriff."

"You should go on home," Concho said. "I'm good. I'll see you tomorrow."

Maria shook her head. "I'll go later. I'll be fine after some coffee." She patted his arm and left the room, nodding in passing to Parkland, who came forward to stand by the edge of the bed.

Concho frowned. "What day is it anyway?" he asked the sheriff.

"Still Monday," Parkland said, coming closer. "You've been out about twelve hours."

Concho took a deep breath and regretted it. He took a shallow one instead.

"Happy to see you alive," Parkland said.

"Happy about it myself. What's the story on Drake?"

"They tried reattaching his hand. Not sure it's going to take. He's in worse shape than you are."

"I'm not too broken up."

"Reckon not. We got some good news. Hoight found Tony right where you left him. He's doing some talking. Doesn't seem he has any scoop on the murders, though."

Concho nodded. "You know, I rather like Tony. A fellow kind of like myself, trying to do a difficult job for a difficult employer."

Parkland hmphed. "We've also put a guard on those Drake Industries trucks. They won't be moving anytime soon and I should have a warrant by the end of the day. We'll search 'em."

Concho told Parkland how he'd discovered the hidey holes in one of the trucks. Then, "As much as I hate it, we may not be able to pin Ben Deer-Run's murder on Drake. Not unless Wayne Quaite talks."

"We'll do what we can do."

"You better look into Coleman Chase, too," Concho said. "He had to be in on the mall thing with Darrel Fallon from the beginning. He could be the one to look to for the bank's missing bonds. I'm pretty sure now he was the one driving the black pickup that ran me off the road on the Rez. Just wearing a mask and a blond wig."

Parkland shook his head. "I wouldn't have believed it. Talked to the fellow several times. A real eager beaver type."

"He was a good actor."

"Looks like he and Jacob Drake both attended a dojo in San Antonio years ago. I'm still getting information. But," Parkland patted Concho on the arm, "I'm going to let you rest. I'll drop by tomorrow. Maybe I'll have more details to fill you in on. Hopefully, good ones."

"Thanks for everything," Concho said, offering the sheriff his hand. Parkland shook it.

"Not a problem," the man replied.

***

Concho closed his eyes when he was alone again. Questions still roiled in his mind, particularly about the role of Hamilton Blackthorne in everything that had happened. But he didn't have much urge to follow that trail right now. Maybe it was the pain meds. He just wanted to rest, not necessarily sleep, but drowse.

The door opened. He turned his head, expecting to see Maria. The young Kickapoo named Bull Knife stood there, wearing buckskin trousers and a beaded shirt. A necklace of polished deer antler had replaced the eagle talons around his neck. Hawk feathers hung from the braids at either side of his head.

Concho stiffened. His mind began to search for any weapons he might have near him. There weren't many he could think of. His hands would have to do. Bull Knife approached but stopped out of reach of those hands. He studied Concho with almost blank dark eyes. His own fists were empty.

"I didn't come to hurt you," Bull Knife said.

"Relieved to hear it," Concho replied.

"Point of fact, I saved your life." The young man held up two fingers. "Twice."

"Once," Concho said. "The first time. I saw you look over my shoulder as a warning, but I'd already figured it was a trap. One you led me into."

"Another age. A century ago. Before."

"Before what?"

Bull Knife shrugged and changed the subject. "When you get out, make yourself available on the Rez. Joseph Big-Pine is hidden but he'll find you. He'll give you what you need to know about the murder of your friend, Ben. It will be enough to convict Jacob Drake."

Concho arched both eyebrows. "And why will Big-Pine do this?"

"Two reasons. First, I asked him to."

"And the second?"

"He believes your magic is stronger than his. He doesn't want to anger the spirits."

"And what about you?"

"I've already angered them." He lifted his head, listening. "The woman returns," he said.

"You hurt her and I'll get up out of this bed to kill you!" Concho said in a growl.

"Not going to hurt her." Bull Knife glanced back at Concho and lifted one finger to his forehead. "Rest well...Ranger."

The man moved swiftly to the door and through it. Maria came in only seconds later. Concho was sitting up, starting to swing his legs out of bed. The woman rushed to him, pushed him back. He let himself be pushed because she was alive and safe.

"Did you see him?" Concho demanded.

"See who?" Maria asked, frowning.

"A young man. An Indian. A Kickapoo."

"I didn't see anyone," Maria said. She leaned down and kissed his stubbled cheek. "Only you."

A LOOK AT: HOT, BLUE AND RIGHTEOUS (CONCHO BOOK TWO)

A routine morning turns deadly as Concho Ten-Wolves, a Texas Ranger working the Rio Grande border between Mexico and the U.S., responds to a bank robbery where shots have been fired. The robbery proves to be the least of Concho's troubles as it opens up a mystery that pits kin against kin and lust against love. Through the heart of it all stalks an elusive figure whose crimes are just coming to light.

Everyone is pushing Ten-Wolves to stay out of it, to let sleeping dogs lie. But Concho has already taken sides and he's about to push back.

AVAILABLE JULY 2021

ABOUT THE AUTHOR

Charles Gramlich lives amid the piney woods of south-ern Louisiana and is the author of the Talera fantasy series, the SF novel Under the Ember Star, and the thriller Cold in the Light. His work has appeared in magazines such as Star*Line, Beat to a Pulp, Night to Dawn, Pedestal Magazine, and others. Many of his stories have been collected in the anthologies, Bitter Steel, (fantasy), Midnight in Rosary (Vampires/Werewolves), and In the Language of Scorpions (Horror). Charles also writes westerns under the name Tyler Boone. Although he writes in many different genres, all of his fiction work is known for its intense action and strong visuals.

Made in United States
Orlando, FL
12 December 2024

55459180R00174